The Fall

Kate Sherwood

Published by Kate Sherwood

Cover Art by Leah Kaye Suttle

Print ISBN #978-1-988752-19-8

Second Edition Issued 2019

CHAPTER ONE

"IT'S NOT like I was expecting an adorable little café. I knew that even Starbucks might be pushing it." Mackenzie tried to loosen his grip on his cell phone before saying, "But Kristen, there's not even a Tim Hortons! There's a donut shop. It's called The Donut Shop. It sells *donuts*. No pastries, no soup, no sandwiches. Just donuts. And coffee." In the interest of full disclosure, he added, "And bagels. I don't know what's with the bagels. But there isn't even a drive-through!"

"You *were* just co

mplaining about having to drive everywhere up there," Kristen replied. Mackenzie could hear the laughter in her voice, and it really didn't help matters. "And you aren't a big coffee drinker, anyway."

"It's not for *me*," Mackenzie said in exasperation. He pushed away from the stone wall he'd been leaning on. "It's for the clientele. I mean, I need support services, right? People aren't going to drive all the way up here for a wedding and not want to get something to eat or do a little shopping. I was excited when I saw that they have an antique store, but, honestly, it looks like my grandma's basement. It's not even kitsch—just crap."

Kristen sounded a little more serious as she asked, "What are you going to do about it? It's not too late to come back, you know. Sell the damn church, get back down here to the land of cafés, and move on with your life."

"I *am* moving on." Mackenzie had given this some serious thought, especially the night before as he'd tossed and turned in his low-thread-count sheets at the local motel. "This business was my idea, not Nathan's. And it's a *good* idea. If I come back now, I'll just sit around and mope. I need to keep busy."

"If you come back now, you'll be looking for work," Kristen corrected. "You don't have a sugar daddy anymore."

"I paid my own way," Mackenzie protested. "I mean, I paid for the essentials. If Nathan chose to treat me to a few luxuries...."

"You haven't paid for rent, utilities, or groceries in almost six years. Stealing clothes from your shoots does not count as paying for the essentials."

"I paid for some of those clothes. And the rest were gifts, not stolen. I can't help it if people want me to be seen wearing their designs."

"You finding much use for your wardrobe up there? Anyone appreciating your bold fashion choices?" Kristen was clearly back to laughing at him.

"*My* people will continue to appreciate me. And soon, my people will be up here. They'll be getting married in my beautiful church, celebrating in the lovely gardens—"

"And picking up donuts in town. *Without* driving through."

"The town needs some work," Mackenzie admitted. "Hard to believe that somewhere two hours from Canada's biggest city could be this backward. But I'm not giving up. No way. I just need to figure a few things out." He looked up at the stone wall he'd been standing next to, then stepped back far enough that he could see the whole front of the church. "It's a beautiful building, Kristen. It's going to be perfect when it's all fixed up."

"A traditional venue to celebrate your nontraditional love," she said. "Is that the one you're going with?"

"Or maybe 'drive two hours out of the city to get married in a total shithole.'"

"I vote for the first one. I'm coming up this weekend, okay? If you don't have a place by then, I can stay at your motel. You've made it sound so appealing I can't resist."

"You'll bring Griffin?"

"Of course. He's pining without you."

"He's not really, is he? He's okay?"

There was a pause, and Mackenzie could picture Kristen leaning down to fondle the goldendoodle's silky ears. Or probably just leaning over, not down, because as soon as Kristen had heard the dog didn't shed, she'd made him into her couch mate and cuddle partner. "He's fine. He was sad for the first five minutes, just like he always is when you leave him. Then I gave him the new toy, and he got over it. But he'll be happy to see his daddy."

"One of them, at least."

"He never loved Nathan like he loves you."

"Good thing." There didn't need to be two of them pining for Nathan. But Mackenzie didn't want to think about that. Luckily, a distraction arrived in the form of a pickup truck with ladders and a variety of tools in the back, and two men in front. There was a Sutton Construction logo on the side. "I've got to go. The contractors are here."

"Have fun. Call me later."

He agreed and ended the call, then squinted at the men getting out of the truck. They were both tall and rangy with angular faces, wearing jeans and work shirts, the driver with a baseball cap and the passenger slipping on a cowboy hat without a trace of irony. Mackenzie kept staring at them. There was something strange going on....

"Yeah, we're twins," the one from the driver's side said with a friendly smile. "But I'm the good-looking one." He held out his hand. "Will Sutton. We spoke on the phone." He glanced over at his brother, who was staring at the church like he thought it might be about to crumble on their heads. "That's Joe. Don't mind him. He's just here in case there's heavy lifting."

"I'm Mackenzie." He extended his hand and braced himself for a painful show of manly strength, but Will's handshake was firm without being crushing. "Thanks for coming by. Do you want to look inside, or...?"

"Outside first, if that's okay. I did a quick look-around when you called me. There's a few things you should have a look at."

"Okay," Mackenzie said doubtfully. He knew nothing about construction.

"It looks like it's in pretty good shape," Will said as he led the way around the building. "Couple broken windows in the basement, but the big windows look okay. You're keeping the stained glass?"

"Absolutely."

Will nodded. "Good. It adds a lot, I think. There's a bit of work to be done here," he said as he brushed at some loose mortar, "and we'll have to take a good look inside to make sure water didn't get in. Gutters need some work, there"—he pointed—"and we'll have to go up and take a look at the roof to see what kind of shape it's in."

"*We* won't be doing that," Mackenzie clarified. "There's no way I'm going up there."

"Joe'll do it," Will said dismissively. "He likes heights."

Joe didn't respond or even look in their direction. Mackenzie was beginning to find the man's silence a little unsettling.

Will continued to calmly point out deficiencies in the building as they toured around the perimeter, and Mackenzie struggled to maintain his positive attitude. "We had an inspection done," he said defensively. "They said there were no major problems. And you just said it was in pretty good shape...."

"It is," Will responded in surprise. "*Really* good, considering. But it's a hundred and forty years old, and it's been empty for almost a decade. It needs some work."

"I'm on a fairly tight budget. Can you prioritize things? Like, tell me what needs to be done right away to keep the place from falling down, what needs to be done in a couple years, what would be nice to do someday? That'd be really helpful."

Will had given him a weird look as soon as he'd said he was on a tight budget, and that was just one more thing for Mackenzie to worry about. The contractors had been highly recommended as people who weren't only good at their jobs but also scrupulously honest, and Mackenzie had really hoped he'd be able to just sit back and let them guide him through the necessary renovations. But if they were looking for someone who'd be able to throw endless cash into the project, he was in trouble. Two months ago, he'd have been happy to oblige, and he probably wouldn't have looked too closely at the invoices, either. Now, though, he needed to be more careful.

"We can figure it out," Will finally said. "You want to go look inside, see what's what in there?"

Mackenzie absolutely did. The outside of the church was lovely, but it was the interior that had really captured his heart. He led the way through the carved wooden doors, through the gracious narthex with its spiral staircase, and into the sanctuary. He took a deep, satisfied breath as he entered. Yes. This room made it all worthwhile. The proportions of the walls and arched ceiling were perfect, the light through the stained glass divine. The wooden pews curved gracefully toward the altar, which was itself rounded and felt like a part of the larger circle. It was a setting that spoke of community and fellowship and belonging, and it was the *perfect* place to celebrate a wedding.

But Will wasn't soaking up the charm quite as deeply as Mackenzie always did. Instead, he was focusing on a collection of whitish-gray... something in the middle of the central aisle. He glanced toward his brother, who shrugged in laconic cowboy fashion.

"Not a tragedy," Will said as he turned back to Mackenzie. "But we need to get this taken care of. It's a mess, but it's also acidic. The floor beneath that spot is probably wrecked. We'll have to try to match the hardwood for the repairs."

"What is it?" Mackenzie asked. "I mean, it looks like bird shit...."

"Bat shit," Will corrected.

And for the first time, the cowboy spoke. "You've got bats in your belfry." He pointed up, and Mackenzie followed his finger. The pile of droppings sat immediately beneath an octagonal hole in the ceiling, an opening Mackenzie had barely even noticed before.

"Bats? And that's my belfry?" He frowned. "What *is* a belfry?"

"It's where the bell goes." Will was back in charge. "But I doubt they'll let you ring a bell, anyway. It's not like you're a real church. Is there even a bell up there? We should check, to make sure it's not going to fall on someone's head."

"It's over in Mossberg," the cowboy told his brother. "In that schoolhouse."

"The converted one on the town line?"

"Yeah. They moved it over a few years ago."

Will nodded, then turned to Mackenzie. "That's Joe's second skill. He likes heights, and he knows weird shit." He grinned quickly and waggled his eyebrows almost suggestively. "I don't know if you want to hear about his *third* skill!"

"Enough," the cowboy said, no humor in his tone, and there was a tense moment when it seemed like Will might push whatever he was doing just a little further. Finally, though, he shrugged as if disappointed in his brother's decision, then turned around in a big circle, looking at the ceiling.

"Probably best to just shut the belfry off entirely, but we'll want to get the bats out too. Might need to hire an expert for that. You'll need to check on their breeding season; they've probably got babies up there now, and you don't want to separate a family." Will glanced over to be sure Mackenzie wasn't going to argue with that, then continued his inspection. "I don't see any water damage from down here, but we'll need to poke around up there to be sure. And we'll want to check the basement, and the windows...."

So the inspection continued without further interaction between the brothers. Mackenzie wondered why the cowboy was even there; he certainly didn't seem too interested in any of the proceedings. Mackenzie had heard this was a family business, but it seemed pretty clear that Will was the brains of the operation. Whatever Joe's mysterious skills were, they obviously didn't involve customer service.

"You want to go set up the ladders?" Will asked his brother when they'd finished poking through the choir loft. "We can check out the basement while you're doing that."

Joe looked almost suspicious at the offered escape, but he nodded and headed outside while Will and Mackenzie made their way to the basement.

"Joe's a good guy," Will said as he tested the stability of the railing on the stairs. "Just takes him a while to warm up to people."

"Okay." It wasn't like it was any of Mackenzie's business. "Can you take a look at the ceiling? There's a couple feet of space in there, and if we could find a way to open that up...."

"They probably lowered it to save heat. You've got a big space here, and you're going to want someone to come in and look at the furnace, wherever it is. It'll probably be worth the expense of updating it as soon as you can. They've got natural gas running by here now, so you could hook up to that and get rid of the propane tanks." He found a rickety chair and stepped up on it to peek into the ceiling. "He's never been much of a talker," he said, his voice muffled.

It took Mackenzie a while to figure out that the man was back to his brother. "Well, that's kind of nice sometimes," he managed. "Gives more space for the rest of us to dominate the conversation."

"Exactly!" Will hopped off the chair and dusted his hands off on his jeans. "Yeah, I think we could raise that ceiling back up. You've got a lot of height down here. More than most old churches. Have you got plans for the space?"

"I'm not sure. I was thinking we could use it for receptions if we had to. There doesn't seem to be anywhere in town...."

"Legion, community center, golf course," Will said thoughtfully. "Or people's backyards. That's where most people have their receptions."

"The golf course?" That was an exciting possibility. Mackenzie didn't golf himself, but many well-heeled people did.

"Out on the highway. You would have driven past it on the way from the city."

Mackenzie searched his memory. "Can you see the clubhouse from the road?"

"Yeah. It's board and batten, kind of a faded green? One story, with the shop in front and a big garage door on the side."

"Huh." Mackenzie couldn't remember the exact building, but it wasn't sounding too promising.

"You want something fancy?" Will guessed. "That ain't it. This isn't a rich area. Industry is pretty much packed up and gone, and farming... it's mostly going large-scale, now. The people who actually *own* the land are probably making good cash, but they live down in the city or maybe even farther away. The ones who live up here are just employees now, not real farmers."

Of course it wasn't a wealthy area. That was why Mackenzie had been able to afford to buy the church. It was located in a picturesque hamlet a few miles outside a two-stoplight town, with quaint historic homes on either side of it and a forest-covered ravine in the back. The setting was beautiful, but remote. If it were located elsewhere, it would have been snapped up at three times the price and converted into a grand residence or weekend home. He sighed. "Let's see if we can find the furnace. And one of the bathrooms has a pretty big shower in it. Does that make sense? Do people shower at church?"

"No idea. Joe might know. Does it work?"

"Seems to."

They continued the walk-through with only a few more bits of random praise or apology for Joe's behavior, then walked outside to find the cowboy himself leaning on the back of the pickup, silver ladders safely stowed away.

"What'd you see?" Will asked.

"Looks good. Steel's in good shape. Maybe a couple hours to fix a few loose spots. A day for a cleaning and a coat of paint. But it's solid."

Will seemed pleased, and that cemented Mackenzie's decision to trust the man. He wasn't trying to pretend the roof needed more work than it did. He was happy to discuss the issue in front of Mackenzie, not trying to control information or manipulate anything. "I'll put some paperwork together," Will said. "I'll prioritize stuff, like you said—what needs to be done, what should be done, what you could do at some point if you felt like it. Okay?"

"Sounds great," Mackenzie agreed. "Thanks for coming by." He held out his hand for another firm but not crushing shake. By the time he'd turned toward Joe, the man was already heading for the passenger door of the truck. Obviously he wasn't interested in any departure rituals.

Mackenzie watched the truck pull away and wasn't surprised to see the door of the house across the street open almost immediately. Lorraine Liverson had introduced herself that morning, inquiring none too subtly into Mackenzie's background, his plans for the church, his plans for himself, his marital status.... He had almost expected her to pry his mouth open for a look at his teeth. Now she was back, her manner exaggeratedly casual.

"Oh, the Suttons came by? I hope they said good things about your project!"

Mackenzie decided it was time for a little prying of his own. He'd heard the recommendations from his local lawyer and his real estate agent, but Lorraine probably had her own collection of data ready for review. "One of them did. Will. I haven't gotten a quote from him yet, though."

"It'll be fair, whatever it says," Lorraine said confidently. She was one of those women who seemed to have gotten frozen in late middle-age. He couldn't have said whether she was in her fifties or her seventies, but her eyes were still bright, and her voice was strong as she said, "The Suttons have been in Falls Creek since the settler days, and they've always been honest. A lot of the last generation moved away, but Will's father stayed, and he started that company... must be coming up on forty years ago now." She smiled, pleased to have found a justification for her gossip.

"The father's retired now? Is Will in charge, or the other one?"

"Malcolm passed about five years ago, along with his wife, Susan. They were lovely people. It was so sad... an icy night, and their car just slid right in front of a gravel truck out on Bayersly Road. All those kids left behind." She sighed, then brightened. "Lucky that Will and Joe were old enough to take care of the younger ones. It would have broken Susan's heart if her brood had been split up."

"A *brood*? How many kids are in a brood, exactly?" Mackenzie had only wanted to know whether the contractors were honest, but now he was finding himself intrigued by the rest of their story.

And Lorraine was happy to share. "Well, the twins, obviously. That's two. Then a bit of a gap, and with the handful those two were when they were babies, I can't blame Susan for waiting a bit. Then Sarah. She just got married this summer, to Dave Henderson. They're a good family too. Dave works for the municipality, Sarah does the office stuff for her brothers." She paused for Mackenzie's encouraging nod and having received it, moved on. "Nick's the next one, and he's away at school. Studying business, last I heard, so I guess he'll probably be staying away, although...." She paused as if there was actually a piece of information she wasn't sure she should share. "That comes with its own set of issues. Then Ally. She's a bit... well, I'd say it's because she was raised by her brothers, but that's only been for the past few years, and Ally's been a tomboy since she was born. Hard to get her out of the barn, as I hear it."

Lorraine seemed done, but it was possible she was just pausing for a well-deserved breath. "So, five of them?" Mackenzie prompted. "That's the brood?"

"Well, that's *that* generation. They've started on the next, as well."

That made sense. Mackenzie hadn't noticed a ring on either brother, but they must be in their late twenties, so it would hardly be surprising if one of them had begun reproducing. "Will?" he guessed. He couldn't imagine the taciturn Joe as a father.

And there was the moment's hesitation again before Lorraine threw caution to the wind and leaned in with a wicked smile. "Nick! When he was still in high school! And *not* with the sort of girl who you'd want raising a little one, if you know what I mean. It wasn't that long after their parents died, so everyone was pretty understanding about his little mistake. And Austin's a complete charmer, bright and happy all the time, and Lord knows the whole Sutton family just dotes on him. So it all worked out okay, really."

"Sounds like it," Mackenzie agreed. "And they all work for the construction business? But Will's in charge?"

"The construction is Will's," Lorraine said, "but Joe helps out sometimes. The rest of the time Joe looks after the... well, folks around here call it the ranch, even if that's a bit of a strange word for this part of the country. But it's over a thousand acres, most of it only good for grazing and logging. You can't really call that a farm, can you?"

Mackenzie had absolutely no idea what he'd call it, and Lorraine didn't seem too concerned about his opinion, anyway. "I don't actually know why he was with Will today, to be honest. It sure wasn't for the sales pitch."

Lorraine snorted. "He didn't seem too friendly? I'm not surprised." She shrugged philosophically. "It's probably the gay thing."

It hit Mackenzie almost like a slap. He'd thought he was prepared for small-town attitudes toward his sexuality and had absolutely considered homophobia as a possible barrier to setting up his wedding chapel somewhere like Falls Creek. But he couldn't believe it was being treated so casually. "You're saying he was rude to me because I'm gay?"

Lorraine looked startled. "No. I'm not sure I'd call it rude, but the way he acts? Distant, kind of? I always figured it was because *he's* gay. You know, he's always been a bit different, so he's never really tried too hard to fit in. He just hangs out on his ranch, being a lonely cowboy...." She trailed off and fixed her gaze on Mackenzie. "But you say *you're* gay as well? I mean, I can't say it didn't cross my mind. But it seemed rude to ask...."

"Joe Sutton is gay." Mackenzie had always prided himself on being able to read people and *certainly* on being able to pick up on that little spark from a man who was noticing Mackenzie's undeniable charms. But he'd gotten none of that from the cowboy brother. "That's confirmed? Or you're just guessing?"

"Well, I haven't been there in the room with him and another fella," Lorraine said with an arched brow, "but it's general knowledge. He's never tried to hide it, not that I ever heard of."

"Maybe he just couldn't be bothered to speak in order to deny it. He doesn't seem like someone who cares a whole lot what other people think about him." Mackenzie was trying to figure it all out. He wanted to find a mirror and make sure he still looked like himself. First Nathan had dumped him for that twenty-year-old, and now a man living in what must surely be a gay desert had crawled right past Mackenzie's bountiful oasis?

"You could ask Nancy Yeats's nephew, if you wanted. Trevor something or other. He lives over in Darton, and I guess the two of them were seeing each other for quite a while." Lorraine's grin was a mix of curiosity and mischief. "If you're interested, I can find out if he's seeing anyone right now. I haven't heard of it, and usually that'd be a good sign that it isn't happening, but like I said, Joe's a bit different. A bit more private than most folks."

Private was not a good enough excuse for failing to pay attention to his surroundings or, more importantly, failing to pay attention to *Mackenzie*. But none of that needed to be shared with a woman who clearly gossiped as a way of life. He smiled brightly. "Oh, no, I'm not interested. You know, not like *that*. I was just curious. I wanted to know what kind of people I'd be doing business with if I had the Suttons do the work on the church."

"The best kind," Lorraine said firmly. "You couldn't do better."

Lorraine started telling a story about the Suttons helping out some poor family that had lost everything in a house fire—well, of course the whole community had chipped in, but the Suttons had done the biggest part—and some people might say that's because they're blood, but really, they'd be third cousins at best—because it was Susan Sutton's grandmother? Yes, grandmother, Maggie Johnson—she was from out in Newfoundland, back before it was even part of Canada, and she'd carried that accent with her for her whole life.... Mackenzie tuned out. Joe Sutton was openly gay. And Mackenzie was a *model*, for Christ's sake. Maybe his career hadn't quite taken off, but that was because Nathan hadn't really liked it. He hadn't been rude enough to try to forbid it, but he'd be grumpy for days before and after Mackenzie went out of town for even a couple days, and there just weren't enough shoots in Toronto to propel someone into the modeling elite. The first time Mackenzie turned down a New York job, Nathan had leased him a silver Mini convertible as a reward. Mackenzie had been thrilled by the symbol of Nathan's affection *and* by the adorable new wheels. But being a good boyfriend had made it a bit difficult to be a good model. So, no, it wasn't as if Mackenzie had set the world on fire as a model. Still, he must be a tastier piece of ass than Nancy Whoever's nephew!

Mackenzie forced himself to pay a bit more attention to Lorraine's chatter, but the biggest part of his brain was still focused elsewhere. He was *not* going to be ignored by some desperate hick pretending to be a damn cowboy. No. Joe Sutton was about to get his world rocked. "Nobody puts Baby in a corner," he muttered to himself, and then he smiled when Lorraine shot him a quizzical glance. "I've got to go," he said without trying to explain. "But thanks so much for catching me up on all this. You've given me a lot to think about."

He beat a hasty retreat inside and went to sit in the sanctuary of the church. A *lot* to think about. And a lot of things to do, things actually based around the important points of building a successful business and keeping himself out of the poorhouse. But his mind kept drifting back to the tall cowboy who'd told him he had bats in his belfry. And then ignored him. What the *hell* was Joe Sutton's problem?

CHAPTER TWO

"WHAT THE hell's your problem, Joe?" Will was driving, which meant he didn't get to use his traditional 'I'll stare at you until you talk' technique. So Joe didn't really feel compelled to speak. He stared out the window at the passing fields. Davidson's canola was at least a week ahead of VanDayn's, even though they'd planted at the same time. Might be a different variety planted, might be different sun exposure. Might be the soil, Joe supposed, although he didn't think he'd seen much difference. He should probably ask Terry Davidson about it. The ranch didn't usually plant canola, but....

Joe's reflection was interrupted as the truck swerved onto the shoulder of the road, kicking up a plume of dust behind it. Damn. They'd just turned onto their own road and were only a couple miles from their driveway, and Joe had begun to think he was going to get away with his escape. But he didn't get to ignore this conversation; Will wasn't messing around.

"I'm serious, Joe." Will was staring at him now. Joe wasn't looking in that direction, but he could feel his twin's gaze drilling into him, right behind his left ear. Experience had taught him it was an irresistible force, and he knew he'd be defeated eventually, but he always resisted anyway. He squinted at the speck on the horizon. Hawk? No, there was another, and another. Turkey vultures. Over by the railroad tracks, it looked like.

"Hey, asshole, I'm talking to you." Will didn't sound mad.

Not even frustrated, really. Just gently amused. He knew Joe was resisting, but he also knew Joe would lose. And Joe knew it too, because the pull was getting stronger, the urge to turn his neck almost irresistible. He looked desperately over the landscape. A fallen tree, too rotten to be any use as firewood, but maybe something interesting living in it. What would Joe find if he dug his fingers into the mealy wood pulp in the middle of that stump?

"Hey, Joe?" Will's voice was light and inviting, and damn it, Joe instinctively turned his head before he remembered he wasn't supposed to. He'd been caught in the trap of his own distraction. And once he was looking at his brother, the game was over. Will was gracious enough to keep his smile from being *too* triumphant. "Joe. Hey. I was just wondering what you thought about the new guy? And the church idea? I mean, gay weddings, way up here— you think that'll work?"

"No idea." That was true enough. Joe hadn't given the issue enough thought to have an opinion, and he wasn't one for thinking out loud.

But Will nodded like he'd said something profound. "Yeah. It's a gamble, for sure. Beautiful building, though. You've always liked that church, haven't you? I know you were sad when it was put up for sale. We thought someone would buy it and turn it into a house, lose all that charm. So this is good news, really. Someone keeping it for more or less its original purpose."

"Guess so."

Again, Will nodded as if Joe was actually contributing to the conversation. "And the guy seemed nice enough. A bit... what's the word I'm looking for? He seemed a bit...."

"Gay?"

"Hey! No stereotypes here. I was thinking more like... flamboyant, maybe?"

Will had dragged Joe to a couple of Toronto's gay pride parades, back when Joe was still figuring things out. They both knew the church guy was pretty damn low on the flamboyant scale. But compared to other people in the area, Will probably had a point. "Didn't notice," Joe said. "The roof looked good. The basement okay?"

"Needs some work if he wants it to be nice enough for a reception, but structurally, it's fine." Will grinned. "I'd say the guy's structurally fine too. Right?"

"I don't know. I didn't check out his basement." Probably a mistake, but as always, Joe had trouble resisting the opportunity for a play on words.

Will seized on the weakness. "You didn't check out any part of him, from what I could see. Good-looking guy like that, single guy like you... seems like you might have at least given him a once-over?"

"Had my mind on the job. I'm a businessman, Will."

"Not usually."

"Turned over a new leaf."

"Yeah? When?"

"Sometime this morning. Right after you said you needed my help on a new project. But...." Joe held out his hand in a vaguely leaflike fashion. "It's not a healthy leaf. It doesn't like growing on me." He crinkled his fingers. "It's drying up... it's dying...." He wiggled his fingers as his hand fell to the seat of the truck, showing the rain of leaf fragments as it dissolved. "It's dead. It was killed by realizing that you don't need my help at all and were just trying to set me up with some guy you'd never met, based on the sole criteria that we both like dick." Joe shrugged. It was hardly a new phenomenon. "Now I'm back to my old leaves, and they want to go home and get some work done. So if you could maybe *drive* the truck instead of just sitting in it, that'd be great."

But Will didn't seem inclined to follow Joe's suggestion. "You need to get out more. You're like a hermit or something. You're not as young as you used to be, you know."

"We're the same age, jackass."

"You wouldn't know it by the way you act."

"I'm not the one who has to pull the car over to have a conversation. I'm still young enough that I can drive and talk at the same time."

"Yeah, you were talking up a storm."

"I had nothing to say."

Will sighed and finally turned to look out the windshield. "He seemed okay," he offered.

But Joe wasn't playing that game. "He seemed like a complete pain in the ass. I bet those jeans cost two hundred dollars and came prefaded."

"But his ass looked good in them."

"Are you *sure* you're straight? They say it's pretty likely for twins to have the same sexual preference."

"Are you sure you're gay? Or maybe you're... what's it called? Asexual."

"Yeah. I think maybe I am. So you should respect that and back the fuck off."

"When's the last time you got laid, Joe? Just how long's it been?"

Jesus, this conversation was getting annoying. Joe smiled at his brother. "It's been a while. But that's just because the guy's dick was so huge he kind of tore me open. Did some serious damage. And now my asshole's all gaping and gross. I shit myself sometimes. I thought you would have noticed the smell. Actually, I think maybe I've got a bit of a load in my jeans right now." He unbuckled his seat belt and shifted around. "Can you smell for me, tell me what's in there?" He moved fast, grabbing Will's head and pushing it down toward the seat. "Smell my ass for me, okay?"

Will resisted, of course, but he was laughing harder than Joe was, and that made him weak. Having the steering wheel in his lap probably didn't help, either. Joe managed to get his brother pretty much horizontal before he hoisted himself up and started aiming his ass in the general direction of Will's face. It was gross and immature, and Joe would never have done anything like it with anyone else in the world, not even the other members of his own family, but this was Will. He and Joe had shared a womb, a cradle, and practically everything else. A little ass-smelling between twins was nothing to get upset about.

"You're fucking sick," Will yelled through his laughter.

"No, not a sickness, an *injury*. I knew I should tell him to stop, but it just felt *so good*...."

"Get off me!" Will struggled, and Joe fought back, and it wasn't until they both stopped for breath that they heard the tapping on the driver's side window.

Joe twisted around to see a familiar face above a familiar uniform staring in at them with an all too familiar expression. Joe stretched out to find the button that would lower the window. "Hi, Andy."

Constable Andrew Stark of the Ontario Provincial Police nodded calmly. "Joe." He peered inside the cab until Will managed to extricate his head from under Joe's right knee, then added, "Will. Good to see you both."

"You too, Andy," Will said, his voice only a little strained by his odd position. "What brings you out this way?"

Andy sighed. "I wish I could say I was called to intervene in another strange fight between the Sutton twins, but I'm afraid it was a bit more serious."

Joe shifted his weight enough to let Will sit up and then swung his own legs around. The struggle had somehow resulted in the two of them swapping positions, and Joe was now in the driver's seat. He wished he could go back to wrestling with Will, because Andy didn't sound like he was joking.

It couldn't be anything *too* bad, Joe reassured himself. Andy had been there the night Joe's parents had died, so Joe knew what Andy's face looked like when he had truly awful news to share. He didn't look like that now. "The Waltons?" Joe guessed. The Suttons' closest neighbors seemed like a fairly normal family as long as the parents stayed off the booze, but when they slipped up, things got really bad really fast.

Andy nodded. "The girls hightailed it to your place, and Sarah called us. I came out to check on Del and Martina, but they were already sleeping it off by the time I got there." He checked his watch. "They must have started pretty early this morning, I guess. Lacey got home from work and saw what was going on, and she grabbed the younger ones and got out of there." It was what they'd told Lacey to do: don't ask questions, don't try to intervene, just get her two sisters to safety and let someone else take care of things. Joe was glad she'd listened to them.

"They're still at our place?"

Andy nodded. "Sarah and Dave are out there with them, said they'd stay until you guys got back. You okay to babysit tonight? I don't want them alone if Del decides he wants his family back."

"Yeah, no problem," Joe said. And just to be on the safe side, he asked, "You took Del's gun last fall, right?"

"Yeah, and I checked around in case he'd got his hands on another one somehow, but there was no sign of anything."

Not completely reassuring, but the best Joe supposed they could expect. He really didn't think Del would get violent, at least not against someone bigger than he was. "We'll keep them until you get back to us, then?"

"Yeah, if you don't mind. I'll call around and see what other options there are, but you know how things are. Those kids'll lie their heads off if it keeps them from getting put in the system."

Joe nodded tiredly. The kids had clearly decided it was better to live together in a less than stable home than to be separated and put into foster care. He remembered how important it had felt for him to keep his own family together after his parents' death and couldn't judge the kids for their current attitude. "We'll keep an eye on them," he said.

"Keep us in the loop, Andy," Will said from the passenger seat. "Let us know if we can do anything else to help."

"Will do." Andy straightened a little, then bent back down. "So I can trust you two to drive straight home, now, without stopping for anymore... whatever the hell that was?"

"I'm the one driving now," Joe said firmly. "No more trouble."

"So it was a driving dispute?" Andy looked like he was pretty sure he already knew the answer.

But Andy was used to being lied to. "Essentially," Joe agreed, and he started the engine as Andy turned away. Joe noticed that Andy stayed in his cruiser, watching, until the pickup had pulled away and driven off without incident. He felt a pang of sympathy for the cop: it was hard to serve and protect people who wouldn't tell him what was going on and didn't want his help half the time anyway. But he didn't need to worry about Joe or any of the other Suttons. They could take care of themselves.

"The Walton situation isn't a crisis," Will said as they turned into their long driveway. "This has happened before, and there's nothing we can really do about it anyway. It's not a crisis. Not a big deal."

Joe cast a quizzical look at his brother. "Thanks for talking me down, there. I was about to get hysterical, but I feel much better now."

"No, what I mean is...." Will sighed in frustration. It was only slightly theatrical. "The Walton drama should not get in the way of my main message, which I'm about to deliver."

"You really want to try delivering a message again?"

"Yes," Will said firmly. He turned to look at his brother as Joe pulled the truck to a stop near the side door of the house. "Because the family is doing well. We've hit some rough spots, but we've pulled through. And I know you were the one who carried a lot of the weight; I mean, I tried too, but you were home more, and you're just... I don't know, you're better at that shit than I am. Calmer. Whatever. But we're all fine right now, and maybe it's your turn to have a little drama, you know? If you want to do something stupid? Take a risk, take a vacation, take up skydiving... take a chance on love... whatever. We'd be here for you if it didn't work out. Okay?"

Joe didn't want to laugh at his brother, but it wasn't easy to resist. "So, what, I have a two-minute window of opportunity here? I should seize the day and do something stupid?"

"It might last longer than two minutes. Or a day. Whatever."

"Nick's been quiet for too long. He's probably building up to something big. And I told you Ally's science teacher called, right? No idea what that's about, but it can't be good." Joe pushed his door open but didn't get out of the truck. "But none of that's getting in my way, Will. I don't do stupid shit because I don't like being stupid. It's that simple."

"Okay, I knew I shouldn't have used that word. I don't mean 'stupid' like setting the barn on fire. I just mean... yeah, like you said, you should seize the day. Live a little. You've got the rest of your life to look after cattle and cut down trees and fix shit."

"I've got the rest of my life to fuck pretty-boy wedding planners too. But I don't plan to start doing it."

"You're not rich enough to be a dirty old man, Joe." Will finally opened his own door. "At least not one that's getting any action. You need to make hay while the sun is shining. We are never going to be better-looking than we are right now, and I really don't see you doing much to take advantage of that reality."

"You and Lindsey still good?" Joe was mostly trying to change the subject, but it had suddenly occurred to him that he hadn't seen Will's girlfriend in at least a week.

"We're hitting a bit of a rough patch," Will said slowly. "But it'll work out."

"Or it won't, and *you* can have the next family crisis." They both climbed out of the truck, but Joe stopped after a step or two and looked across the hood at his brother. "You okay?" he asked, his tone gentler. "Anything we can do?" Will usually told Joe everything without prompting, and it was a bit strange to realize something had been going on that Joe hadn't known about. And he felt guilty that he hadn't noticed any weirdness, hadn't even noticed Lindsey's absence. He needed to pull his head out of his ass and pay more attention to his family.

"It's fine," Will said firmly. "Just sorting through some stuff. Figuring out what the next level is." And he arched an eyebrow in Joe's direction as they started toward the house. "That isn't something you'd know anything about, of course, since you never let things get past the first level."

Of course it circled back around to Joe and how he was doing everything wrong. "Maybe I'll give Del Walton a call and ask him for his advice on a lasting relationship," he said in a voice he was sure wouldn't carry to any other ears. "There's a couple that took some chances, and look how well it worked out for them!"

"Well, you're neither an alcoholic nor an asshole, so I think you might pull things together a bit more smoothly than they did." Will caught Joe's arm just before he pulled the mudroom's screen door open. The three dogs waiting on the other side of the door squirmed impatiently, but both men ignored them. "I just want you to be happy. Okay? I want you to have some fun, and I want to know that the family isn't getting in the way of all that."

Just then an excited squeal came from inside the house, and a pint-sized body sped toward them. "Joe! Joe!" Austin pushed his way through the canine crowd and stretched up to reach the latch on the door. "Will!"

"Hey, buddy." Joe dodged the edge of the screen door as it swung toward them and crouched down to welcome Austin into his arms. He was quick, swooping the blond four-year-old up before the dogs closed in for their own greetings. "Hey, guys," Joe said, using his free hand to ruffle a few silky ears. Then he looked over at his brother and said, "You really think all this is something that makes me *un*happy?" He pressed a kiss to Austin's temple. "You think I need to escape from this?" He shifted Austin around until he could see the boy's face. "What'd you do today, buddy? Anything fun? Did you make me dinner?"

"We swimmed. There was...." Austin searched his mind for the new word, then smiled as if it didn't matter. "There was something. And a dead frog, and a fish kissed my toes."

"Nice. Sounds like a good day. Now what about dinner? Did you at least *help* make me dinner?"

Austin shook his head sadly. "Sarah said no."

"I said he had to wash his hands first," Sarah said from the kitchen. She leaned into the doorway, her smile warm if a little tired. "Apparently that was out of the question."

Joe gave Austin his sternest look. "You've got to wash your hands, buddy. Nobody wants to eat dirt." He shifted his gaze toward Sarah. "Is there anything left for him to do?"

She shrugged. "I guess the salad could use some more veggies."

"Hear that, buddy? The salad needs work! Let's go wash up, and then we'll make the salad special, okay? Maybe some extra... cucumbers?"

Austin was clearly torn between his no-washing philosophy and his desire to do important things with his uncle. "Not cucumbers," he finally said. "Peas."

"Peas, huh? Okay, that sounds tasty, if we have any. Let's wash up, and then we'll look in the oven."

Austin shook his head as Joe headed for the bathroom. "Not oven. We look in the fridge."

"The fridge? For vegetables? No, I don't think so. We should look under your pillow." Joe turned on the faucet and lifted one leg so Austin could sit on his knee while they both ran their hands under the warm water.

"Not pillow! Fridge!"

Joe sudsed up his hands and wrapped them around Austin's perfect, tender fingers. "Maybe in the barn?" he suggested.

Austin threw himself back into Joe's chest, his giggles so deep and real his whole body vibrated. "No!" he shouted. "The *fridge*."

"Wash, buddy," Joe directed quietly. "Scrub those fingers, get all the dirt off." As Austin leaned forward, Joe lowered his head until their cheeks were touching, and Austin pressed his soft face against Joe's rough stubble for one moment of pure affection. Joe would never take this for granted, but he forced himself to record the memory and then push forward. "Good washing. Let's dry those hands and then go find the vegetables in the clothes dryer."

"*The friiiiiidge!*"

Joe held the towel while Austin mangled it. "Oh. The fridge." He tucked the towel back into the rack and shifted Austin back up to his hip. "Yeah. I think we should look for puppies in the fridge!"

Austin's eyes were wide with glee. "Not puppies! Vegetables!"

"If that kid puts a dog in the fridge, I'm blaming you," Will said as they headed past him.

"There's only one kind of dog that goes in the fridge," Joe said seriously, his gaze locked with Austin's. "What kind of dog is that?" He waited, got no answer, and added, "When they come out of the fridge, we might put them on a stick and roast them over the fire...."

"A hot dog!"

"Yeah! Hot dogs go in the fridge. Not real dogs. Right?"

"Right!"

Joe carried Austin into the kitchen and set him on the floor in front of the refrigerator. "Okay, Mr. Clean Hands, find us some vegetables." He turned to his sister and quietly asked, "Where are the Waltons?"

"Down at the lake with Ally and Dave. They were looking kind of frayed; I figured a bit of sun and exercise might do them good."

Joe nodded. "I'm glad you were here." He gave her a half hug and kissed the top of her head. "You staying for dinner?"

"No. Dave and I want to have some newlywed time. But there's two meatloaves in the oven, baked potatoes, salad, and whatever vegetables you pull out of the freezer."

"Nice. Thanks."

"How was the church?" Sarah was paying a little *too* much attention to Austin, and her question was working pretty hard to sound casual.

Joe groaned loudly enough that Austin glanced up at him before returning to his vegetable quest. "You weren't in on that, were you?"

"Not in on it. But I don't think it was a terrible idea. I mean, maybe not *that* guy. But *a* guy. That'd be nice for you. I mean...." She turned to look at him. "Nick's gone, probably for good. I'm married and have my own place. Will... you know Lindsey wants them to move in together, right? He's dragging his feet, but if he went, and then if Ally goes away to school next year, it'd be just you left. It's a big house for just you. Won't you be lonely?"

"Just me?" Joe crouched down next to Austin and looked up at Sarah. "Me and the vegetable man!" He didn't want to listen to Sarah detail the dissolution of their family and didn't want to think about Will moving in with Lindsey, or what it would mean if he *didn't* move in with her. He absolutely didn't want to wonder why Sarah knew something about Will that Joe didn't. No, he didn't want any of those thoughts taking up space in his brain. Instead, he reached into the fridge and pulled out a block of cheddar. "Carrots!" he said happily.

"No, that's *cheese!*" Austin replied with a delighted snort, and the game continued. Joe and Austin had their own little world. It was a strange land of misidentification and grubby fingernails, but Joe liked it there. Everyone else should just mind their own business.

CHAPTER THREE

"I'LL TURN it back into an office eventually," Mackenzie said self-consciously. "This is just short-term."

Kristen nodded and looked around the small room. Mackenzie had bought a metal bedframe and mattress at the thrift store and was using an old wooden shelf from the back of the church as a bedside table. The few clothes he'd brought with him were carefully tucked into a dresser he'd picked up at the same time he bought the bed. It probably looked like a monk's cell, but Kristen smiled at him. "It's not quite as nice as Nathan's condo," she acknowledged with gracious understatement, "but it's all yours."

"Ours," he said as he ruffled Griffin's ears. The dog had been trotting all over the basement, sniffing everything he could reach, but had never let himself get out of sight of his master. He was clearly not interested in being abandoned again, and Mackenzie was feeling just as attached. Nathan had never wanted the dog on the bed with them, but Mackenzie knew he'd be snuggling up with Griffin that night. "Let's go upstairs. I can show both of you the best part of the place."

The back stairs were closer, but they were utilitarian and opened into a sort of service area. Mackenzie wanted

Kristen to get the full impact of the church, so he led her back through the basement to the front of the church and then up the stairs to the narthex. He was startled when he realized someone else was already there. "Will. Hi."

"Joe," the man corrected, and then he crouched to Griffin's eye level. "Hey, pup," he said softly, and he extended his hand, fingers curled underneath. Griffin gave the hand a cursory sniff and then charged forward to greet the man with enthusiasm that did credit to both his golden retriever and his poodle ancestry. "Hey, there," Joe said easily, his hands confident and gentle as he ran them over Griffin's body.

Joe Sutton. The bastard was giving more attention to a dog than he'd ever given to Mackenzie. There were fifty other things Mackenzie should be worrying about, and over the past week he'd managed to do a pretty good job of forgetting the irritation from his first meeting with the Sutton brother, but now it flared back up. But he wouldn't get anywhere by expressing it. "You're working today?" he asked sweetly. "On a Saturday? We were just going to have a quick look at the church and then go have a drink in the garden. Why don't you join us?"

The man looked as if he'd rather drink poison. "Better not," he said. "I've got work to do."

"Oh, great! What are you working on?" Mackenzie was trying to sound interested, but he was pretty sure he was just coming across as a bit of a dip. And rude, he realized as he felt Kristen shift behind him. "Oh, sorry! Kristen, this is Joe Sutton. He's doing work on the church, obviously. Joe, this is my friend Kristen. She's visiting for the weekend, and she brought my dog up for me. You've already met Griffin."

Joe straightened up, still resting one hand on Griffin's

adoring head, and nodded at Kristen. He wasn't wearing his cowboy hat, and he didn't actually *say* ma'am, but the effect was still there. Then he glanced in Mackenzie's direction. "I'm putting a tarp under your belfry."

It took Mackenzie longer than it should have to realize the man was answering his original question about what work was being done that day. "Oh. Okay. That's a job worth coming out on a Saturday for?"

"I was in town anyway, and Will wants to get that cleaned up on Monday." Joe spoke as if each word was used against his better judgment. Now that Mackenzie was looking more closely, it was pretty easy to tell the brothers apart. There was the different level of friendliness, of course, but Joe also carried himself differently. Will was a dog and Joe was a cat, Mackenzie decided. A big cat, tall and powerful, but definitely feline.

But he needed to postpone that sort of musing for another time. He tried to bring himself back to the topic at hand. "And will you be working on the rest of the jobs? It's nice to see you, but I was expecting Will to be in charge."

"Will's in charge." For the first time, Mackenzie saw a hint of personality in the man's impassive face as he twitched his lips in apparent amusement. "But he's not good with heights. So I'm doing the tarp."

There was something appealing about that tiny hint of a smile. Something intriguing about the man's quiet reserve. And something maddening about his total lack of interest. "Do you need any help with anything? I don't want you to get hurt...."

"I'll be careful." Joe looked down at the dog. "See you later, pup." He nodded in Kristen's direction. "Nice to meet you." And that was it. He turned and walked away, heading into the nave of the church without a second glance toward Mackenzie.

"He's *hot*," Kristen breathed when Joe was barely out of earshot. "Good face, *great* body! Those shoulders? Damn. And he's got a twin? One gay, one straight?" She waggled her eyebrows in Mackenzie's direction. "Both single? Get on the phone, baby, and get that brother over here!"

"There is no way you get to have the straight brother when I can't even get the gay one to *look* at me. No chance."

"Selfish," Kristen said lightly, but she didn't seem too concerned. "Now, show me your beautiful church. If there happens to be a beautiful man somewhere inside, that's just a cross we will have to bear."

"This is ridiculous," Mackenzie muttered. "I'm good at flirting! But I have no idea how to do it when the other person won't flirt back...."

"Sweetie, if the other person isn't doing it back, it's not flirting. It's harassment." Kristen paused long enough for the message to sink in, then smiled. "So show me the church."

Mackenzie did, and Kristen was suitably impressed. "I might actually *go* to a church like this. Not for the sermons, but just to soak up the atmosphere." She eased into one of the curved pews and ran her fingers reverently along the smooth wood.

"Well, not enough people around here felt that way, obviously. They closed the place because of low attendance."

They sat quietly for a while, watching Joe climbing his ladder in four different parts of the church to install ropes in the rafters. He was efficient, with no wasted movement or effort, and it was almost hypnotizing to watch him move, his muscles shifting under his worn T-shirt, his jeans snugging around his legs when he stretched in the right way, giving just a hint of the strength underneath.

"Yeah, he's a fine-looking man," Kristen said admiringly. "But you're right, I didn't get a gay vibe at all. Well, except that he didn't pay any more attention to me than he did to you." She shifted sideways in the pew and stretched her arms out to the side, arching her back to press her breasts against the front of her skimpy halter top. "Am I not worthy of a little ogling?"

"I'd ogle you all day long, if that was my thing," Mackenzie assured her.

"Maybe he's involved with somebody, and he's just *really* faithful." Kristen sighed. "That'd be so romantic."

"Lorraine said he isn't, and I'm pretty sure Lorraine knows what everyone in this whole town had for breakfast."

"Well, damn. I guess you're just not his type. And neither am I." She looked up at the arched ceiling, and in a dreamier tone of voice, she asked, "Are you really going to be able to save this place? Can you make it work? 'Cause I'm serious, I want this church available for *my* wedding, and I'm not even dating anybody right now. But it's just gorgeous. Absolutely perfect."

Mackenzie flopped against the back of the pew. "I have no idea. The whole project was so much easier when I had Nathan's deep pockets to help me out. I mean, I would have reno'ed the basement right away, hired a team of gardeners to restore that jungle outside...." He held up his blistered hands and showed the ground-in dirt that had resulted from his own attempts at gardening. "Had money for an ad campaign...."

"But you still would have been stuck in a nontrendy area. Unless Nathan was going to go into the hotel business, you still would have been working someplace where guests can't stay over, which means they can't really drink at the reception, which means... good luck getting anyone to have their reception here. And even if you figure that out, you're still someplace where there's nothing for guests to do in between the wedding and the reception. What was the plan for all that back then?"

"The plan was to not care all that much," Mackenzie admitted reluctantly. "I was supposed to be a pampered boy toy who ran a quaint gay wedding chapel as a hobby. I didn't need to make a living; I would have been happy just to break even."

"Maybe it's time to walk away," Kristen said gently. "Circumstances have changed. Maybe you need to change with them."

"But then what happens to the church?" Mackenzie was surprised to realize how strongly he felt about this. "I mean, it didn't cost that much. I could cover the mortgage payments while I wait for it to sell, especially if I'm back in the city, working. But who's going to buy it? Is someone going to turn it into a house? Because that's not what this place should be. It should be somewhere for the community to come together, somewhere for... it doesn't have to be worship, but it should be about connection, right? It should be... it's special, and it should stay that way."

"Have you talked to the chamber of commerce?" It was a new voice in the conversation. Joe Sutton was still halfway across the church, but his words carried to them with volume and clarity that made it clear he must have been able to hear everything they'd been saying since they'd entered the room. He stepped closer, and there was another twitch of his lips, another near smile as he watched them realize how much he'd heard. But he didn't comment on that. Instead, he said, "Will's part of it. Local businesses working together. Something like this could bring a lot of money to the area, so they'd probably be interested. You need somewhere for people to stay, so maybe there could be B&Bs." He shrugged. "And there's people doing crafts up here." He caught Mackenzie's gaze with a look of warning. "Not just grandma crap. Potters, and wood carvers, and a guy working with glass over near Mossberg. They sell down in the city, mostly, so your trendy friends wouldn't be slumming too hard. There's folksy stuff too—quilts or whatever. You could set up a studio tour for people, between the wedding and the reception, and collect a commission from the artists. Get a cut from the B&B people too. Maybe you could handle the bookings for them and earn a bigger percentage that way." He stopped talking almost abruptly, like a monk remembering his vow of silence. Then he shrugged as if he'd decided he could afford to share a few more words. "You're right.

This shouldn't be somebody's house. It should stay special."

"The chamber of commerce?" Mackenzie asked. He tried to sound less like an excited kid. "They could help with all of that?"

"They could help with some of it." Joe took a step backward, out of the conversation. "They meet every other Tuesday night. You should give Will a call; he'd know more."

"Those are great ideas," Mackenzie said as Joe retreated. He wanted the man to stay, to share more ideas and local knowledge. It was no longer annoying that Joe wouldn't admire Mackenzie as a sex object; now it was annoying that Joe wouldn't keep helping him with the business plan. "Thank you. Look, you heard what we were saying, and I'm sorry if you were offended. But, seriously, no subtext. We're going to have drinks in the garden, and it'd be great if you could join us. We could bounce ideas around. You know what I mean about this church being special; it'd be really useful if you could help us keep it that way."

For a moment it felt like Mackenzie had won. But then Joe shook his head. "Sorry. I've got a lot of work to do today. I just stopped in here to do this one job."

Mackenzie couldn't think of a way to counter that. "Okay," he conceded. "Thanks for the ideas. I'll definitely be giving Will a call. And sorry again, about... you know."

"Don't worry about it." And there it was, the little spark of connection, the recognition of a common trait as the man grinned at Mackenzie. "Never hurts to do a little ogling." But the connection shut down just as quickly as it had been made. Joe was back to business as he said, "Another ten minutes in here, probably, and then I'll be done."

"We'll leave you to it," Mackenzie suggested, and Kristen stood up obediently. "But we'll be in the back if you need anything."

Joe nodded his understanding and immediately returned his attention to the task at hand. Mackenzie and Kristen went back downstairs to pull their bottle of wine out of the ancient fridge in the church's spartan kitchen. Mackenzie grabbed two plastic cups, then added another, just in case.

Kristen grinned at him. "Optimist."

"Did you see him when he smiled?" Mackenzie was barely whispering, newly paranoid about the acoustics of the building. "I thought I might pass out."

"He has a very nice smile," Kristen admitted at normal volume. "And a tight tushy, broad shoulders, and... oh my God, a brain!"

"Yeah," Mackenzie said regretfully. "One that tells him I'm not his type." He bent down to get a consolation kiss from Griffin. "At least *you* love me, right?"

"I don't know if you're talking to me or the dog, but, yes, we both love you. Now let's go drink."

They made their way out to the patch of garden that Mackenzie had gotten mostly under control and sat on lawn chairs as they drank their wine. Mackenzie had his eyes closed, relaxing in the sun's warmth, when a sudden yelp was followed by a drawn-out series of pained yips coming from somewhere at the back of the property.

"Griffin!" he yelled. His wine glass tumbled to the ground as he jerked himself out of the canvas chair. He looked around wildly. "Griffin!" He saw no sign of the dog. Mackenzie ran to the top of the ravine at the back of the garden, peered around a decrepit shed that was on his list for destruction, and saw Griffin on the ground, rolling and rubbing his face. At least he was moving. But as Mackenzie drew closer, Griffin raised his head and Mackenzie gasped.

"Are those quills?" Kristen asked from behind them. "Oh my God, are those from a porcupine?"

"Oh, baby," Mackenzie said. He barely had the presence of mind to look around for the porcupine before approaching his whimpering dog. "Oh no, Griffin." He looked back at Kristen. "What do we do? We can't... we need a vet, right?"

She glanced back over her shoulder, and her whole body relaxed. "Oh, thank God," she said to someone coming around the side of the shed. "Griffin's hurt."

Joe Sutton appeared a moment later, took one look at the dog, and shook his head. "Damn," he said. "That's a good nest of them. He must have gone back for a couple tries." He squinted a little. "He's got some in his paw too. I guess he took a swat at the thing, or maybe it caught him with its tail." He looked at Mackenzie. "We can try to pull them out, but there's a lot of them, and near his eyes. I'd take him to the vet. Have you got one up here?"

"No," Mackenzie said, trying not to cry. He couldn't stand seeing any living creature in pain, and when it was one he loved it was much, much worse. "Do you?"

"Yeah, sure." Joe crouched down next to the dog and held his hand out cautiously. "Some dogs bite when they're scared, but he doesn't seem like the sort. Which is good, 'cause we'd have a hell of a time getting a muzzle on him through all those quills." He looked at Mackenzie, and his voice was gentle as he said, "This isn't a big deal. It's scary, I guess, but dogs get into porcupines all the time. The vet'll sedate him, pull the quills, and maybe give you painkillers and antibiotics or something. He'll be good as new in a few days."

Mackenzie nodded and tried to collect himself. Joe knew what he was talking about. This would all work out. "Okay," he said. "What should I do?"

"Can you carry him? Keep him from pawing or rubbing; he'll just push them in deeper. I'll call the vet and let them know we're coming." Joe checked his watch. "I think they're still open."

"What if they're not?" Mackenzie wasn't sure he wanted to hear the answer.

But Joe didn't look too concerned. "I can call Tim at home. He owes me a couple favors. But he's probably still working."

Mackenzie knew what he was supposed to do. He was a

grown man, and he should thank Joe for his help, say he could take care of it, and then do so. But Griffin was *trembling*, staring up at him with confusion and need in his big brown eyes, and Mackenzie had to use all of his strength and self-control in order to properly comfort his dog. So he didn't object to Joe's mastery. He just wrapped his arms around Griffin's thin body and lifted him as gently as he could. Kristen fussed around them, useless but concerned, and Joe pulled his phone out as they walked to the car.

"Trish? Hey, it's Joe Sutton. ... Hi. I've got a dog with a face full of porcupine quills. Can Tim take care of it? ... No, not Red. Not this time. He's a friend's dog. ... Yeah, thanks. We'll be there in about five minutes."

They were at the parking area by then, and Mackenzie paused in indecision. But Joe was still in charge, pulling open the back doors of his crew cab pickup truck. "I'll drive. Mackenzie, let me hold him for a second while you climb in, then I'll pass him to you. Kristen, can you just keep an eye on his paw and his head, make sure he isn't brushing the quills against anything? They're barbed, so the deeper they go in, the harder they'll be to get out."

Mackenzie tried to smile as he let Joe lift the suffering dog from his arms. "Thank you," he said.

"He's going to be fine." Joe waited for Mackenzie to scramble into the back of the truck, then carefully maneuvered the dog in through the door. Kristen watched from the side, then raced around to the passenger door and jumped in.

Joe made sure Mackenzie had a good grip on the dog before he swung the door shut and climbed easily into the driver's seat. It only took them a few minutes to get to the vet's, and then there was a blur of activity as Mackenzie carried the dog inside and held him while he was examined.

"We're going to give him a full anesthetic," the vet said. "It'll make it easier to remove the quills and less traumatic for him. He'll wake up with a sore face and a bit of a hangover, but no memories of people hurting him. You can stay while we're putting him under if you like, but then you'll need to go to the waiting room."

"I can't stay with him?" He looked down at the paperwork the assistant had handed to him and signed it without reading.

"We'll be more efficient without you," the vet said bluntly. "And once he's asleep, Griffin won't know whether you're here or not."

"Joe's in the waiting room," the assistant said. She smiled softly. "He'll keep you company."

Mackenzie wasn't sure what relationship the assistant was imagining between himself and Joe. "He thinks I'm an idiot, getting this upset about a few porcupine quills."

The assistant's laugh was more like a snort. "There are people up here who might judge you for that, but Joe Sutton is not one of them. The man looks after his animals like they're his babies."

"And looks after that baby like he's the future king of England," the vet added with a smile of his own. He and the assistant were busy with their hands as they chatted, preparing whatever solutions they were going to use, shaving a little patch of fur off poor Griffin's front leg, and finally slipping a needle into that naked skin. Mackenzie could feel Griffin's body relaxing almost immediately.

"We'll probably be about forty-five minutes," the assistant said, "and then a while longer for the anesthetic to wear off." She had her hand on Mackenzie's shoulder and gently guided him toward the door. "We can keep him overnight if you want, but that's not really necessary as long as there's someone at home to keep an eye on him. He'd only be getting checked on every other hour here, so if you can be with him—"

"I can be," Mackenzie said fervently. He wasn't sure he would ever let the dog out of his sight again. "And I can call you if anything goes wrong? Is there a list of things I should be looking out for? Is there an Internet site you'd recommend, or some reading about aftercare, or... anything?"

The assistant smiled. "We'll give you a sheet to take home, and it'll have emergency numbers on it. If you want any other details on helping dogs recover from quills...." They were in the waiting room now, and she smiled sweetly in Joe's direction. "You've got an expert right there."

Joe didn't stand, just nodded laconically in her direction. "It's getting so I don't need you at all, Trish. And without Red... no more overtime pay for you."

"I could survive." Her tone got a bit more businesslike. "We're looking at an hour or so. You're all going to wait?"

"We drove over together," Joe said.

Shit. That was true. Joe had said he had things to do, and instead he'd been hijacked into this adventure, and now he couldn't leave because he was the only one with a car. "We could go back to the church," Mackenzie said reluctantly. "While he's asleep. You could drop us off and we could come back in one of our cars."

"But what about all my expert advice on post-quill care?" Joe asked lightly as the assistant backed out of the conversation and closed the door behind her.

"And what if we need his help at the church?" Kristen added. "Getting things set up for Griffin's comfort, or... I don't know, really, but it seems like it'd be nice to have a local at hand. Right?" Her prompting was a little too transparent, and it made Mackenzie tired.

"No, we'll be fine," he forced himself to say. He'd love it if Joe insisted otherwise, but he had already taken up far too much of the man's time. He didn't want to play his game anymore, didn't want to seduce a cowboy or treat a decent man like a sex toy just to soothe his own bruised ego. Joe had done the right thing by helping out with Griffin, and Mackenzie should do the right thing by releasing him from his responsibility as soon as possible.

"They said there was a sheet I can read and emergency numbers on there. There isn't much more to be done, is there?"

Joe shook his head slowly. "Not really. He'll probably be groggy tonight. You should just let him rest. If you usually feed him kibble, you might want to pick up some canned food, 'cause if he got any quills in his mouth, he'll be sore for a bit. Other than that, I don't think there's much to worry about."

"Okay," Mackenzie said with more confidence than he felt. He was trying not to think about Griffin getting quills inside his poor mouth. "If you don't mind giving us a lift back to the church, we can come back over in one of our cars." He turned to Kristen with a firm expression. "Right?" he said, but his tone made it clear he wasn't really asking a question.

She nodded reluctantly. "I guess. But this is a new outfit—I don't want Griffin-blood on it!"

Mackenzie was pretty sure she'd have waded through a vat of entrails if it helped Griffin get better, but he appreciated her efforts to distract him. And Joe took her more seriously, saying, "Shouldn't be any blood. Some scabs, but if there's blood, call those emergency numbers." He looked at Mackenzie. "I'll leave you my numbers too." He pulled one of the vet's business cards from the reception counter and reached behind it to borrow a pen. "We don't get great coverage at the house, so if the cell doesn't work, try the home number." He wrote the numbers on the card, then handed it to Mackenzie. "You can call me if there's something subemergency that you're still worried about. Okay?"

That was something, at least, and Mackenzie carefully stashed the little piece of cardstock in his pocket. "Thank you," he said sincerely. "For everything."

"Hey, the service isn't over yet," Joe said with a grin. "You want a ride back out to the church, don't you?"

"I guess so, yeah." Mackenzie had already discovered there was one taxi serving the entire town, and it only ran when the owner felt like going for a drive. Getting a lift from Joe would be a much better idea. "I'll thank you again when we get there."

"It's not a big deal, man." Joe's voice was a little softer. "It's nice to see people caring about their animals."

"Even if it makes them scared and useless?"

"You weren't useless. If I hadn't been there, you would have figured all of this out on your own. Taking a hurt dog to the vet isn't rocket science."

"I think you might be giving me too much credit," Mackenzie said as he reluctantly left the vet's office and headed toward the truck. "My hands are still shaking."

"Nah," Joe said as he climbed into the driver's side of the truck. Kristen got the front passenger seat, so Joe had to turn around to look at Mackenzie. "Your hands *just started* shaking. It's your body wearing off the adrenaline now that it knows you don't need it. You were steady when you were carrying the dog around and when you were in the exam room with him."

It was true, Mackenzie realized. He'd done what he had to when it had counted. He'd been scared, but he'd handled himself. And Joe had noticed. "Thank you," he said again, and this time Joe didn't brush the appreciation away. He grinned, then turned around and drove them back to the church.

CHAPTER FOUR

JOE DIDN'T do the rest of the chores he'd planned for that day. Instead he went back to the ranch, whistled for the dogs, and headed straight for the barn. Normally he'd go find Austin first thing, but right then he wanted a little time alone.

Well, not quite *alone*, he thought as he leaned down and ran his fingers over Red's grizzled face. The dog was a Chesapeake Bay Retriever, stocky and tough, and he'd been Joe's companion since he was a pup. Now he was gray around his muzzle, and his eyes were starting to get cloudy, but he still ruled the farmyard and kept the younger dogs in their places. Joe tilted the dog's head a little and squinted down at the scars on his muzzle. "How many times have you gotten into the porcupines? Huh? How come you can't learn?"

The dog pulled his head loose and then butted his nose into Joe's hand, inviting less inspection and more affection. Joe obliged briefly, then said, "I'm going for a ride. You should stay here." There had been a time when the dog had gamely raced alongside whoever Joe was riding, but if he tried it these days, he ended up sore for a week. Joe blinked back a sudden and surprising surge of emotion. No need to get worried about Red's mortality, for Christ's sake. The dog was fine. He was a tough old bastard, and he wasn't going anywhere.

But Joe still sank to his knees and wrapped an arm around Red's burly shoulders. Things were changing. Everyone was leaving. First Joe's parents, then Nick went away to school, then Sarah got married, and now Will was thinking about moving in with his girlfriend. And Joe had returned the call from Ally's science teacher to find that he wanted to nominate her for a special science school. She'd spend her last semester of high school traveling around the world, having different experiences at different scientific facilities. The program was heavily sponsored by a government program to encourage female scientists, but it would still be expensive. But it was a once-in-a-lifetime opportunity, and there was no way Joe could get in the way of Ally's participation, especially not just because he didn't want his baby sister to move out seven months earlier than he'd been prepared to lose her. Sarah had been right; Joe was getting left behind. "You don't get to go anywhere, Red. Okay? You have to stay with me. Right?"

Red licked Joe's chin in apparent agreement, and Joe smiled as he stood up. "Okay, you can come with us today. We don't have to go fast."

Joe saddled up Misery, his cantankerous gray mare, and the three of them went for a relaxed tour of the property, the other two dogs using them as a mobile base for their own, wider-ranging explorations. The ranch was almost all rolling hills, about a third forested and the rest grassland, too steep for crops but perfect for grazing cattle. Joe had been riding the same paths since he'd first sat on a horse, and every inch of the huge property felt like home to him. He had to have an excuse for his ride, so he checked three different herds of cattle, even though he'd already done that in the morning, but mostly he just let the sounds and the smells and the sights wash over him, let the warm afternoon sun work the kinks out of his shoulders as the familiar rhythm of the horse's slow jog massaged him into a relaxed trance. Everyone was leaving him, that was true. But they were leaving him *here*, so it was okay. The land would never get old and die, never move away, never fall in love and start a new life or a new family. Joe would look after the land, and the land would look after him in return. It was a comforting thought, and he was in a much better mood by the time he turned Misery back toward the barn.

Red's ears pricked toward something in the tree line, and Joe tried to see anything moving in the area. His mind flew to the possibility of another damn porcupine—he *liked* the slow-moving, gentle herbivores, personally, but Red obviously did not. "Or maybe you like them a little *too* much. Is that it, buddy?" He looked down at the dog, who wagged his tail back, agreeing to ignore whatever had caught his attention in the forest. "Are you trying to make friends with them? Even though you know it's not a good idea, you just can't resist?"

And, of course, that brought Joe's mind back to the biggest thing he was trying not to think about: the church guy. He wasn't really that much of an asshole. Not an asshole at all, maybe. He cared about his dog, at least. And about the church. Hard to dislike someone who liked animals and historic buildings. But if Joe didn't dislike the man, then he didn't have a reason to ignore the fact that the guy was pretty close to perfect, physically. Blonder than Joe and a little shorter, but still over six feet, and absolutely put together well. His face was mobile, changing expressions with practically every sentence he or anyone else shared. At first Joe had thought it was annoying, like the guy was being overdramatic. Flamboyant, like Will had said. But now it was starting to seem like Mackenzie really *had* each of those emotions, really felt things that quickly and that sincerely. He wasn't putting on an act; he was just brave and honest enough to let his feelings show instead of hiding them away.

But Joe wasn't a farm dog, sticking his nose into a porcupine even though he'd been quilled countless times before. Sure, the quills weren't usually a serious problem, but that didn't mean they didn't sting, and it would be stupid to forget that.

But at least Joe would get some pleasure before the pain began, a part of his brain reminded him. Red was stupid to keep going after porcupines because he never even got a bite of them, just a mouthful of quills and instant suffering. Joe's adventures.... He felt a stirring down toward the saddle and knew he'd better change his train of thought if he didn't want a very uncomfortable ride home. It was enough for him to acknowledge that he generally got some significant physical rewards to compensate him for his emotional distress. So maybe he didn't need to give up on the physical altogether. Maybe he just needed to get better at keeping his emotions out of the picture. "If you could eat porcupine steak without worrying about the quills, you'd be stupid not to do it, right, buddy?"

But Red had been asked too many questions and wasn't even going to try to answer this one. He kept his gaze fixed on the next hill, trotting steadily alongside Joe without acknowledging his presence.

"You showing me how it should be done, buddy? I can be in the same place as someone... hell, the same bed... and not think about them all that much. I can do that. Right?"

The dog still didn't respond. Maybe he was just tired of hearing the same justifications, the same well-intentioned plans Joe had made before, only to ignore them as soon as he was actually involved with someone. "It's just not the way I'm made," Joe admitted. "I'm a big softy. Right, buddy?" And Joe was going to insist on an answer to this one. He stopped the horse and swung down to the ground, then crouched to let the dog approach and snuggle in against his body. "I'm a softy. Right? Right?" Red butted his forehead against Joe's chin in agreement. "Yeah. You know it and I know it." Joe wrapped his arm around the dog's shoulder and whispered into his ear, "But don't tell anyone. Okay?"

Red licked his chin, and Joe stood up and started walking. They weren't far from the barn, and he wanted to be able to let his fingers tickle along the top of Red's head as they walked together. Misery trailed along behind, the reins loose between her bit and Joe's hand. The mare had a habit of trying to bite Red's wagging tail, so Joe had to make sure he was between the two of them, but that was fine. He was in the middle of his animals, and they were in the middle of his ranch. He couldn't imagine wanting to be anywhere else. And he would damn well ignore the little voice that told him the situation might be just a tiny bit better if he had a bit of human companionship to go along with the animals.

When he got back to the barn, he led Misery straight to her yard and took her saddle and bridle off there. She hadn't worked up a sweat and wasn't the sort of horse who enjoyed being groomed or fussed over. She wasn't the sort of horse who enjoyed much, really. She worked the cattle with a calm, grumpy brilliance, like an office manager who did her job not because she loved it but because she didn't trust anyone else to be competent at it. She didn't seem to bond with anyone either, human or animal, although she did Joe the courtesy of not trying to bite him as often as she went after others. But sullen respect was not affection, and Joe knew it. Misery just wanted to be left alone.

Joe was pulling the mare's gate shut behind him, juggling her saddle and bridle, when Will approached from inside the barn. "Nice ride?"

"I was checking the cattle," Joe said defensively.

"They any different from this morning?"

Damn it. Since when did Will pay such close attention to Joe's activities? "About the same," he admitted.

Will nodded. "You got a call while you were out. Mackenzie wanted to say thanks again. He said Griffin is home, sleeping it off." He paused. "I thought he was using some sort of code or something. But I guess Griffin's his dog?"

"Seems like," Joe agreed.

"And Griffin got quilled. And you saved the day."

"I drove them to Tim's. *Tim* saved the day."

"That's not how Mackenzie sees it," Will said. His smirk was beginning to grow. "You just happened to be there when it happened?"

"You *asked* me to put up a tarp, asshole. I would have thought you were playing your stupid matchmaking game again, but I know what a pussy you are about heights, so I figured it was legit. Don't make this into something it isn't."

"But he's a pretty nice guy, right? I mean, after you spent some time with him?"

"It wasn't a *date*, Will. I drove his hurt dog to the vet."

Will sighed deeply. "I like him. I've spent three days working on the church so far, and he's been there, and I like him."

"I hope the two of you are very happy together."

Will didn't say anything for a while, just trailed after Joe as he lugged the saddle to the barn and put it away. Finally, Will said, "Lindsey wants us to move in together. Get a place in town, probably."

"Yeah. I heard." And then just because it had been bugging him, Joe added, "From Sarah. Seems like she's known about it for a while."

There was another long pause, enough time for Joe to rinse his bit and hang the bridle up on its hook. They were on their way through the wide barn door when Will said, "Sometimes it's not easy to talk to you."

It was strange how that twisted in Joe's gut. He wasn't a big talker, maybe, but he'd never thought of himself as a bad listener. And this was *Will*, for Christ's sake. They were twins, and they'd always been close. They didn't talk much, but that was because they didn't need to; they could just figure things out without bothering with words. Or at least that was what Joe had always thought. Maybe he'd been wrong about that.

He hadn't been planning on feeding the mare, but he needed something to occupy his hands, so he measured out a half scoop of sweet feed and sloshed it into a bucket. "You looking for a place? Have you got enough money to buy, or are you thinking of renting?"

"We haven't gotten that far. We're still working it out." Will sounded like he knew the conversation wasn't going quite where he wanted but had no idea how to get it back on track.

"Well, let me know. If you need help moving, or whatever."

"I'm not sure I want to do it," Will said.

"Oh." Maybe Joe was supposed to ask why. Maybe he was supposed to be the understanding sounding board for Will's angst. But he really didn't feel like it. "Look, Will, if you want to move in with her, you should move in with her. It's your life; it's your call. But if any of this is about me—if your stupid matchmaking bullshit is because you think I'm going to pine away on my own if you move in with your girlfriend—you need to get over yourself. I'm fine now, and I'll be fine when you're gone."

"And you're ready to look after Austin all on your own?"

"I do that most of the time anyway. Sarah helps out more than you do, and she doesn't even live here anymore." Joe stopped talking long enough to force a smile onto his face. "Lindsey's a great girl. I like her. You guys are good together." Maybe that wasn't all completely true, but it would be rude to say anything else. "This is a decision you need to make based on what's best for you, not what you think is best for me." He shook his head. "This isn't about me."

He shook the feed around in the bucket and walked slowly out to the paddock. Misery was watching him with her ears pricked forward. She was a good keeper and didn't get grain often, but that didn't mean she didn't recognize the signs.

"I think maybe I'm going to do it," Will said from somewhere back toward the barn.

Joe didn't turn around. Mostly because he didn't want to look at Will, but also because Misery was most likely to bite when she noticed someone wasn't paying attention to her. "Congratulations," he called back over his shoulder. "Like I said, let me know if you need any help moving."

"Joe," Will said, moving a little closer, "have you ever asked *me* for help with anything?"

"What?" Joe opened the gate wide enough to get the bucket inside and hooked it onto the post, then stepped away from the fence. "Have I ever...?"

"Have you ever asked *anyone* for help? You like helping other people—you help the family, you help friends, you're a volunteer firefighter, for God's sake. You're the king of helping everyone else, but when does anyone else help you?"

"What are you getting at?"

"It's okay to need people, Joe. You don't have to do everything on your own."

"You're giving me a headache. What the hell does any of this mean? I get help when I need it! This farm isn't a one-man operation."

Will wrapped his fingers around the top board of the fence and stared at his hands for a moment before turning back to Joe. "The farm's a great example. 'Cause I've seen you before a cattle drive or haying or any big job where other people are involved. You *hate* asking, you insist on paying everyone but me—which means they're not helping you, they're *working for* you— and you fuss around this place like a general preparing for D-Day, making sure everything's going to go smoothly so no one's inconvenienced." He took a deep breath and let it out slowly. "You don't let people close to you. I mean, it's great that you're independent. Great that you *can* look after yourself. But it makes it hard for other people to... I don't know. People want to be equal, right? It's not equal if you're giving all the time and we're only ever taking."

"You're really on an anti-Joe kick, aren't you?" Joe stepped away from the fence, far enough so he knew he wouldn't be able to take a swing at his brother if the next lines out of his mouth were as frustrating as the last ones had been. "I'm a pathetic loser who can't look after himself or get laid without your help, people can't get close to me, I need to change and be more like you are because there's something wrong with the way I am now. Is that a pretty good summary of this conversation? No, wait, is it a pretty good summary of every conversation we've had over the past couple weeks?" He shook his head and took another step backward. "I have no idea why you've suddenly got a problem with me. But you need to back the fuck off before *I* start having a problem with *you*. Okay?" Will's mouth opened, but no words came out, which was just as well. "You want me to ask for help? Okay, here goes: it'd help me out if you'd back off with this shit. You want to sit over there and judge me? Fine, go for it. But don't bring your judgments to me and expect me to act on them. You want us to be more equal? Stop asking me to do stupid shit. If you don't want my help, don't ask me to check the church roof or hang your fucking tarp because you're scared of heights. Okay? Instead of me changing to be more like you, maybe you could change to be more like me. Or maybe we could both just be ourselves and leave the other one alone."

Joe turned back to the horse. He was pretty sure his brother stood there for a while longer, but by the time Misery finished her treat and Joe retrieved the bucket, Will was gone.

Joe put the bucket away, checked the barn, and made his way back to the house, trying to think peaceful thoughts. Sarah was sitting in the old rocker on the front porch, watching Austin slap dandelions with a miniature golf club.

"Where's Ally?" Joe asked, settling onto the porch steps at Sarah's feet. "It was her turn to babysit."

Sarah gave Joe a strange look. Maybe his tone had been a bit accusing, because she sounded defensive when she said, "She did, most of the day. But there's a barbecue tonight over at the Waltons', and she wanted to go."

"The Waltons?" Mrs. Walton had come to pick the kids up the morning after they'd arrived. She hadn't discussed the reason the kids had needed to sleep over, just thanked Joe and Will for their hospitality and said she hoped the kids hadn't been too much trouble. It was a strange situation, and a part of Joe wanted to do something more, but a bigger part told him it was just the way the world went: families weren't perfect, but that didn't mean they should be torn apart completely. Still, Joe wasn't sure he wanted his baby sister spending a lot of time in that atmosphere.

And Sarah seemed to sense his hesitation. "It's not fair to the Walton kids if we treat them like a leper colony. Ally knows to come home if things get weird. And it's usually a few weeks, at least, between benders, right?"

Joe sighed and forced his shoulders to relax. "She's got her phone? Do they get coverage over there?"

"Better than we do. Good enough for a quick call. You're home tonight? You can go over if she needs you?"

"I'm going to be hanging out in the tree line spying on them with binoculars."

"You've got Austin too. I'm not sure he'd be much good at wilderness surveillance."

And as if to prove her point, Austin looked up from the weed he was about to destroy and greeted the new arrival to the porch with a joyful yell. "Joe! Joe! I hit the dandidelions! I'm helping!"

"You sure are, buddy. Keep at it." Joe looked toward the parking area and then up at Sarah. "Will's gone? And you're heading home? It's just me and the little man for dinner?"

Sarah nodded. "We ate that chicken for lunch, so if that was your plan, you'd better find another." She looked at him for longer than was usual, then said, "Did you and Will have a fight? He was a bit weird when he left."

Joe thought about it. "Not a fight, really. I think he's just kind of... I don't know. I guess I'm not being who he wants me to be."

Sarah frowned. "That doesn't sound like Will. I think he just wants you to be *you*, doesn't he?"

"Apparently not. Seems like there's a pretty long list of things

I'm doing wrong." Joe ran one hand through his hair, front to back, then back to front, leaving it feeling ruffled and spiky. Maybe he wasn't being fair. "He wants me to be happy. I get that. He just...." Joe twisted around so he could look at his sister more directly. "People are built different, right? Like horses are. We don't have to know exactly what's going on in Misery's brain to know she's best on her own. We've tried putting her in with other horses, and she just beats the crap out of them or comes up against someone tougher than her and gets beat up but won't back down. She's not... it's not a question of whether she's happy or not. It's just what she's suited to. She's not a horse that does well in a herd. It doesn't do any good to keep pushing her at other horses. She's a loner. That's the way she is."

Sarah nodded quietly. Then she slid off her chair and settled next to Joe on the step. "That's the way she is," she agreed softly. "The thing is, Joe, I don't think it's the way *you* are. I mean, if I look back to all the times I've seen you being really, really happy— you're with other people. The family, mostly, but Trevor too. You guys got along really well. You were happy with him. Right?"

"You can't see me being really happy when I'm alone because *you're not there*, Sarah. That's what *alone* means."

"No," she said confidently. "I don't buy it. I mean, I believe you're happy on your own. But I know you're happy with other people too. You're not like Misery." She leaned over enough to rest her head on his shoulder, and they were quiet together for a while, watching their nephew wage war on the yellow invaders. Then Sarah said, "You never talk about Trevor. He was just around one day and then he was gone. What happened?"

Sarah's voice was tentative; she knew she was treading on dangerous ground. But enough time had passed now, and Joe just sighed. "We wanted different things."

"He's moved down to the city, right?"

"Yeah."

"He wanted you to go with him?"

"Yeah."

"And you couldn't. Ally was only sixteen, Austin was three. You had commitments here. You gave up on that because of the family, and you wonder why me and Will feel guilty about *not* giving up on stuff? Why Will isn't sure he should be moving in with Lindsey and leaving you alone with the kids? When Mom and Dad died, you and Will could have given up on us, shipped us off to relatives or foster care or whatever. When Austin was born, you could have told Nick to put him up for adoption or take care of him himself, but you didn't. You've given up a lot for this family, Joe, and it makes us sad that you had to give up on Trevor too."

"I didn't give up on Trevor because of the family," Joe said firmly. "I meant it: he and I *wanted different things*. He wanted to go to the city; I wanted to stay on the farm. Seriously, Sarah, can you see me in the city? Not visiting for the weekend, but living down there? No horses, no space, trying to get Red to walk on a leash and not beat up every new dog he meets, swimming in a chlorinated, peed-in pool instead of a lake, everyone crammed in together and hating each other...." He shrugged his shoulder enough that Sarah had to straighten up, then turned so he could look at her. "I love my family, and it's absolutely part of the appeal of this place. But I didn't give up on some big-city dream, Sarah. I like it here. This is where I want to live. There's nothing for you to feel guilty about." He frowned. "And I haven't given up *anything* for this family. The family's a good thing. Keeping us all together, taking care of Austin... that's *good* stuff. It's stuff I wanted to do, not stuff I had to."

She nodded slowly. "Yeah. I believe that. But it's *all* you want?" Her raised eyebrows gave Joe the warning he needed before she said, "You don't even want to get *laid*, Joe?"

Having that conversation with Will was bad enough. There was no way he would have it with his little sister.

But apparently Sarah didn't feel quite the same level of

discomfort that Joe did. "Come on, Joey! It'd make me and Will feel so much better if you'd get a little action. You'd be more relaxed, *we'd* be more relaxed. It'd be good for everyone." She grinned as Joe tried to squirm away, wrapping her thin arm around his broad shoulders. "Seriously, Joe, you've convinced me that you're not really making many sacrifices for the family, so it's about time you started! And you can do that by going against your better judgment and getting yourself a piece of ass. Will has found a suitable candidate for you, but I'm willing to be a bit more flexible. I won't *specify* who you need to bone, I just want you to get out there and get laid. By anyone. Just once is fine, although I think once you try it you're going to remember you kind of like it...."

"This is not an appropriate conversation," Joe protested. He raised his voice a little. "Austin! Austin! Your aunt's being crazy! Come save me!"

Austin ran over, giggling, and he wrestled Sarah away from Joe and then shrieked as she held him by his ankles and turned him upside down. Joe sat back and watched. This was what he loved. It was what he wanted. But maybe, just maybe, Sarah had a point. Maybe there was room in his life for just a little bit more.

CHAPTER FIVE

IT WAS probably crossing a line. But Mackenzie had searched his soul, and he was sure his intentions were as pure as the organic, handcrafted chocolates on the seat next to him. He wasn't trying to seduce Joe Sutton; he just wanted to thank him. And maybe get to see that glowing smile just one more time. And if the smiling led to laughing, and laughing led to touching.... Okay, his intentions weren't completely pure. But even the chocolates had gooey caramel centers.

Will Sutton had given him directions to the farm, but he'd been a bit hesitant about it, and Mackenzie really wasn't sure why. Had spending time with Mackenzie made the contractor change his mind about matchmaking? That was a bit insulting. But Will had been nothing but friendly and helpful, both at the church and at the chamber of commerce meeting the night before. Maybe Mackenzie had imagined the reluctance.

He came to a long gravel driveway, just as Will had described—the only opening in a dense patch of forest at the road. But the trees soon thinned, and Mackenzie found himself driving between two large fields, both with tall grass waving in the breeze. After that the driveway was lined with a post-and-rail fence, horses grazing peacefully on one side, and finally Mackenzie could see the house. Or the homestead, maybe, because this really did feel like something out of the Old West. A big, old wooden house with a wraparound porch, several small outbuildings Mackenzie wanted to believe were bunkhouses for the cowhands, and a hulking barn perched halfway up a gently sloping hill. The property wasn't palatial, but it seemed prosperous enough. Well cared for without being overly manicured. It felt like a home, Mackenzie decided.

He pulled into a broader patch of gravel next to the pickup he recognized as Joe's, then gave himself a moment to deal with the flash of self-doubt. Was he invading the man's privacy?

No, this was just a social call. How many people had knocked on the church door and invited themselves in since Mackenzie had arrived? This was the country way of doing things.

He grabbed his chocolates and headed for the front door of the house. Then he remembered how many of his visitors had come to the back door of the church. Was that a church-specific custom, or was the front door only used for formal occasions in the country?

He was standing in the gravel, dithering, when he saw a familiar shape up the hill by the barn. Mackenzie had only seen two men with shoulders like that since he'd arrived in Falls Creek, and he'd just left Will working at the church. Mackenzie had found his target.

He was about halfway up the hill when the dogs noticed him. There were three of them, none taller than Griffin but all chunky, solid, farm-dog-looking creatures, and they were approaching at great speed with quite a bit of barking. They probably would have eaten Griffin for breakfast. It was entirely possible they were about to eat *Mackenzie* for breakfast.

"Hey!" came an authoritative voice from up the hill. "Knock it off."

The dogs stopped running and barking, at least, but they still stared at Mackenzie with malevolent fascination. He forced himself to keep walking and tried to look nonchalant about it all.

"Hi!" he called, and one of the dogs, a grizzled, old reddish-brown brute, growled as if Mackenzie had just insulted his mother.

"Hi," Joe said, walking down the hill toward him. Joe tickled the top of the angry dog's head with his fingers as he passed, and the animal responded as if the man had flipped a switch on his personality. The rage disappeared and was replaced by indifference as the dog trailed along, his gaze on his master as if waiting for the next command. "Everything okay?"

"Yes," Mackenzie said. He didn't plan to take his eyes off the dogs quite yet, but he managed a quick smile. "I hope you don't mind my coming out. I just wanted to say thanks, again." He held out the wrapped box of chocolates Kristen had overnight-mailed from the city. "For helping with Griffin, but even more for your idea about the chamber of commerce."

"Will said it went well," Joe said. He took the box from Mackenzie's hand but held it between two fingers as if it might be full of snakes. Then he held up his other hand, covered in some sort of green slime. "I'm cleaning out the water tanks," he explained. "The algae grows fast in the heat of the summer."

"Oh." Mackenzie really didn't think he had anything to add to a conversation about water-tank algae. "I guess the work never ends on a place like this."

There was a moment's pause that made it clear Joe was thinking about something. Then he wiped his hand on his jeans as if it were symbolic of some great decision. "It's kind of a relief to know you'll never be able to finish all the work; it means you don't have to keep trying to get it all done. So the workday ends when you say it does." He glanced down at his watch, then made a face. "Or at least you take breaks when you say you should. You want to come down to the house and get something to drink?"

Mackenzie wasn't sure why he was surprised by the invitation. It was just about exactly what he'd been hoping for. But he still stuttered a bit as he replied, "Uh, yeah, that'd be great, if you have time...."

Joe didn't answer, just started down the hill toward the house. Mackenzie turned quickly enough to earn a suspicious glare from the obedient dog and followed Joe down the gravel path.

"You stay out," Joe told the dog, and then he turned to Mackenzie. "He comes in at night, but he's better off outside during the day."

It sounded almost like an apology, and Mackenzie quickly said, "Sounds like a good life for a dog. I know Griffin would be outside all day if he could be."

"You didn't bring him?"

"I thought about it," Mackenzie admitted. "But I wasn't sure of the etiquette. I'd never think of bringing a dog with me to visit someone in the city, so it seemed a bit weird to do it here."

"Probably just as well. Not because of the etiquette, but because we'd have to tie Red up. He takes the top dog job pretty seriously." Joe led the way through a crowded but tidy mudroom into a bright country kitchen. Mackenzie waited while Joe washed his hands in the kitchen sink, then tried to keep his eyes off the man's denim-clad ass as he leaned over to look in the fridge. "Lemonade, milk, water, or beer," he said as he straightened. "Or I could brew some iced tea if you're okay waiting a few minutes. Or regular tea. Or coffee."

"Whatever you're having," Mackenzie said.

Joe checked his watch again, then said, "Too early for beer?"

"It's past noon. But how much work do you still have to do today?"

Joe shrugged. "I don't think a few beers will get in the way of my ability to clean water tanks."

"A *few* beers, now." Mackenzie's good intentions were fading fast. This man was gorgeous, he was finally being friendly, and they were about to consume alcohol together. There was no way Mackenzie would be able to turn off his flirting instinct, and for the first time he was getting the feeling there was a chance of reciprocation. The gaydar that had failed him at the church was suddenly pinging at full strength, and he felt a new sense of confidence. Farm etiquette, angry dogs, and algae might be beyond his experience, but flirting with hot men was his specialty. "This is sounding like more than a little break. I'd better get comfortable."

"You can get as comfortable as you want." It should have sounded sleazy, but there was something about the delivery that made the line work. Maybe it was the appreciative gaze Joe was *finally* sending Mackenzie's way or the easy, relaxed movements as the man pulled two bottles out of the fridge and twisted off both lids before handing a bottle to Mackenzie. Yeah, something had definitely changed, and whatever it was, Mackenzie liked it. A lot.

"Here?" he asked, running his fingers along the back of one of the kitchen chairs. "Outside?" He said the words slowly enough, kept his gaze level enough that it was clear he was wondering about the best location for any activity Joe might want to take part in.

"Upstairs?" Joe suggested, his voice so casual Mackenzie actually wondered if it was possible he'd misheard the word. But there was no mistaking the look in Joe's eyes or the seductive slowness with which he raised the beer bottle to his lips and took a deep swallow. Damn, country boys moved fast.

"What changed?" Mackenzie hadn't planned to ask the question. Now that it was out, he really hoped the answer didn't interfere with whatever was going on in that kitchen.

Joe looked down at the bottle in his hands, then back up at Mackenzie. "You just caught me in the right mood, I guess."

"And what if I'm not in that mood?" Jesus, what was he doing? The words had been spoken flirtatiously, but what was the point in flirting when the deal was already so clearly ready to be closed?

But Joe didn't seem upset by the coyness. He just took another long swallow from his bottle. He was half done with the beer, and Mackenzie still hadn't taken a sip. "If you're not in the mood, we should go outside and sit on the porch. It's a nice day."

"It's a bit hot," Mackenzie said, and he finally lifted the bottle to his lips. He wasn't a big beer fan, but the bitter taste helped clear his mind a little. "And I have fair skin. I don't do well in the sun."

Joe stepped closer, his gaze trailing down over Mackenzie's face toward the skin exposed by the opening of his V-neck shirt. Joe nodded. "Maybe we should stay in, then." Another step and he was close enough to slowly reach out with his bottle and press the cold glass against the skin of Mackenzie's neck.

Mackenzie drew in a quick breath and felt goose bumps rise as Joe slid the bottle slowly down, along the top hem of his shirt and up to his neck on the far side. They were closer now somehow, close enough that when Joe spoke Mackenzie could feel the faint puff of breath along the cooled skin of his neck. "But not here. No one's home, and no one *should* be home. But I don't want to get walked in on. Upstairs or outside."

More touching or no more touching. It wasn't a difficult decision. "Where are the stairs?"

Joe pointed his chin toward the front of the house, and Mackenzie pressed on. He could sense Joe close behind him, but there was no contact, no words. It was all so efficient, so strangely impersonal, that Mackenzie began to feel a bit like one of the cows he imagined Joe herding all day.

"First on the right," Joe said as they reached the top of the stairs. Mackenzie took a couple steps and pushed the door open, stepped inside, and heard Joe close and lock the door behind them.

The room was bright, with crisp white curtains fluttering in front of an open window. Joe didn't have much furniture: a bed, a dresser, and a bench by the window that looked like it might have been carved from a single log and then not polished up all that carefully. Rustic, Mackenzie supposed, but not really to his taste. It felt like the bedroom of a teenager, not a grown man. At least there weren't posters on the wall, and he had a full-sized bed. Maybe even a king. Still, it wasn't what he was used to. It was nothing like Nathan's ornate master suite, with its cool modern furniture, fireplace, and wall of floor-to-ceiling windows. But that was the point, he reminded himself. Joe wasn't Nathan. Joe wasn't a cheating bastard who had dumped Mackenzie for someone he'd be better able to push around and manipulate.

And Joe apparently wasn't quite as arrogantly insensitive as Nathan, either, because when Mackenzie turned around, Joe was leaning against the door, watching Mackenzie judging the room and clearly recognizing that he wasn't impressed. "You still with me?" he asked quietly, then shifted so he wasn't blocking the only exit. The invitation to leave was so clear it was almost a dare.

"*You* still with *me?*" Mackenzie stepped into Joe's space, noticing again that the man was a little taller and a little broader in the shoulders. Nathan had been shorter than Mackenzie and very slender, almost delicate. A person might have found him effeminate if they hadn't seen the way he moved or heard the way he spoke to those around him. Absolute alpha male. Possibly a bit of a Napoleon complex. But Mackenzie wasn't talking to Nathan, he was talking to Joe, and it honestly looked like the man was considering his question.

"No. I'm not with you. Not like this." Joe didn't move, but somehow his whole body shifted back to its former unreceptive status. "Not with you thinking about someone else."

Okay, that was a bit too accurate for comfort. Mackenzie thought about denying it but shrugged instead. "So make me forget about him. That's what I'm here for."

Joe nodded slowly. "Yeah, that explains it," he agreed. "You're trying to forget somebody else, and I'm trying to prove something to people who shouldn't be involved in my sex life at all." His grin was slow and not entirely kind. "Ain't we a pair."

Mackenzie was pretty sure he should hear a bit more about the whole 'proving something' thing, but before he could ask for details Joe surged forward and shoved Mackenzie a step backward until he hit the wall. It had happened fast and smooth, and it definitely got Mackenzie focusing on what was happening inside the room, especially when Joe followed through with his own body, using it to pin Mackenzie against the wall. He lifted Mackenzie's unresisting arms above his head and held them there with one hand while he slid the other down to cup Mackenzie's jaw.

"We're doing this?" Joe asked with an intriguing growl.

"Hell yeah," Mackenzie breathed. His mind flew back to Nathan. The man had dominated him just as confidently as Joe was, but there had been no physical superiority there, just psychological power. With Nathan, Mackenzie had always known that if he wanted to, he could resist and refuse, as long as he was prepared to deal with the unpleasant consequences. There had been times he'd almost done it, but never quite. With Joe, that safety valve wasn't there, but somehow Mackenzie was even more confident that he wouldn't be pushed further than he wanted to go. Joe would stop as soon as Mackenzie asked him to. The knowledge was intoxicating. Joe would act like he was in control, but, really, Mackenzie held all the cards. But Joe was frowning at him again. "You're right," Mackenzie admitted before the accusation had to be spoken. "I *was* thinking about him. But not in a good way. Does that help?"

Apparently it did. Joe pressed forward again, working his thigh between Mackenzie's and then grinding upward while he touched Mackenzie's lips with his for the first time. No affection in the contact, just dominance and desire, an insistent tongue that claimed Mackenzie's mouth and left him gasping. And Joe was busy with his free hand as well, working his way inside Mackenzie's shirt and up over his ribs, finding his nipple and tweaking it almost painfully. There was so much going on it should have felt frenzied, but Joe was clearly in control of it all.

Mackenzie was just trying to keep his balance and soon lost the ability to catalogue individual sensations. He had no idea when his shirt had been lifted over his head, no idea how his arms had been lowered and then somehow trapped still in the sleeves of the half-off shirt, but he knew he was frustrated when he tried to reach for Joe's strong chest and couldn't get to it. And he could tell from the light in Joe's eyes that the man had noticed the frustration and found it exciting.

Joe pushed away a little farther, just enough distance so he could get a good view, and Mackenzie imagined what he must be seeing. A man trapped by his own clothing, his lips wet and kiss-swollen, his eyes wide with excitement... his cock straining against the fabric of his jeans....

It was the final point that seemed to catch Joe's attention, and he reached down to run his fingers firmly along the visible bulge. Mackenzie let his hips push forward and leaned out to try to capture Joe's mouth and persuade him with a kiss, but Joe grinned and shoved him back against the wall. "A pampered boy toy," he said musingly. "That's what you called yourself that day in the church." He squeezed Mackenzie's cock through the denim while he slowly scratched his way down Mackenzie's chest with the fingernails of his other hand. "I'm not going to pamper you. But I definitely don't mind playing with you a little."

"Just get on with it," Mackenzie groaned. The pressure on his cock was halfway between torture and ecstasy, and the strain between the two extremes was too much to handle.

"Patience," Joe murmured.

It went against years of conditioning, but it felt really good when Mackenzie squirmed his arms out of his shirt and brought his hands around to catch Joe by the hips. "Fuck patience," he said, and then it was his turn to spin them around, his turn to press in with his body and wedge his thigh just right, and when he pressed up, it was his turn to hear his partner gasp.

The breathless chuckle that came from Joe was new to the mix, though. "I guess we're both playing," he said.

"Take your shirt off." Mackenzie leaned back enough to give Joe room to comply and was rewarded with obedience and the sight of a broad, toned chest with a light covering of dark hair. The contrast with Mackenzie's own carefully waxed body was intriguing, and he let himself lean forward to rub the different textures together.

"Pants?" Joe suggested, and Mackenzie dropped to his knees as if he'd been shot. He licked his lips in anticipation as he worked on Joe's fly. Even through the clothes he could tell the man's cock was going to match the rest of his body in size, but he wanted to see the details. And when he eased Joe's pants and underwear down and off, he was greeted with a sight that exceeded his expectations. It was hard to say why some cocks were beautiful and others were ugly, but this was definitely one from the first group. Long and straight, smooth skin just a bit darker than the rest of Joe's body, head plump and well-defined, with just a tiny glistening of moisture at the tip…. Mackenzie tasted, and then he went to town. He loved sucking cock, and everything about Joe's was perfect. There was even the right scent—a tiny bit of muskiness that suggested the man had been working that day, but nothing overwhelming. Mackenzie swallowed as deeply as he could, eased off, then worked his way back on. He licked, he sucked, he let his teeth graze ever so gently along the tender skin. God, he could suck this cock all day.

So why were Joe's hands in his hair, pulling him away? He glanced up resentfully and saw Joe's tight face looking down at him. "If this is all we're doing, keep going," Joe said. "But if you want to do anything else…."

Oh. That was a good point. And a surprisingly hard choice. Mackenzie had come upstairs thinking in terms of a good hard fuck, but damn, he really wanted more of this too. He wanted to taste Joe, wanted the thrill of knowing he had power over this man's pleasure. But, God, the intensity of feeling that perfect cock stretching him open, plunging deep inside him… that would be wonderful too. Clearly this needed to be more than a one-time event, because there was a lot Mackenzie wanted to do with the body he was kneeling in front of. For now, though, he was undecided.

That was when Joe said, "I want to fuck you."

"Yup," Mackenzie agreed quickly. It was an excellent idea. Hard to argue with, really. He gave the tip of Joe's cock a quick good-bye kiss, then stood up and kissed hello to Joe's lips. Their bodies felt natural as they pressed together, both warm and strong, soft skin over hard muscle. Joe made quick work of their remaining clothes and then came back to the kiss. He wrapped his fingers tight around Mackenzie's cock, his callouses and scratches rough and tantalizing as they moved against Mackenzie's most sensitive skin.

They didn't rush. Just a half step followed by a few deep kisses, then another half step, until finally Mackenzie bumped up against the side of the bed. His breathing was already heavy, his senses overloaded by too many sensations, but everything got even more intense when Joe boosted Mackenzie up onto the bed and pushed him backward. He ended up lying on his back with his ass on the edge of the bed and his legs wrapped around Joe's tight body. He could feel Joe's cock, not trying to push inside but sliding easily along the crease of Mackenzie's ass, a comfortable, tantalizing hint of what was to come.

Joe looked down at him. "Like this?" he asked. "You good?"

"Perfect," Mackenzie replied, and he used his legs to pull Joe in a little tighter. But Joe pulled away. He didn't go far, just leaning over and stretching to the side, but it was absolutely the wrong direction. Then Mackenzie heard the sound of a drawer being pulled open and let his legs relax a little. Joe was just taking care of things. Taking care of both of them. He wasn't trying to get away.

It only took a moment before Joe's attention was back on Mackenzie. Something cool dribbled onto his ass, then Joe teased at his opening with a slippery finger. "Just fuck me," Mackenzie moaned. "I'm not a virgin!"

"Shhh," Joe replied, and slipped his finger just inside before pulling out and going back to teasing around the rim. Then in again, a little deeper, and maybe this *was* more prep than Mackenzie needed, but damn it felt good. And it felt good to look up and see Joe looking down at him, watching his expressions, reading his body's reactions and trying to do more of whatever Mackenzie seemed to be enjoying. It made the word *lover* flash into Mackenzie's mind, but he fought to dismiss it. It was a stupid word to start with, and even if it were a better word, that wasn't what this was. *Trick, fuck buddy, sex partner, this guy I know.* Any of those would be more accurate, and Mackenzie needed to remember that.

And then the pressure from Joe's finger was replaced by something much larger. Mackenzie didn't have to work at keeping intrusive thoughts out of his head anymore because there were no thoughts at all, just the instinctive mental sigh that came from feeling the exact right thing at the exact right time. He tensed and relaxed in a slow, perfect rhythm, resisting and then welcoming the intrusion, and Joe moved in the same pattern, easing his way deeper and deeper inside. Mackenzie let his head flop back against the mattress and gave in to the sensations. He tried to choke back his moan of pleasure but then remembered he wasn't with Nathan anymore; he didn't have to worry about the old rules. Releasing that last bit of inhibition took Mackenzie somewhere even better than he'd already been, someplace where he didn't even *know* if he was making noises because he was barely even in his body, just floating away from everything in a peaceful sea of sensations and pleasure. He could feel the waves building, knew that as good as they would feel, they would also wash him back to shore and back to reality, so he held off, tried to maintain his relaxation as long as he could. But the building pressure was too much, Joe's cock and hand insisting Mackenzie give in, and finally it washed over him, rushed him along, wave after wave of pleasure coursing through his entire body and driving him along.

He was just beginning to find his bearings, just struggling out of the crashing surf, when he felt Joe's rhythm falter. He forced his eyes open so he could watch Joe lose his focus and take his own journey through the waves. The condom had been a good idea, but Mackenzie found himself resenting it. He wanted to imagine Joe coming deep inside him, his seed spreading even farther than his long cock had been able to reach. Mackenzie wanted Joe to be leaving something behind. As it was, when Joe straightened up and slowly pulled out, Mackenzie was left feeling nothing but empty.

Well, empty and satisfied. Relaxed. Joe was fussing about, using someone's underwear to clean up, and Mackenzie hoped it wasn't his, because he didn't want to go home commando. But he couldn't be bothered to check. When he felt his legs being lifted he managed to help a little, shifting around so he was in a better position for sleeping, and maybe there was something warm being wrapped around him, but he didn't pay any attention to what it might be. He didn't pay attention to anything until a gentle hand shook his shoulder.

"Hey, man, wake up." Mackenzie opened one eye to see Joe crouched next to the bed. "Sorry, but... people are going to be getting home soon. Probably best that you're not here... or at least not upstairs...."

Joe sounded apologetic. And he damn well should. Mackenzie was comfortable, lying there in the big old bed with cool air gently blowing in from the window, the heavy old-fashioned quilt wrapped around his shoulders.... "I like this room," he mumbled.

"Yeah, okay." Joe sounded like he wasn't sure what to do with that tidbit of information. "You can come visit it again sometime if you want. But I don't want Austin confused about anything, so it'd be good if you weren't in my bed when he gets home."

It took Mackenzie longer than it should have to figure out who Joe was talking about. "Austin's your nephew?"

"He's four. I don't... none of us do... we don't introduce him to people we don't... you know. He doesn't understand that some stuff is just casual. And my baby sister's the one picking him up from day care, and she's only seventeen. I don't introduce *her* to casual fucks, either."

Well, that cleared up any potential misunderstandings, and it was stupid for Mackenzie to feel hurt by the quick classification. He'd probably spent less than an hour with this guy, total, before jumping into bed with him. Of *course* it was a casual fuck.

He forced himself to sit up and swing his legs over the side of the mattress. His clothes had been gathered up and neatly placed within easy reach at the foot of the bed. Joe Sutton was pretty damn efficient at getting strange men out of his bedroom. Mackenzie wanted to flop back and say he was too tired to leave, wanted to try to seduce Joe back into the bed, wanted to do *anything* to mess up the sequence of events that now felt so mass-produced and impersonal.

But it was hard to claim the moral high ground over a man who was just trying to protect his family, so Mackenzie obediently pulled on his underwear—*not* the pair Joe had used for cleanup, thankfully—and then stood up and stepped into his jeans. Joe was waiting patiently, not really watching but not ostentatiously looking away. It was like changing clothes backstage at a runway show, but with less frantic haste.

"This was fun," Joe said quietly as Mackenzie pulled his shirt over his head. "And I had one of the chocolates—really good. Thanks."

Fun. Mackenzie was pretty sure he'd just had the best sex of his whole life—certainly the most intense orgasm. Maybe that had partly been because of the drought before it; not only the recovery period since Nathan had left him but also the entire too-disciplined, Nathan-satisfying expanse of their relationship. And before that Mackenzie had been just a kid, having sex with other kids who maybe didn't really know what they were doing. Maybe Joe Sutton wasn't some sort of super sex god. Maybe he was just an adult man who knew how to please his partner. "Yeah, it was fun," Mackenzie said. "If you want to do it again sometime, let me know. Maybe at my place next time, so I can keep sleeping." He managed a wry grin, enough to show this was all fine and he wasn't feeling rejected.

"In a church? Seems kind of sacrilegious...." Joe's tone was teasing, but there was still a distance to his manner.

"It's been deconsecrated." Mackenzie looked around for his sandals. "And as long as I'm living there, it had better get used to being the site of at least a little gay sex." And then, because the point needed to be made, he smiled sweetly and said, "Whether it's with you or with someone else."

Joe nodded in slow acknowledgment. "There's not that many guys up here who are out. Probably not that many who are gay; they tend to move down to the city. But I'm sure you wouldn't have any trouble finding someone if you were looking for a little variety."

"Because this is a one-time deal, you and me." Mackenzie wasn't sure why he was pushing for the final rejection; maybe it would just be better to have everything out on the table.

But Joe shrugged noncommittally. "This is a *casual* deal, as far as I'm concerned. If it happens again, great. If it doesn't... okay."

Well, at least 'happens again' had ranked slightly higher than 'doesn't' on the reaction scale. But Mackenzie was done with this conversation. He still had a little bit of happy afterglow from the sex itself, and he didn't want to wipe it out with more of this guy's noncommittal bullshit. "All right, then. I'd better get out of here before the family arrives."

They headed down the stairs without talking, and Joe guided Mackenzie back to the mudroom door and out onto the porch. The dogs greeted them cheerfully this time; Joe had probably left enough of his scent on Mackenzie's body to make it clear he wasn't a stranger. Which wasn't a thought that should send blood rushing to Mackenzie's cock.

Damn it, he'd wanted to seduce the cowboy as a way to move

on from one unbalanced relationship, not to start into a whole new unhealthy dynamic. What was he supposed to do now, throw himself at *another* man in order to forget this one?

There was no good-bye kiss and no promise of future contact. When Mackenzie got back to the church, Will was still working, and the man's knowing smirk was about the only evidence Mackenzie had that anything had even happened with Joe. Other than a pleasantly sore ass.

He was supposed to be concentrating on the church, he reminded himself. His bank account was shrinking rapidly, and while the response from the chamber of commerce had been encouraging, it had mostly been in the form of "we'll see what we can do" and "maybe I'll give so-and-so a call about that." Damn it, if the chamber of commerce didn't come through, Mackenzie wanted at least some of his chocolates back. Then he thought about his afternoon, the way Joe had checked to be sure Mackenzie was on board with everything, the simple care he'd taken to respond to Mackenzie's body, the mind-shattering orgasm, and the gentleness with which the quilt had been wrapped around him. Okay, Joe could keep the chocolates.

But he could shove his postsex attitude right up his well-muscled ass.

Chapter Six

"The idea was for you to be in a *good* mood after you got laid," Will said blandly. They were washing the dishes while Ally was upstairs reading Austin his bedtime stories, and it was the first time Will had been able to get Joe alone since Mackenzie's visit that afternoon. Will smirked a little. "Could you not get it up? Was there some other disaster?"

"Do you like to go down on Lindsey first, then fuck her? Or does she just like a good hard banging right off the top?"

"What?" Will looked at his brother as if he was wondering whether it was time to start swinging.

"Oh. Is that none of my business? Was it kind of disrespectful for me to ask that?" Joe nodded slowly. "Yeah. I can see that it would be. I guess there are some boundaries that should be respected. Sorry about that." He handed the dish he'd been drying back to Will, who was supposed to be washing. "There's still some cheese in the corner, there."

"Okay, a woman who I'm in a relationship with... a woman I might *marry*, for fuck's sake, someone who could bear my children... she is not the same as one of your one-night stands."

Joe didn't respond, just examined another dish from the drainboard and handed it back to his brother. "Cheese on that one too. You need to use the scrubby thing."

Will was still giving Joe a dirty look, but he glanced away long enough to find the plastic scrubber. "You didn't used to be so touchy," he finally said. "You're changing the rules."

"Lots of things change. It's the way of the world."

"Just so I'm fully caught up, then... this is it? I can't ask about anything having to do with your sex life anymore? I mean, I can't check in on things, make sure you're doing okay...."

"That sounds perfect," Joe said with feeling. "Yeah. You should just not even think about it, if you can manage it. If you've got to think about it, you can keep it to yourself." He squinted down at the dish Will had just placed back in the drainboard. "Also, you should probably learn how to wash a fucking plate. There's *still* cheese on that." He handed the dish back and said, "You and Lindsey are looking for a place with a dishwasher, right? A really good one?"

"I'll put it on the wish list," Will responded. He picked at the overcooked cheese with his fingernail. "You're sure you're okay with it? You and Austin are good on your own once Ally's gone? Even if she goes early for the science thing?"

"You're not planning to leave the country, are you? I mean, you'll be like Sarah, living somewhere else but still helping out around here. Right?"

"Yeah, absolutely. I mean...." He looked like he wasn't sure he even wanted to bring up the idea, but he pressed on. "Lindsey said we should offer to take Austin. If you wanted. It'd be easier with two of us...."

"No." Joe wiped the bowl in his hands with a little extra enthusiasm, then forced himself to rein it in before he broke the china. "He's good here. He knows this house, he knows me. He loves the animals and the space." And then it was his turn to say something he wasn't sure he should. "Lindsey's a bit conservative about some of that stuff. She probably thinks a kid needs a mom and a dad and all that. Right? Family values?" He saw the look on Will's face and set down the bowl he was drying. "Shit. She's not...." He'd never really warmed to his brother's girlfriend, but he hadn't had reason to believe she was.... "She's not trying to get him away from his *gay* uncle, is she?"

"Not like that," Will said quickly. "She's not homophobic, not herself. But she hears people talking. She just thinks it will be a bit hard for Austin. You know, if people judge him for it or tease him or whatever...."

They both turned at a noise at the door to the front hall. Ally was standing there, thankfully without a little blond companion, but still not looking pleased by what she'd overheard. "Maybe you should ask one of the *other* kids raised by a gay man how that worked out for her," she said, staring Will down. "Maybe you should ask *that* kid whether people judge her or tease her about it."

"Maybe we should," Joe said softly.

"They do, a bit," she said without taking her eyes off Will. "Just like they tease Margo for her dad being such a nerd and tease Tony about how everyone in his family looks exactly the same. They call him Tony Clonerson instead of Anderson. And they bug Matt about his big ass and Kelli about how thin her hair is. Sometimes they're nice, sometimes they're kind of mean. But none of it really matters. Not compared to coming home and knowing I've got people who love me and look after me and give me the freedom to be who I want to be. I wouldn't trade this family for the world and neither would Austin." She turned to Will. "And Lindsey should damn well know that, and if you can't find the balls to tell it to her, then I absolutely will."

"Okay, bruiser," Joe said. He set down the dishcloth and walked over to give his sister a one-armed hug and a kiss on the top of her head. "I wouldn't trade this family for anything, either." Then he tugged on her ponytail. "Unless there was a family that was exactly like this in every way *except* that the youngest daughter didn't keep forgetting to empty the bucket on the tack room dehumidifier."

"Oh shit!" Her eyes were wide. "I forgot *again*! I'll go do it right now...."

"I already did. But you're the one with the show saddle—if it gets moldy, you're cleaning it up yourself."

"Teaching me responsibility," Ally said with an approving nod. "Using natural consequences to reinforce your rules. Very nice parenting there, Joey."

"That psychology class really stuck with you, huh?"

"I'm still going to be a vet. But I think psychology will be my hobby."

"God help us," Will said from the sink. Then he looked at his brother. "But you're both right. Austin's lucky to be here. And Lindsey knows it. She's just a worrier."

Ally raised an eyebrow that suggested she thought maybe there was a little more to it than that, and Joe gave his sister's shoulders another affectionate squeeze. He had a good team on his side. Even Will, for all his nagging, was trying to look out for him. "You guys want to sit out on the porch for a while?" He looked at his little sister. "Maybe have a beer?"

She grinned widely. "I love the way you make it sound like I couldn't get a case of beer all for myself anytime I wanted."

"That's forbidden beer," Joe said, trying to sound wise. "Isn't there some psychological theory about this? Sneaking around and drinking with your friends is one thing—and if you get busted for it, you're going to be facing some more of those 'consequences' you're so impressed by—but an officially sanctioned beer, as a symbol of your impending membership in the adult side of the family? Come on, that's got to taste just a little better, doesn't it?"

Ally cocked her head, then started toward the fridge. "I'll let you know in a couple seconds." She pulled out three bottles and handed them around, then twisted the top off hers and took a cautious sip. "Wow, you're *right*," she said, her eyes impossibly wide. "That is a *delicious* beer. I might want to have more than just one of those...."

"Don't get carried away," Joe cautioned. Then the three of them went out to the porch and watched the sun setting over the land they all loved. And they didn't squabble about anything the entire time they were out there.

JOE WAS up early the next morning, as usual. He loved being outside as the new day started, the night animals scurrying away to their nests while the day animals began their louder, more obvious lives. He supposed that would be one thing he'd have to give up, at least for a while, if he was the only one looking after Austin. The little man loved the outdoors and was learning to at least sit on a horse, if not ride in the truest sense, but he was absolutely not a morning person, so far. He tended to wake up cranky and stay that way for at least an hour, and Joe was pretty sure it would be better to give up and stick around the house than to have his morning rides ruined by a grumpy preschooler. But there was still time before Ally was supposed to go away to school; maybe Austin would get over his morning blues by then. And if he didn't, Joe would just have to find other ways to enjoy the sunrise.

For some reason that made him think of Mackenzie. What would it be like to wake up together, to roll over in bed and watch the sun come up, then roll a little more and find other sources of enjoyment?

It had been a long time since Joe had spent the night with anyone; even with Trevor it had been a rare occasion. Trevor had never slept over at the farm, and Joe had rarely wanted to spend a night away from the place. It wasn't just the kids, but also the very real possibility of a problem with the livestock. Joe didn't have a nine-to-five job he could leave behind at the end of the day; Trevor had never really accepted that. "If you *wanted* to come, you'd find a way to come," he'd said on more than one occasion, and Joe had to admit it was true. He'd liked Trevor and enjoyed the ways their bodies worked together, but he hadn't loved him, and Trevor had known it. "I'll stay if you ask me to," Trevor had said just before leaving for the city. Joe hadn't asked.

He wondered if he should add that little tidbit to Sarah and Will's understanding of his romantic past. It would probably just set them off on a whole new tangent, raving about how Joe couldn't commit even to a fantastic guy like Trevor, how he was too walled off from everyone, how he was damaged and defective and wrong. Ironic that his family was so accepting of his homosexuality but seemed to have so much trouble understanding his need for independence.

He took Misery out to check the grass the cattle were on; it was good for another day or two, but he'd need to move them soon. It wasn't a huge job, just herding them through a gate into the next enormous field, but he'd get Ally to help him with it anyway. She liked working the cattle, and she was trying to train her horse into some of the skills Misery just seemed to have by instinct. He gave the mare an affectionate pat on the neck, and she responded with pinned ears and the little hop that was as close to a buck as she was allowed to get while he was riding her.

By the time he got back home, the house had clearly woken up. He was pretty sure he could smell bacon all the way up at the barn, a suspicion he confirmed after he put Misery away and headed for the kitchen. Will and Ally were sitting with Austin at the table, but there was an extra inhabitant working the grill.

"Nick," Joe said to his younger brother. "Hey, man, good to see you." Judging by the tension in the room, Joe was pretty sure something else was going on, but he wasn't sure what it was and hoped he'd be able to avoid getting involved. Then Austin turned to look at him, his face tear-stained and threatening to break into a new wave of sobbing, and Joe had at least a little more understanding. Nick was Austin's biological father, but he'd been too young to raise him and had happily signed guardianship over to Joe and Will. And he hadn't spent much time at the house since then, having left home to go to school when Austin was a toddler and only coming home for Christmas and maybe a week over the summer. But he still seemed to feel a sense of ownership over the boy and expected some level of love from him. Usually the family knew when Nick was coming and got Austin psyched up beforehand, but this wasn't a planned visit, and Austin was clearly not taking the surprise very well.

"Hey, little buddy," Joe said. He moved to the boy's side and laid a comforting hand on his shoulder. "Having some breakfast?"

Apparently that was the wrong thing to ask about because Austin's trembling lip sagged into a full, open-mouthed sob. He raised his chubby little arms in an irresistible plea, and Joe lifted the boy out of his chair and let him wrap himself around his uncle's body.

"What the hell?" Joe mouthed to Will.

"Apparently there's a new rule," Ally said, her eyes shooting daggers in Nick's direction. "Apparently Austin has to clean his plate, even when somebody gave him food he doesn't like."

"Bacon, eggs, and toast... who doesn't like those things?" Nick asked, frustration clear in his tone and body language.

Joe glanced down at Austin's plate. "Scrambled eggs or soft-boiled in the shell, so he can dip his toast. Not sunny-side up." He shrugged. Austin's sobs were already subsiding. This wasn't a tragedy. "And we generally don't push him for much new effort in the morning; he's not good until he's totally awake." Another shrug, this time with a smile in Nick's direction. "It's not a big deal, man. No way you could have known."

"Oh, there's a way," Ally said pointedly. "'Cause *we* all know. Maybe if somebody moves out and never comes to visit, somebody should listen to the people who *do* live here when they try to tell him how it's done!"

Well, she wasn't wrong, but Joe wrinkled his nose at her anyway. "Enough with the *somebody*, okay?" He bounced Austin a little, then said, "It's good to see you, Nick. I don't think we need to worry about him finishing his breakfast, do we? Or maybe you want some fruit, little man? An orange to give you superpowers for the day?"

There was a tense moment when it seemed like Austin might be choosing to use his superpowers to raise the roof, but then he nodded. "Orange," he snuffled into Joe's now damp shirt collar.

"Magic word?" Joe asked as he moved toward the fridge.

"Orange, please," Austin said promptly. The meltdown was clearly resolved.

But Nick was standing in front of the fridge, his arms crossed, staring at Joe. "You're completely undermining my authority, Joe." He shook his head. "I already went through this with Will. It's important that Austin develop some respect for rules. The world isn't always going to revolve around his stupid preferences."

"He respects rules. The ones he knows. We don't have a clean-your-plate rule because we want him to enjoy his food and enjoy his mealtimes. And he's a good eater. Nobody's asking you to cook him another egg; I'm just asking you to get out of the way so he can eat an orange."

"And I'm asking you to respect the boundaries that I've established with *my son*."

Nick could be crusty, but he wasn't usually a total asshole. Whatever was going on here was going to take a serious hashing-out, and that wasn't something Austin needed to be around for. So Joe bounced the little boy again and said, "Oh no! We need to buy more oranges! We should go to the hardware store!"

Austin lifted his head to squint at Joe, then slowly shook his head. "Grocery store," he said softly.

"Grocery store? No, we're not buying nails!" He headed for the mudroom and pulled his wallet and keys out of the pocket of his jacket. "Maybe the dollar store?"

"Grocery store," Austin said more insistently.

"No, we don't need cheap stuff. We need *oranges!* Let's go buy them at the gas station!"

Austin giggled as Joe carried him down the steps, and then they both turned as the door banged shut again and Ally stormed out. "I'm either coming with you, or I'm staying here and killing him," she said.

"Coming with us sounds like a good option. We're just going to the gas station to get oranges."

"*Grocery* store!"

"Oh, the grocery store," Joe responded. "Okay. Let's go to the grocery store and get some feed for the horses." He shifted Austin into his car seat and started playing with the buckles, then glanced toward his sister. "Did he say why he's back?"

"Let's go to the feed store," Austin suggested. He loved the place, for some reason Joe hadn't really been able to figure out. "*And* the grocery store." He cocked his head. "And ice cream?"

"He didn't say," Ally responded from the front seat. Then she reached behind her and tweaked Austin's bare toes. "And no ice cream this early in the morning. Morning is for oranges."

"Or berries." Normally Joe would suggest that they get ingredients for a smoothy, but he wasn't sure he wanted to drag Austin back into whatever was going on in that kitchen. Or what he *hoped* was going on. Will and Nick had always gotten along pretty well, so this should definitely be Will's problem to solve. Joe would deal with the better-behaved kids.

They made it to the grocery store and ended up getting a cartful, as they seemed to do every time they walked in the door. They grew their own vegetables and raised their own beef and still managed to go through more groceries than an entire city block should need. Partly it was because both Will and Joe still seemed to have their teenage metabolisms and ate everything in sight, but it was also because the house was a comfortable home, and they did a lot of casual entertaining: family dinners; Ally's friends coming over for a swim and a snack that turned into a meal; people dropping by and staying for a few hours. It was the way it had always been and the way Joe liked it. He wondered if it would change when it was only him and Austin there to lure people in. The kindergarten crowd didn't do a lot of dropping in on people, at least not as far as Joe had seen. And he had to admit it was pretty rare for anyone to come to the house just to see him. One more thing to worry about, but not right then.

Right then, he was busy keeping track of Austin. The little guy loved wandering through the grocery store, and he'd been well trained that he wasn't allowed to touch things without asking, so Joe tried to shop at off-peak hours when a loose kid wouldn't get in everyone's way and then let the little guy go. Early morning definitely qualified as off-peak, and Austin was in visual stimulation heaven. "Can you find an S, buddy?" Joe asked, and the boy started scanning the packages on the shelves. It gave Joe time to check a few prices and stack cans in the cart.

"S," Austin announced triumphantly, pointing.

Joe crouched down to inspect the label. "Good job, buddy. That's an S, for sure! And then with the O, U, P after it, the word is 'soup.' Soup starts with 'S.'" He gave the letter a little extra hiss, because that was Austin's favorite.

Ally came back with an armful of ingredients and said she'd make dinner that night, and they shopped on. When they neared the checkout counter, Ally held her hand out, and Joe passed her the credit card without comment. She knew where he'd be, and Austin was already tugging impatiently on his hand.

The little boy led him to the corner of the store reserved for plants and flowers, then dropped his hand and walked forward as if in a trance. It wasn't a very big store, and the selection wasn't huge, but there was always something new, and even the old favorites had their appeal to a four-year-old. Joe had thought about taking the kid down to the city and showing him one of the big flower markets, but there was no point blowing his mind when he was so clearly still enthralled by something closer to home.

Austin ran his fingers through the air just above each plant, looking back guiltily on the one occasion he slipped up and touched the corner of a leaf. He paced along the row of flowers, stopped to carefully smell a few bouquets, and then finally came to rest in front of a modest collection of irises. "Purple," he said, and then he peered more closely before adding, "and yellow."

"Are those the ones? Those are your favorites today?"

Austin gave an agonizing look at a tall arrangement of orange-red glads but then turned back to the irises and nodded. "These ones."

"And who are they for?" It'd be nice if the kid said Nick, but Joe was pretty sure he wouldn't, and he'd never prompted Austin's choices at this. The whole point of the gift was the sincerity of the giver.

"Ally," Austin declared.

"Very nice. I'm sure she'll like them. Do you need help?"

Austin looked over to the customer service counter where a familiar face was smiling back at him. He knew that lady, and she knew the drill. He shook his head to refuse the offer of help as Joe peered at the price of the flowers and then handed Austin a ten-dollar bill.

The boy walked confidently to the counter and handed the bill to the lady, then turned decisively around. Joe had been ready for that; Austin wasn't great at multistep transactions yet. "Get your change, buddy," he prompted, and Austin turned back with a sheepish grin.

"Those are lovely," the lady at the counter said as she handed the change back to the boy. "Who are they for this time?"

Austin looked over to where his teenage aunt was waiting by the exit, then turned back to the lady who'd helped him with flowers on so many occasions. The struggle was clear, but so was his final decision. "For you," he said firmly, and he handed the flowers across the counter.

She seemed startled, then looked to Joe as if for guidance.

"We tell him he can give the flowers to whoever he wants," Joe said with a smile. It was an extravagance, but none of the flowers in the store cost all that much, and it was a nice tradition to maintain. "If he wants to give them to you...."

"For you," Austin repeated, standing on his tiptoes to push the flowers closer to the woman.

"Oh, sweetie. Thank you so much," she said with a quaver in her voice. "Nobody's given me flowers in a very long time. These are lovely. Thank you."

Austin beamed at her. "You're welcome," he said. "They're purple and yellow."

"Yes, they are. And those are lovely colors."

Austin nodded, then turned back to Joe with his hand outstretched. He'd done his thing and now it was time to move on.

"I was about to say that he's going to be a heartbreaker," the woman said, clutching the flowers in one hand while the other fluttered over her chest. "But I think he already is."

There was a moment when Joe was afraid she might be talking literally, but she took her hand away from her heart in order to wave good-bye to Austin, and she wasn't falling over or anything, so it seemed safe to head for the exit.

That was when he saw Mackenzie standing between the checkouts and the exit door with his own cloth bag of groceries, watching the whole exchange. The guy probably could have snuck out, slunk away without being noticed, but he hadn't, and Joe wasn't sure if he was impressed by that or not. It was one thing to be casual and not treat an acquaintance as if there was something awkward between them, but surely Joe had made it clear that one-night stands didn't meet the family.

But business associates certainly could. Joe put on a friendly smile as he led Austin across to the doors. "Hey, buddy, this is Mackenzie. He owns the church Will's been working on. That nice church that was empty for a long time?"

Austin hid behind Joe's leg. The shyness had just started a couple weeks ago and was fairly intermittent, as the kid's smoothness with the flower lady had shown. Maybe he only worried about brand-new people. But then Ally joined them, and Joe went through the introductions again, and by the time that was done, Austin was peeking out.

"Hi, Austin," Mackenzie said quietly, and the boy ducked back behind Joe.

Ally shook her head. "I think we're supposed to ignore it? If we comfort him and try to lure him out, that'd be positive reinforcement, right?" She shrugged in Mackenzie's direction. "If he doesn't want to meet new people, he doesn't get to make new friends." Her smile was warmer as she added, "He doesn't get to meet the guy who's saving that gorgeous church. Joe and I used to talk about buying it ourselves, just because we both love it so much, but we couldn't figure out what to do with it. It's great to see you having such fresh ideas."

Mackenzie looked amused. He arched an eyebrow in Joe's direction and said, "You thought about buying it yourself? I don't think you ever mentioned that to me."

"For about five minutes, maybe. I was probably drunk."

Ally rolled her eyes. "Joe doesn't really have that entrepreneurial spirit. Not a big fan of taking chances." She looked down to where Austin was sneaking out again, obviously fascinated by the shine on Mackenzie's brown shoes.

It was nice that Ally was helping train Austin out of his shyness, but Joe really wished she'd found someone else to use as the bait. It was pretty awkward trying to come up with topics of conversation, and he wasn't totally enjoying the 'analyze Joe's personality' approach she seemed to have settled on.

But he wasn't quick enough to do anything about it. "It's probably a family dynamic," Ally said thoughtfully. "Will's the businessman, so Joe's the domestic one. I mean, maybe there's a reason why marriages traditionally got divided up that way, right? Not that it should always be men making money and women being homemakers, but it's kind of nice to have one of each in a family, isn't it?"

Mackenzie seemed much more amused by all this than Joe was, but that made sense: it wasn't Mackenzie who was being used as an example of traditional roles within a marriage. "I guess each person could take responsibility for some part of each job," Mackenzie speculated. "Like each person could be half moneymaker, half homemaker. Or whatever ratio worked out for that family."

"I make money," Joe protested. "The cattle are profitable!"

"I'm not saying you aren't valuable!" Ally's eyes were wide enough to make it clear that she was putting on a bit of a show. "But in *addition* to the money, you give us beef, and you heat the home with firewood, and we love the vegetables and maple syrup and fish and eggs and chicken... but the only one of those things that actually gets *sold* is the beef, right? Your contributions are primarily domestic, in the economic sense. Like, if we were a country, you wouldn't have a lot of exports. *That* kind of domestic."

"I don't think you should go to school anymore," Joe replied. "Your brain is getting big, and kind of weird. You should stay at home and help with the domestic stuff."

"I think your brain is great," Mackenzie said to Ally with apparent sincerity. He looked down at Austin, who was running his fingers just above Mackenzie's shoes with the same reverence he used for the flowers. "And your brother is pretty great too," he said. It was clear which brother he was referring to, but Joe still squirmed a little. What the hell was wrong with him? Why was he feeling so torn? None of this was supposed to be happening... Mackenzie shouldn't be anywhere near either of the younger

Suttons. But he was, and Joe wasn't hating it. He was actually glad they were getting along. And if he was totally honest with himself, he had to admit that maybe he wouldn't have hated it if Mackenzie *had* been referring to him when he'd spoken of a great brother. Damn it, the rules were getting messed up. He'd known it was a mistake to let his guard down around Mackenzie, and now his confusion was the price he had to pay.

"We should get going," he said. He gently nudged Austin with his toe. "Ready, buddy?"

"But I haven't even had the chance to hint about wanting a tour of the church," Ally protested. "I haven't seen inside for years, not since I was too young to really appreciate it!"

Mackenzie laughed. "Anytime," he said. "I love the place, and I love showing it off."

"Are you going home now?" Ally asked hopefully. "If you aren't, don't worry about it. But if you are... it's hardly out of the way at all, right, Joe?"

He should have been quicker, should have had an excuse ready. But given that he'd left the house in order to avoid getting in a fight with his brother, he couldn't very well pretend he was in a big hurry to get back. "We bought milk," he said lamely. "It should go in the fridge."

"Ten minutes won't hurt," Ally scoffed.

Mackenzie raised his eyebrow again, clearly mocking Joe's lack of a ready excuse. Then he smiled sweetly in Ally's direction. "I *am* going home now. Can you follow along behind? Make sure your brother doesn't get lost on the way?"

And for the first time Ally seemed to realize there was a little more to this interaction than she'd thought. As they walked to their respective cars, she quietly asked, "Is this a bad thing? Is there some reason you might have wanted to get lost on the way?"

Joe shook his head. There wasn't any real reason, and wanting to avoid an awkward day-after with the previous afternoon's quick fuck wasn't something he wanted to get into with his baby sister. And he was the only one being awkward about it, he realized. Mackenzie wasn't being weird, wasn't flirting or making any allusions to anything; he was treating the sex as if it had been just as casual as Joe had insisted it was.

He was doing it again, he realized as he loaded groceries into the back of the truck. He raced ahead of things in the first part of relationships, caring too much too fast, getting too involved when there was nothing to be involved *with*. And then he ran out of interest before he got to the finish line. He was the hare in the relationship race, and there were tortoises out there doing much better than he was. So he tried to stay out of the race, and when he couldn't, he tried to *act* like the tortoises did. And this time the act had been good enough that he'd even fooled himself, at least for a little while. But here he was, behaving like an uptight idiot around some guy he barely knew, just because they'd spent a little time together naked.

"It's a beautiful church," he said as he settled into the driver's seat and turned around to check that Ally had buckled Austin in properly. "You should definitely see it. Maybe you'll give up on this vet thing and turn into an architect."

"If I was a vet, I'd give you a *big* discount for all the animals."

"Well, then, maybe we really shouldn't go see the church. I don't want to get in the way of my discount." He grinned at her. "Of course, by the time you're done with all that school, I'll probably be retired and won't have animals anyway."

"You'll always have animals," she said with quiet confidence. He couldn't argue with that, and they drove the rest of the way to the church discussing the relative merits of the possible career choices.

Austin thought she should be an astronaut.

CHAPTER SEVEN

THERE WAS no mirror in the upstairs part of the church, and Mackenzie didn't have time to run down the stairs to check himself out in the bathroom. Damn it. He'd dressed for a quick trip to pick up cereal, not an encounter with a man who was somehow looking even better today than he had the day before. Maybe it was because Joe smiled more when he was around the younger members of his family. Lord knew the man had a beautiful smile.

Mackenzie tried to make his own expression as attractive as possible as he stood in the doorway with Griffin frolicking at his feet as they both waited for Joe to unbuckle the little boy. Mackenzie'd been a model, after all. He knew how to make himself look good. Then he frowned and let his pose relax a little. Why was he trying to impress this guy? Was he tying himself up in knots in hopes of earning another round of afternoon delight? He was that desperate?

Hell no. He focused his attention on Ally as she made her way up the walkway, already beaming in anticipation. "Does it still have those curved pews?" she asked excitedly. "I loved those!"

"See for yourself," he responded, with a somewhat grandiose arm gesture toward the double front doors.

Her eyes danced, and she scampered past him.

"Sometimes she's a bit of a kid," Joe said from surprisingly close. Mackenzie turned to see the man standing next to him, Austin perched on his hip. "Then two minutes later she sounds like a wise old lady. Two minutes after that, she sounds like a *senile* old lady...."

"Sounds like fun," Mackenzie said.

"Yeah," Joe admitted. "It kind of is." Austin squirmed, and Joe bent to set him on the ground. The boy headed straight for the perennial beds as Joe watched with fond amusement. "We don't have many flowers at our place. My mom had beds, but no one's really maintained them. I figure that can be his first job when he gets big enough to be useful—he can be our groundskeeper."

"Everyone has their own jobs? Their own areas of responsibility?" Mackenzie had been raised in a household where his only chore had been making it home before curfew. He was curious about the way this family seemed to be run.

But Joe was frowning, as if the question had brought up a sensitive subject. "Everyone used to. But they're moving away now, so I just kind of... I don't know, I guess I decide what needs to be done and what I can let go. But then everyone chips in for the big jobs."

"No extensive staff? No cowboys living in the bunkhouses, even? You're shattering my illusions."

"No bunkhouses," Joe said. "We've got quite a few outbuildings, but most of them are empty—I guess a couple might have been for sleeping, at some point. My dad knew more about the farm's history, but...." He shrugged. "That's kind of lost, now."

"You should just make it up. A void is a kind of freedom, right? You can fill it with whatever feels right to you, and if you repeat the stories often enough, people will start believing them."

"You think I should spin a complicated web of lies about the history of an Ontario farm?" Joe raised an eyebrow. "I'll put that on the to-do list, but it's going to be pretty close to the bottom."

"Your loss." Mackenzie stretched his arms in an exaggerated shrug, and if he happened to know the pose would make his body look long, lean, and irresistible—well, no reason not to show Joe what else he stood to lose in all this.

But as usual, Joe showed no reaction. He seemed to have lost all interest in Mackenzie, really, and was crouching down to greet Griffin and peer at his snout. "He looks good. Those little marks will probably go away, and if they don't... they give him character."

"Yeah, he's a tough guy now. Won't go anywhere near that shed, though."

"He's actually got some sense, then. Maybe we *should* introduce him to Red, try to teach that old bastard a few new tricks."

Mackenzie took a quick look around to make sure there were no kids within earshot, then said, "I really don't like to introduce Griffin to the dogs of my casual tricks. I think it just confuses him."

Joe snorted, then grinned. "Yeah, that's a good point."

Damn, there was something special about Joe's smile. It made Mackenzie feel like he'd earned something, been granted membership into an exclusive club. People Earning Joe Sutton's Amusement. PEJSA. They could sell T-shirts. "You want to go inside? Make sure your sister hasn't passed out from the beauty of it all?"

Joe turned to the little boy peering through the weeds, searching for blossoms. "Austin, you ready to go inside? You'll like the inside too. It's very nice."

Austin looked reluctant but obediently trotted over and took his uncle's hand. And damn it, that was another stupidly appealing thing about Joe. Mackenzie didn't think he had a paternal bone in his body and generally tried to avoid children whenever possible, but there was something really, really sexy about the way Joe treated the little guy: attuned to the kid's needs and reactions. Gentle and respectful while still firm and in charge. Well, yeah, that kind of solved the mystery of why it was sexy, although it was a bit weird to think that the qualities Mackenzie had liked about Joe in the bedroom were the same ones that made him a good parent. Probably not something Mackenzie should think about too much, so he fell in behind Joe and Austin as they walked into the church.

The family wasn't there long, but Joe seemed to relax enough to not be looking for every possible escape; the milk wasn't mentioned once. And when they'd finished their brief tour and Ally was getting Austin buckled into his car seat, Joe stayed back a little with Mackenzie. He kept his eyes on the truck as he said, "You doing anything tonight? Want some company?"

Mackenzie knew what he should say. He needed to get some power in this damn relationship, needed to make it clear that he wasn't a toy sitting on the shelf, waiting for the mighty Joe Sutton to pick him up and play with him when convenient. At the very least he should make a comment about two days in a row not being all that *casual*. Instead, he told the truth: "I don't have any plans. Company would be good."

"I should put Austin to bed, and then I need to make sure someone else is staying home with him. That shouldn't be a problem, but if it is, I'll give you a call, okay? Otherwise, around nine, maybe? Here?"

Mackenzie nodded with as much nonchalance as he could muster. "Okay. If something comes up for me, I'll let you know. Otherwise, nine works."

Joe finally looked at him, and something about his expression made Mackenzie feel like he was about to be kissed. Which was ridiculous. No way would Joe do that, not out in the open, in front of his family... no chance.

And sure enough, Joe started moving away, but he maintained eye contact as he went. "I'll see you tonight," he said quietly, and on that note, he turned and headed for the truck.

Mackenzie stood and watched as the truck pulled away. Ally was waving happily from the passenger window.

He went back inside the church and tried to distract himself. He put away groceries, responded to e-mails, worked on the marketing plan, and then went outside and weeded the garden. There was a lot to do, but he couldn't keep his mind on any of it.

Should he have something ready to eat or drink when Joe came by? What should he wear? Should he be daring and seductive? He could skip clothes entirely, or maybe just wear his robe... but was that seductive or just sleazy? What would Joe like? Mackenzie tried to put himself in the other man's shoes. He'd found someone reasonably compatible: Mackenzie liked to bottom, and Joe was pretty damn good at topping. About the same age, neither one prudish or resistant to the idea of sex between acquaintances. They were both good-looking, although in different ways. Did Joe *like* it that Mackenzie was smoother than him? Prettier, less rugged? Or was that a turnoff? Was Mackenzie getting action because of what he looked like or in spite of it?

He had too many questions and no idea how to answer any of them. He'd known all these things with Nathan, known what Nathan liked and expected, what parts of himself Mackenzie should accentuate and what parts he should disguise. But Joe was new, and Mackenzie was pretty sure he wouldn't have the same taste as Nathan, at least in most areas.

He yanked on a particularly tough clump of grass in one of the flowerbeds, then wrapped both hands around it and pulled again, harder this time. He could feel little rootlets breaking, but it didn't seem to affect the central mass. He put his whole strength behind it, pulling until he was afraid something in his back was going to pop, and the clump was still exactly where it had been to start with.

"You need to do it in little bits," a female voice said from behind him.

He turned to see Lorraine Liverson smiling at him, her amusement plain. She was wearing a short-sleeved blouse tucked into her elastic-waist jeans, some sort of rubber shoes, and, most intriguingly, gardening gloves. She stepped forward, nudged him aside without actually touching him, and bent to wrap her fingers around a few blades of the tough grass. A practiced pull and the grass was being tossed into the battered wheelbarrow he'd found in the back shed. She looked up at him to be sure he was paying attention, then brought her other hand into action, wrapping and pulling, then both hands at once, picking the clump apart like a nervous anorexic destroying a dinner roll. Wrap, pull, toss. Wrap, pull, toss. The clump was gone in a matter of seconds and Lorraine straightened to smile at him. "You don't need to fight it. Sneak up on it!"

He nodded ruefully. "Thank you."

She looked at him a moment longer, then said, "You need a hoe."

"Pardon?"

"A hoe," she repeated. "Long tool with a sort of blade on the end."

Oh. Not the first meaning that came to mind when he heard that word. He tried to regroup. "It's good for getting rid of weeds?"

She shrugged. "There's those who swear by it. I've never seen the point myself—it takes off the tops but leaves the roots behind, so the weeds just grow right back."

"So why do I need it?"

"Because it's good for frustration. If you had a woodstove, I'd say you need an ax—chopping a cord of wood will put a man in a much more relaxed state of mind. But you don't have a woodstove. *I* do, but I started buying my wood presplit two years ago, and I haven't looked back. But hoeing is almost as good as chopping. You spend a few hours hacking away at the soil, and you'll be surprised how much better you feel."

"It's that clear? The frustration?"

"This was supposed to be a fun little project, wasn't it? I saw you when you came up with the real estate agent and that older man. You saw the church, you liked it, you bought it. Didn't even look around to see what else there was in the area, just… jumped in. But now you're having to work at it." She squinted at him. "You don't strike me as someone who's done a whole lot of work in his lifetime."

He wanted to argue, but didn't think he could. "Not a whole lot," he admitted.

"Well, you're working hard now, and that's something. Sometimes that's what's needed." She nodded at the grass in the wheelbarrow. "But sometimes you just need to work smart. And sometimes you need to ask for help from people who know what they're doing."

"I did!" he protested. "I went to the chamber of commerce! They said they *might* be able to do *something*…."

"And they've already started," she said with a warning look. Apparently Lorraine was a defender of the chamber. "Dale Aithers called me yesterday afternoon and asked who I knew that might be interested in setting up a bed-and-breakfast. He specified it had to be people who wouldn't have a problem with a gay couple staying with them, if it came to that. I gave him a few names. A few single ladies who would *only* likely be interested in either gay men or men traveling with women. You know, ladies who wouldn't feel safe with a single, straight man in the house. Not that I think there are that many single, straight men who'd want to stay in a bed-and-breakfast."

"Wow. That's great. Thank you."

"I'm not sure it's going anywhere, but we're meeting at Sharon Thompson's tomorrow evening to discuss it. She's got the only B&B in town, currently, so we're going to see how it's done. See how much work it would take to get set up." She gave him a challenging look. "We can't afford to spend a whole lot of money fixing up our houses for guests who never actually arrive. People are going to be looking for some sort of assurance that this church is going to work out."

Mackenzie nodded. That made sense. But he wasn't sure

what he could say. "You've seen me working at it. You know I'm committed, right?"

She shrugged. "You've been working. You've put some money into it. And Will Sutton does good work—I'm sure it'll look beautiful when it's done. But are you going to stick around? Can you afford to, if it takes a while for this to get off the ground?"

Damn, Lorraine was sharper than he'd been giving her credit for. "I plan to," he said. "I'm not sure what assurances I can give you beyond that."

"Well, you might want to give that some thought. Right now, people see you keeping to yourself. You don't seem like you're settling into the community. I saw those Suttons coming for a visit, and that was a good sign—seemed like you were making some friends, maybe growing some roots." And again, she pointed toward the demolished clump of grass. "All clumped together like that, you couldn't pull that grass out. That's why it grows that way. One or two stalks all by themselves... easy weeding." She smiled. "You don't want people to think you're going to be easy to weed."

"You are milking that metaphor for all it's worth, Lorraine."

"I used to want to be a writer," she acknowledged. "But don't tell me it doesn't fit."

"Oh, it fits. I understand what you're saying. Thank you." But understanding what she was saying wasn't the same as knowing what to do about it. He cocked his head. "Would you like a glass of wine, or a cup of coffee? We could drink it out here, where everyone driving by would see me enjoying my friendship with a local citizen...."

She smiled at him. "First, we work. You've been putzing away at this garden for a couple weeks now, and you're barely keeping up. You need some help, and you need a strategy. That's why I came over. *After* that, yes, I'd like a glass of wine. And then you can get cleaned up and eat some dinner and come over to my place. It's nothing fancy, but I'm having people over for euchre tonight.

Probably ten or fifteen people... Lord knows the numbers never work out perfectly. You can meet them and show them you're part of the community."

"Euchre?" he said carefully. "I'm not even sure what that is."

"Do you play bridge?"

"No. I don't... they're both card games, right? I don't really play cards."

She looked at him like he was a Martian. "Well, we are going to need to do something about that." She looked at her watch, then nodded decisively. "Two hours in the garden. Then you get cleaned up, come over and help me set up. We'll have sandwiches for dinner, and I'll teach you to play euchre. You don't need to be great, but you need the basics. Then you'll be ready for tonight."

Networking. That was what she was talking about. Nathan's golf games, his glamorous social events, his weekends away... well, possibly those weekends had a different reason, if Mackenzie was being honest with himself. But still, the rest of it was part of being a businessman. In the city, it was one thing. Up here, it was euchre. Mackenzie could learn that, surely. Hopefully. But that wasn't his only challenge. "What, uh... what time will this run to, do you figure?"

"Oh, do you have other plans?" Lorraine's eyes were bright and overly innocent. "I shouldn't have assumed you were free!"

Just because she'd seen his car in the driveway every other night since he'd arrived.... "Not really," he said. "I just... you know, I want to know what to expect."

"It won't be a late night," she said. "We'll probably wrap up around nine or so."

Nine. He could do it. Do his job *and* be home when Joe arrived. He wouldn't have to cancel Joe's visit. Yes, now that he knew he wouldn't have to choose, it was easy to pretend the decision would have been that easy. Of course he would have gone with the event that would help the church. He wasn't so enamored with Joe Sutton, not so desperate for contact that he'd turn down a chance to follow a business plan that really seemed to make sense. "Great, yeah, if that's okay. I don't want to put you out."

Lorraine beamed. "A new face at the table? And a *young* face? I'll be the brightest star of the evening!" She turned back to the garden, hands on her hips. "Now, why don't you keep doing what you've been doing, working on a small area and getting all the little fiddly bits out, and I'll do a wide sweep and get the worst offenders out from the whole garden. Much more satisfying to end up with a huge pile of weeds, and it'll make things look much more presentable, more quickly."

"I bow to your expertise."

"Excellent idea."

They spent the afternoon and evening as Lorraine had planned. Mackenzie managed to pick up on most of Lorraine's euchre instructions and had the fun of producing a right bower at just the right moment to thwart his opponents' plans and earn the glee of his partner. He wasn't sure how much good he was doing for the church project, but surely he wasn't doing it any harm. And he wasn't sitting around at home trying to distract himself from thinking about Joe. Wasn't watching the clock, even, up until about quarter to nine. He'd left a note and hadn't locked the church door—he had to hope that'd be enough to keep Joe around if he arrived early.

But as the evening dragged on, it got harder and harder to pay attention to the cards. The final game was a close one, both sides advancing by single points, and Mackenzie's competitive spirit wasn't enough to keep him from thinking about throwing the game and getting the hell out of there. But his partner was Mavis Wickens, a spirited octogenarian who was clearly taking great pleasure from the close battle, and he just couldn't let her down.

He left as soon as was polite after the last hand and almost jogged across the street. In the moonlight he could see a pickup parked by the side of the church. Good. He wasn't too late. He just hoped Joe wouldn't be angry or sulk like Nathan used to whenever something got in the way of his time with Mackenzie.

He looked in the cab of the truck as he passed, but it was empty. Joe must be waiting inside; it wasn't like Griffin was much of a watchdog. Mackenzie let his mind wander a little, imagining what Joe would be doing. He had his handle on the doorknob when Joe's voice came from the shadows behind one of the church's buttresses.

"You stood me up for euchre, huh?" Mackenzie was pretty sure he heard amusement in the tone, but sometimes Nathan had been like that too... acting as if it were funny when really he was being bitingly sarcastic.

Mackenzie turned with an apology on his lips but didn't get time to make it. Before he could speak, Joe was there, tall and solid and pressing Mackenzie back against the stone wall. Joe put his right hand flat on Mackenzie's chest, scissoring two fingers around his nipple; he grabbed Mackenzie's hip with his left hand, steering his body to just the right angle. His grin was dangerous in a much different way than Nathan's had ever been. "Did you win, at least?"

Mackenzie tried to answer, but it was a little difficult when Joe's body was pressed against him like that, when Joe's lips were so close to his own. "A couple games," he gasped. He could barely even remember what they were talking about.

Joe finally kissed him, strong and confident and in control, and Mackenzie could feel his whole body reacting. It was like his muscles lost their strength while his nerve endings became supercharged. The cool night air felt colder, and Joe's body was a warm blanket. Every touch sent shockwaves of pleasure out, and when Joe drew his mouth away, Mackenzie's lips felt swollen and hot.

"You going to invite me in?" Joe's gaze was level, his lips curling to show he already knew the answer to the question.

"Absolutely," Mackenzie managed to say. Then he pushed the door open and led the way inside.

CHAPTER EIGHT

"HE'S NOT planning on going back? At all?" Joe was trying to understand what his twin was telling him. It had taken Will several days to work through Nick's nonsense and posturing, and now he was reporting back to Joe so they could figure out a plan. As usual, they had their serious conversations away from the house; this time, they were riding along the long ridge on the far side of the lake. Joe had deliberately left Misery behind and was riding Devil, a pure black quarter horse who did *not* live up to his name. Will was on Angel, a light-gray gelding of uncertain lineage but very reliable temperament. The horses were happy to do as they were told, so the men were able to focus their attention on the problem at hand. "We've already paid a chunk of tuition, right?"

"A few hundred dollars." Will shrugged. "A waste of money, but not a huge deal. But he's spent two years on this degree, and now he's planning to walk away without finishing it."

"Well, that makes more sense than spending another two years in a program he doesn't like, just to get a piece of paper at the end."

Will frowned. "But he *did* like it, up until now. Sounds like he took some course on entrepreneurship at the summer session, and it's got him all turned around. He says the way to make *real* money is to go out on your own, and he doesn't need a degree to start his own business."

"The degree might help him get a start-up loan."

"I think he's got his eyes on a different source of funding."

Oh. "The insurance?" Joe waited for Will's nod. "He's already pulled more out of that pot than anyone else."

"But there's more in there, and he knows it."

"The plan was to pay for everyone's education and then dole out whatever was left."

"Yup. That was the plan."

Joe didn't like it when Will was the laconic one. "What are you thinking? Does he even have a business in mind, or is this all just preliminary?"

"He's got a few ideas, but I'd say he's still in the preliminary stages."

"But he's definitely not going back to school?"

"He says it would be a waste of time and money."

"Then why don't we wait and see on the business stuff? There's no time crunch on that, right? But if he's not going back to school, this isn't a vacation, and he needs to get off his ass and find *something* to do. He can help you, he can help me, he can get a job somewhere else... but enough of him just sitting around."

"Well, that brings up another topic." Will sounded much more careful about this, and Joe halted his horse and turned him around so he and Will were face-to-face. Will's expression was bleak. "He's talking about wanting to be more of a father to Austin."

"More of a father? What does that mean?" Joe tried to keep his voice level. "And how does that tie in with Nick finding something to do with his time?"

"He was talking about pulling Austin out of day care." Will looked like he was braced for an explosion.

Joe managed to contain himself. But placid, boring Devil was prancing beneath him like a thoroughbred on the way to the starting gate, clearly reading his rider's agitation. "Austin *likes* day care. It's his routine. If Nick was going to commit to being around long-term, then, fine, we could break the routine and start a new one. But what about this entrepreneur idea? He's going to start a new business *and* provide full-time child care? Seriously?"

"Kindergarten starts in a week and a half. I was thinking maybe we should let Nick try it for that long. Let him get it out of his system."

Joe turned his horse and let him jog forward. He didn't like this. Will's plan wasn't bad, necessarily, but it felt risky. "We should just tell him to mind his own business."

Will brought Angel up alongside, and Joe grudgingly slowed to a walk. "Austin *is* his business. He's the kid's father."

"Only in the strictest technical sense. The most responsible thing he ever did was when he realized he was too young to raise a kid and signed him over to us. If he wants to be a daddy, he can go knock up some other sixteen-year-old girl and ruin *that* baby's life. Austin is our responsibility, and we need to protect him."

"No one's life is going to get ruined. But we need to be careful. We're the legal guardians, but Austin was underage when he signed those documents, and we were *his* guardians too. If he wanted to challenge it and say he was coerced or something... I'm not sure he wouldn't win."

"Coerced? He was *begging* us to help him out. It was this or adoption. There was no way Nick was going to raise that kid."

"You know that and I know that." Will sounded like he wasn't confident a judge would see it the same way. "Look, you're right. Austin's our responsibility. But so's Nick. He's family too. We need to try to make this work for everybody."

Joe wished he was riding Misery. The mare's attitude would be a closer match to his own mood. "This is bullshit," he said to the world at large. He had a sudden, frightening urge to get off his horse and go find Mackenzie. They'd spent most of the night together after Mackenzie had returned from his euchre party, and it had been really... easy. Yeah, that was the right word. Being around Mackenzie was easy, as long as Joe didn't start thinking too much. But after he'd slipped out just before dawn, on the drive home, he'd realized how dangerous it could be to feel that comfortable around someone. He'd let his guard down, and that wasn't a good idea. So he'd made himself stop thinking about the other man, and he certainly hadn't gone back for another visit. It had been three days now, and the urge was still there, but surely that would fade away. Or at least turn back into simple lust, instead of whatever the hell Joe was trying so hard not to feel.

"We'll figure it out," Will said as they turned back toward the barn. "Just play it cool. If he wants to try looking after Austin for a few days, let him. He'll realize it's hard work and find something else to do."

Joe didn't like it, but he didn't have a better idea. They put the horses away, and Joe kept his mouth shut through dinner with the family and then went back to the barn and worked until well past dark.

He was sitting in the kitchen, trying to decide whether it would be a mistake to have a drink, when Nick shuffled in and opened the fridge door.

"I'm hungry," he groaned. "I wish there was someone who'd deliver pizza out here."

Joe knew he shouldn't poke, but he couldn't help himself. "Have you got *money* for pizza?"

Nick turned and squinted at him. "I'm a little low on cash. But I've got a 20 percent stake in a trust fund worth almost six hundred grand. Maybe I'll use some of that."

"You've got less than 20 percent," Joe corrected. It felt good to get all this out in the open. "We paid your tuition and living expenses for the past two years out of that fund. Nobody else has used nearly that much."

"I'd like to work out the math," Nick said, jutting his chin out. "And I'd like to do it right. It doesn't make sense that my rent counts against my share when everyone else has been living in this house, which is also 20 percent mine, rent-free."

"Rent-free, but contributing to the upkeep of the place," Joe said.

"But the place has also been contributing to their food. Twenty percent of whatever you pulled off this land should be mine. The beef, the vegetables...."

"Make sure you factor in labor costs. If you really want to do this *right*."

"And I should look at the cash income too. All the beef you've sold in the last five years... fine, I'll take out labor costs. But whatever's left, I should get a cut of."

"There's not going to be much left." Joe snorted. "You may end up owing *me* money." He was probably going to say a bit more, even though he knew he shouldn't, but his pager went off, saving him from his own bad judgment. "Shit," he said. He had the same reaction every time the antiquated device activated. It meant he was needed at the fire station where he volunteered, and that meant that somebody, somewhere, was having a worse day than he was. He glanced down at the readout. "Fuck," he said, figuring out the address in his head. He turned for the door.

"What's going on?" Nick asked, his snarkiness replaced with concern. He followed Joe outside.

"Fire at the Waltons'," Joe said as he headed for the truck. "Sounds bad. They're calling in trucks from other towns." Those three kids. Maybe in bed by now....

"Do you need help?"

"No, stay here. The fire department's on the way."

"But we're closer."

"You're not trained. Stay here." Joe jumped in the truck before

Nick could argue any further. He pulled the flashing green light out of the glove box and slapped it on the roof as he sped down the driveway. He wasn't likely to see any other drivers on their little road at this time of night, but he could leave the light flashing on the truck once he got to the site; it would make it easier for the others to find him, since they might not know the property as well as he did.

It took only a few minutes until he was pulling into the long driveway. His stomach churned when he saw the house. One side was almost fully engulfed, the other end billowing smoke.

A shape ran toward him from a pickup parked well back from the house. "I called it in," the man said. He didn't look familiar. "I was just driving by, and I saw it...."

"Has anyone come outside?" Joe demanded. "There's two adults and three kids living there." He scanned the property and saw the Waltons' battered pickup parked near the back door. Damn. He'd been hoping they might have been away.

The man was shaking his head. "I haven't seen anyone. I yelled, but no one answered, and there's fire by the door."

Joe nodded. He wished he had his gear with him, but it was stowed on the fire truck, and the truck wasn't even close enough for the siren to be heard. So there was no use wishing for the gear; he'd have to make do with what he had. He grabbed a flashlight from the glove compartment. The fire department rules were pretty clear that he wasn't supposed to enter a building on his own, but there were *kids* in there.

"If I don't come out, make sure the guys know... two adults and three kids in the family, plus one firefighter. Okay?"

The man's eyes were wide, but he nodded, and Joe jogged toward the house. He'd already figured out his plan. The front door was engulfed in flames, and the stairs wouldn't be safe... but there was a shed roof on the nonburning side, with windows above it. He could at least poke his head in there and see where he was.

He pulled himself up onto the bed of the Waltons' pickup, then vaulted onto its roof. One advantage of not wearing his protective gear was that he was a lot more mobile, but he could feel the heat radiating out from the building, hitting his exposed skin like a force field, and he knew he'd willingly give up some speed in exchange for protection.

There were rules about not introducing more oxygen to a fire, but Joe ignored them as he used the flashlight to shatter the closest window. He swept the plastic flashlight around the edge of the window, clearing out the shards of glass, then took a deep breath and threw a leg over the windowsill. He eased inside, then toppled through the smoke as he tripped on some miscellaneous furniture and landed on the floor. His flashlight was having trouble cutting through the haze so he felt around, keeping his right hand on the wall so he wouldn't get lost. There was something soft... a blanket. A mattress. He was in a bedroom. He launched himself at the bed and almost immediately found a small body, curled up as if asleep. God, please let her just be asleep.

He didn't take any of the usual precautions for transporting someone who was unconscious, just grabbed her and headed for the window. "Hey," he bellowed, and then he slipped out onto the roof and yelled again. "Hey! Come catch her."

He saw the man start to move and let the girl slide, shoving her down the roof until she disappeared, hopefully into the man's waiting arms. One out. Which one had that been? The youngest, he was pretty sure. Eight or nine years old. Damn, he couldn't remember her name. But this house was small, probably only three bedrooms. The youngest kids were likely to share. He took a deep breath of marginally fresher air, then struggled back through the broken window. He felt a slice of pain on his shoulder and realized he must have left some glass in the window frame, but the injury didn't interfere with his movement. Still with hardly any visibility, he groped around the room, this time with his left hand on the wall, hoping the second bed would be opposite the first. His shin banged something, and he bent over to find another mattress. His fingers found something soft, but this wasn't a child... a dog. He forced himself to keep going, leaving the furry creature at the foot of the bed, and he found skin. An arm. He grabbed the girl and slung her over his shoulder, and then he turned and grabbed the dog by the scruff of its neck. He couldn't just leave it there.

This time when he struggled out onto the roof, there was another flashing light on the ground. Not the fire department, though. Cops. Still, it was something. Joe slid a bit down the roof and saw Andrew Stark waving frantically at him. "Get off there," the constable yelled. "There's fire underneath you; the roof's not going to hold!"

Joe lowered the girl into Stark's uplifted arms, then dropped the dog on top of her.

He believed Stark. The fire was beneath him, and that meant the roof was likely to collapse, and if it did, he'd be trapped, engulfed by flames, burned alive....

But he turned and fought his way back toward the house. Lacey was still in there. Ally's friend, the brave girl who looked after her younger sisters when her parents lost control of themselves. Lacey needed someone to look after her now, and Joe wouldn't let her down. He slipped once, his hand landing on the metal roof of the shed before he jerked it back with a burned palm. Yes, there was fire beneath him. He needed to get off the roof. But he had to get Lacey out first.

It was quick work to break the other window and climb inside, but then the torture of groping around the smoke-filled room, feeling his lungs filling with smoke instead of oxygen, feeling the dizziness clouding in on him, and along with it the realization that he had failed. He not only hadn't saved Lacey, but he was going to die there himself. Maybe he still had enough time to make it out, but could he live with himself if he left her? Then he felt the building shake and heard a crash from outside. He didn't go to the window, but he knew the shed roof had collapsed. His escape route was gone.

That was when he kicked something soft but solid on the floor. He bent down and his outstretched fingers found a mass of hair, and then the rest of the girl. She wasn't on the bed, but on the floor. She must have woken up and tried to get away....

He grabbed her under her arms, but he was weak and her weight made him stumble. It wasn't like he had anywhere to go, but he dragged her anyway. They headed for the window, because there was no way the stairs would be passable. Maybe he could find the strength to throw her past the burning rubble of the shed. Maybe something. Maybe somehow. He had no real plan, but couldn't give up. He wanted to see Austin again, just for a couple minutes. Wanted to say good-bye to Will and tell him to take care of the rest of the family.

He didn't understand what was happening at first. A bright light, a change to the texture of the smoke... and then a spray of water right across his face, hard enough to almost knock him back down to his knees. A fire hose. And the light was a spotlight. The department had made it.

He pushed himself the extra step to the window and leaned out to see his comrades quickly extending a ladder over the newly soaked wreckage beneath him. Someone was climbing it even before it was anchored, someone who grabbed Lacey from Joe's arms and dragged her down the ladder.

Joe managed to slide out the window, but everything was backward. He went out headfirst, and his arms were weak, and he just slid down, then tumbled off somewhere near the bottom and got dragged clear by two firefighters, one grabbing each of his arms.

They pulled him all the way to the back of the truck, and someone fastened an oxygen mask over his mouth and nose. He tried to breathe deeply, but the effort sent him off into a fit of coughing.

"Take it easy," a familiar voice said. "You know the drill." Vince

Deacon was the captain of the department and probably should have been directing the efforts to put out the fire, but Joe was glad to have him nearby. "Breathe easy." Vince squirted some saline into Joe's crying eyes, helping to wash away the grit and smoke.

"The girls?" Joe choked out.

"The team's working on them."

"Their parents...."

"Nobody else is going into that house," Vince said firmly. "And when you're feeling better, we're going to have a serious discussion about *you* going in." His tone softened, and he looked over at the blaze. "We've got three trucks here, another on the way. We'll get the fire under control and then worry about the parents."

"Water?" Joe asked.

Vince knew what he meant. There were no hydrants that far from town, so they had to refill the pumper trucks from whatever source of water was nearby. "Map says to get it from the creek down the way, but it's looking pretty shallow."

"Dry year. Use the lake." Joe tried to control his shaking arm as he gestured weakly in the appropriate direction. "The gate across the road. Pasture. Lake at the back."

"You got cattle in that pasture? We need to worry about the gate?"

"No cattle," Joe said. Then he let his head sag back against the fire truck and tried to concentrate on breathing. He wasn't sure if he should ask more questions about the girls or whether it would be better to not know. But he should absolutely get back to work with his team. It sounded like they'd given up hope of any more survivors, so there would be no heroics, just the demanding job of containing the flames before they spread to the outbuildings or, worse, to the dry forest surrounding the house.

"Stay with me, Joe," Vince growled. "I need to know you're conscious."

Joe forced himself to open his eyes and cautiously took a deeper breath from the oxygen mask. He felt an uncomfortable tightness in his chest, but he was able to fight back the coughing. "I'm good. I'm okay. Go see about the water."

Vince looked at him doubtfully, then looked around the scene as if trying to find someone who had time to babysit Joe. That wasn't a good use of anyone's efforts, so Joe pushed the oxygen mask off and dragged himself to his feet. "I'm good," he said again. "See?"

"Don't be a hero, Sutton." Then Vince looked at the house and shook his head. "Too late for that, I guess. But don't be a hero *again*."

"I'm fine." He looked over to where a cluster of adults had gathered around three unmoving shapes on the ground. Damn it, he couldn't think about that. "I'll go with the water truck, make sure they don't have any trouble." His argument would have been stronger if the wave of coughing hadn't hit him like it did, doubling him over. He was barely aware of Vince guiding him back to the truck and fastening the mask back on his face, but after a while the coughing faded and he looked up at his captain.

"You're done for the night," Vince said firmly. "You need to go into the hospital to get checked out. You can hitch a ride with the paramedics. I'll have someone drop your truck off at the ranch, and you can call Will to pick you up at the hospital."

Joe wanted to stay busy, not get poked and prodded at the hospital. He tried to focus on breathing and resolutely refused to look in the direction of the ambulances that raced away with the girls inside. At least they were racing, he told himself. They wouldn't be in a hurry if they didn't think there was a chance.

When another ambulance arrived, Joe reluctantly let Vince drag him over to it. If there was any urgency to the fire scene, he would have fought harder to stay, but it was pretty clear that the department had given up on survivors *and* on saving the house; now they were just making sure the fire didn't spread. The dog Joe had pulled out of the fire was still being given oxygen, but they were bundling him up for a trip to the vet; if they were looking after the animals, they'd run out of hope for the humans. The team would make sure the fire was out, secure the scene, and wait for daylight to start the recovery work.

He let the paramedics check him out, but he resisted when they wanted to put him on a stretcher and take him to the hospital. "I'm fine," he insisted.

"My shift's over," Constable Stark said from nearby. "My partner can take the squad car back, and I can drive Joe in to the hospital in his truck. I live in town; I can walk home from there. And I can cuff him if he gives me any trouble about it."

It was better than an ambulance, at least. Joe found his cell phone in the truck and reluctantly handed his keys to the constable.

The ride to town was quiet until Andy said, "Do you think the parents were drunk? Got careless and started the fire somehow?" Joe couldn't answer the question, and finally Andy said, "I should have *made* them tell the truth. They could have been living in a safe foster home somewhere, not...."

Joe leaned his head against the cool glass of the window. "Yeah. And I should have kept a closer eye on them. And you or me or somebody should have beaten the shit out of Del Walton for even thinking about taking a drink, knowing what he turns into when he's drunk." He started coughing then, and gasping for breath was a pleasant reprieve from the darkness of his thoughts.

Andy didn't say anything more, but when they got to the hospital, he parked the car and came inside with Joe. Neither of them mentioned Joe's need for medical care, not until Andy had found someone to tell them how the girls were doing.

"They're being worked on," the middle-aged nurse told them. She sounded as exhausted as Joe felt. "They're in serious condition. We're not sure if they'll regain consciousness; if they do, we're not sure if there'll be brain damage from the oxygen deprivation."

Joe thought of his own scorched lungs and how quickly he'd become dizzy and disoriented in the house. How much longer had the girls been breathing that crap?

"I've told the doctors you're here, and they want me to take some blood—we'll test it to see if you've inhaled anything too toxic. But they won't be able to get to you for a while." The nurse was writing something on a clipboard as she spoke, but she seemed busy, not inattentive.

"I don't really need to be here," Joe tried, but he could see she wasn't going to buy that. "Or I could come back tomorrow...."

She smiled. "Dr. Michaels said you'd say that. And she said to tell you to sit down and read a magazine. No going home."

Andrew nodded in support. "You could barely breathe for a while there, after you got out."

The nurse raised an eyebrow. "I'll add that to the notes." She pointed to a stretcher with curtains on either side. "Sit. Stay." Then she strode off.

Andrew's lips twitched, but he just said, "You want some company? I can stick around and drive you home after, if you need."

The constable looked almost as tired as Joe felt. They were both used to sleepless nights, but something about guilt and failure drained energy away faster than any exertion. "I'm fine." Joe caught the look and held up his hands in surrender. "I meant I was fine to stay on my own, not that I don't need to stay. I'll stay. Get checked out." And try not to watch the nurses too closely, try not to guess about the girls' status based on the staff's behavior. "You should go get cleaned up. Get some sleep."

Andrew nodded. "Okay. Call if you need me, though. Does Will know where you are?"

Joe held up his cell. "I'll tell him."

Andrew looked like he wasn't sure he could trust Joe to do that, but finally he nodded. "Fine. You're sure you don't need anything?"

Joe nodded, and Andrew headed out. Joe was left behind staring at his phone. He always called after a fire, always called if he wasn't coming straight home from an accident scene. That was the deal he'd made with the family when they'd wanted him to quit the department altogether.

He waited until Andrew was gone and the nurse had given him a hospital gown and taken her vials of blood, then hit the button to dial Will. He'd been hoping the call would go to voice mail, but Will picked up after the first ring, and he didn't sound sleepy.

"It's Joe. I was at a fire, and I'm fine, but I won't be home for a bit. I'm just getting checked out at the hospital."

"You want me to come in?" Will asked. "Nick said it was the Waltons?"

"Don't come in. I'm fine. But, yeah, the Waltons."

"How bad?"

Will might as well hear it. "The parents... if they were home, they're dead. The girls...." Joe took a deep breath and didn't continue until he was sure his voice was under control. "They're at the hospital. They... I don't know. It doesn't look good."

"Jesus." Will didn't say anything for quite a while. When he did speak, his voice was soft. "Get checked out and come home. I'll clear the family out if you want. Or you can walk right by us and go for a ride. Something. But don't do your driving-around thing tonight."

"I'm okay. Don't tell Ally about the girls yet, okay? Wait until there's more information."

"She's going to see it on Facebook as soon as she wakes up."

"Shit. You could pull the plug on the Internet and tell her it's broken...."

"This is Ally we're talking about. She'd troubleshoot that in about five seconds."

"Yeah." And it wasn't like Ally couldn't handle the news. Just because Joe wanted to live in denial didn't mean Ally needed to. And he didn't have the energy to deal with this anymore. "I'll be home later. I'm fine."

Another long pause, then Will finally said, "Yeah, okay. But check in if you're still gone at breakfast time, okay? Austin will want to know."

Playing the Austin card. Will knew all the tricks. "Okay," Joe said tiredly, and then he disconnected the call. He really didn't want to stay still. He never did, after a bad call. Usually it was accident scenes that set him off, but a fire like this... another family that had lost its parents and might be about to lose a hell of a lot more.... Some of the guys could work on something like that and just go back home, sleep for a couple hours, and go back to work as usual. Joe didn't react like that, and he definitely didn't want to bring his mood into the family home. Usually he'd just drive north or west until he hit one of the Great Lakes, then sit and stare at the water for as long as it took. He made sure he was calm enough to cover whatever he was feeling and then got back to his life and let the emotions work out of him in their own time.

But being stuck in the hospital, knowing he was waiting because the doctors were fighting to save the lives of three young girls he hadn't rescued in time... he couldn't stay calm there, couldn't keep the emotions from trying to fight their way free. The nurse had hooked him up to oxygen as a precaution, and he made himself resist the urge to pull the cannula from his nose. If breathing some extra oxygen would get him out of the hospital faster, he needed to do it. And he didn't want to be the petulant patient who distracted the staff from more important tasks. But, damn, he wished he could move around.

Finally, Dr. Michaels arrived and smiled tiredly at him.

"How are the girls?" Joe asked, afraid of the answer.

But she just shrugged. "We've done what we can for them, for now. Time will tell."

That didn't sound like enough, but he knew the doctor and trusted her judgment. So he tried to keep his concerns to himself and just said, "I breathed some smoke, but I'm fine. I just need a quick checkup."

Another tired smile. "I've looked at your blood work. There are elevated levels of some chemicals you aren't exposed to working on the farm; I assume they're from the fire, but I want you to come in next week for another blood test, to make sure you're cleaned out. And there was elevated carbon monoxide—again, safe to assume it's from the fire, but we'll test again next week. It wasn't at a level that causes me concern for your current health. But let me take a look at you, and we'll see where we are."

She tutted over the scratch on his shoulder. "This could use stitches. But there's no point if you're just going to move the arm and pull them out."

"Obviously I'm going to move my arm... it's my *arm*. I kind of need it."

She shook her head. "I heard Nick was home. Couldn't he take over for you for a few days? It won't *kill* you if I don't stitch it, as long as you're careful to keep it from getting infected, but it won't heal as well, and it's much more likely to leave an ugly scar."

Joe wouldn't trust Nick to move his truck, let alone run the ranch. "I heard chicks dig scars."

"Now if only you dug chicks," she said with a wry eyebrow lift. "But, okay. I've cleaned it out. I suppose I can't trust you not to shower, either."

"I smell like melted pig shit."

"Well, that's very descriptive. So...." She reached behind her for something from the counter. "I'll put a wound dressing on it, tape the edges together as tightly as I can, and you'll go shower and ruin all my work. But have someone tape it up for you afterward, the same way. And keep an eye on it. If it's not scabbing well after a couple days, come back in and we'll do something more drastic."

"Thanks," Joe said, ready to slide off the table.

"Oh, no you don't," the doctor said, placing her hand firmly on his chest. "Take the gown the rest of the way off. I see some burns on your back... flying embers, probably? They're not serious, but there might be something worse somewhere else."

Joe thought about arguing, but it was quicker to go along. The doctor's inspection was efficient, and when she got to Joe's hand, she raised her eyebrows at him. "Were you planning to mention this?"

"It's only first degree, right?" He grinned at her. "I'll just put some butter on it."

"No butter!" She turned his hand over so she could see it better, and then poked and prodded a little. "There's a few patches of second-degree burn. I'll clean it out, and you need to *keep* it clean. If you really won't take a few days off, at least take some surgical gloves home with you and wear them under your work gloves. Gauze, surgical glove, work glove. I'll give you antibiotic cream, as well." She gave him a serious look. "You need your body to be in good condition, fully functioning. An infection would get in the way of that. In order to be fully functioning, you will do what is required to prevent infection. Understood?"

"Yes, ma'am."

"I'm serious, Joe."

"Me too. I'll do it, I promise."

She still looked skeptical, but she finished her examination and loaded him down with creams and pills and dressings and extras before letting him get dressed in his smelly, charred clothes and shooing him out the door. He supposed he should have paid for at least some of that stuff, but the firefighters always got special treatment when they came in with work-related issues, and Joe wasn't going to complain about it.

He eased in behind the wheel of his truck. Now that the doctor had pointed them out, he was aware of all the tiny burns on his back and shoulders, and his hand throbbed enough that he popped one of the pain pills she'd given him. He'd taken them before and knew they'd make him groggy, so he couldn't do his usual driving-around trick.

And somehow, that was okay, because this time he didn't really want to drive around. He didn't want to be alone to think about the three girls he was driving away from. He knew where he wanted to be; he just hoped he'd be welcome when he got there.

CHAPTER NINE

THE BUZZING of his phone pulled Mackenzie out of a deep sleep. He had customized ring tones for all his frequent callers; if this was a telemarketing call, he was going to be pissed. He was only slightly mollified when he saw the name on the call display. "Joe? It's the middle of the night!"

"Sorry to wake you. Can I come in?"

"Come *in*? Where are you?"

"Your driveway."

"My...." Mackenzie shook his head and tried to wake up. Joe Sutton was in his driveway and wanted to come inside. It was the middle of the night. Those were about the only facts at his disposal. He sighed. "Meet me at the door."

He stumbled through the dark, Griffin bouncing excitedly at his side. As soon as he opened the door he was met with an acrid stench and wrinkled his nose until he saw Joe's face. The harsh glare of the overhead security light was never kind, but there was more than that making Joe look so drained.

"The smell gets in your clothes...." Joe said apologetically.

Was Mackenzie supposed to know what was going on? "Why is there a smell? What have you been doing?" The entire situation was inexplicable.

"Fire. I'm a firefighter. Part-time. Sorry."

"Sorry that you're combining two sexy stereotype jobs into one? You're a cowboy fireman. Seriously?" But Joe didn't seem like he was quite ready for humor. He looked more like he was ready to collapse. And he'd come here, looking for... something. "Strip down," Mackenzie ordered. He wanted to be compassionate, but he didn't need that smell in his home. "Leave the stink outside, come in, and get in the shower."

Joe's quiet obedience was one more sign that all was not right. Mackenzie was so preoccupied he barely even had lustful thoughts at the sight of Joe's broad, toned chest, and was hardly tempted to reach out and touch as Joe stumbled out of his jeans and headed for the bathroom. He was still wearing his boxer briefs, but the rest of him was on display, and there were some disturbing changes to his body.

"What happened to your shoulder? And what are all those little red marks?" Mackenzie asked.

Joe lifted his hand to touch the bandage on his shoulder. "Glass. I should have cleaned the windowpane out better. The red marks are burns. Flying embers. I wasn't wearing the right gear."

"And your hand?" Mackenzie demanded, squinting at the clean white gauze wrapped around the hand Joe wasn't using.

Joe looked down at the hand. "Burned it." He frowned. "A metal roof, with the fire beneath it. Got pretty hot."

"Jesus, Joe! You've already seen a doctor, right?"

Joe nodded. "I'm cleared. But... can you put the bandages back on for me? If these get wet in the shower?" He frowned, then walked back to the front door and burrowed through the plastic bag he'd been carrying until he found what he was looking for. "I can wear the glove, to keep my hand dry. But I'd really like to wash my head, and that'll get the shoulder wet...."

"Yeah, of course. Do you have the gauze and everything, though? I don't really have any first-aid stuff."

"You should," Joe said seriously. "It comes in handy."

"Most of my houseguests don't show up injured."

"But they might *get* injured while they're here."

"This is a bit of a side topic. Let's focus on getting you cleaned up."

Joe nodded and continued on to the bathroom.

Mackenzie wanted to do something, but he had no idea what. He settled on gathering Joe's discarded clothes and dumping them in a plastic bag. He didn't have a washing machine in the church, and he wasn't sure the clothes were salvageable anyway. A smell like that would be hard to get out, and there must be holes in the clothes since there were holes in Joe's skin. Mackenzie went to the bathroom with the intention of scooping up Joe's underwear and adding it to the bag, but he changed his plans when he saw Joe still partly dressed, staring at the shower curtain as if it were a portal to another universe. The man's brain was clearly as fried as his body.

Mackenzie leaned past him and turned the water on, then reconsidered his temperature setting and dialed back on the heat. It would sting Joe's injuries no matter what, but at least cooler wouldn't burn as much. Then he pulled off his own shirt and dropped it on the floor. Joe didn't even look over as Mackenzie shrugged out of his pajama pants and underwear. He did wake up a little when Mackenzie hooked his fingers into Joe's underwear and tugged them down over his ass, then let them drop. "Okay, cowboy, in you go." Mackenzie stepped into the shower and tried not to wince at the tepid water. He reached for Joe's nonburned hand and tugged him in.

Joe stood quietly as Mackenzie sudsed up his hair and leaned under the spray to be rinsed when prodded to do so, but he didn't say anything, didn't seem to notice the naked body next to his, a body that had previously shared quite a bit of pleasure with his own. Mackenzie squirted body wash onto a sea sponge and gently scrubbed Joe's body. He knew from personal experience that the texture of the sponge was absolutely perfect against the tender skin of his cock, but Joe didn't react to that, either, just stood there and let Mackenzie fuss over him.

When Joe was as clean as he was going to get, Mackenzie put down the sponge and stepped around so he was directly in front of Joe. He brought both of his hands up to frame Joe's face and then kissed him gently on the lips. "I'm worried about you," he said quietly. "Are you okay?"

Joe sighed deeply. "I'm fine," he said. "I'm always fine. It's other people...." He stopped talking then and stepped as far away as he could get. The shower stall was a good size, but there were two full-grown men in it, and Joe didn't get far. Mackenzie shifted around so Joe could make it out the door without going through him, then reached out and hooked his hands around Joe's neck. He didn't pull hard, just tugged a little. Joe resisted for a moment, then gave in, shuffling forward until his body was pressed against Mackenzie's, their water-cooled skin slick and smooth. Mackenzie slid his hands down until he was in better hugging position, and finally Joe relaxed, letting his head fall onto Mackenzie's shoulder, his cold nose nestling into Mackenzie's neck.

They stayed like that until the hot water ran out, and then Mackenzie turned off the shower and dried them both off. He guided Joe over to the bed, peeled off the wet bandage, and tried not to react to the long gash marring Joe's beautiful skin. Joe sat quietly while Mackenzie sorted through the contents of his hospital bag and reapplied the dressing. Then he pushed Joe to lie down on his side and snuggled in behind him. Griffin immediately hopped up on the bed and stepped delicately around them until he was beside Joe's chest. He lay down, his back pressed tight against Joe. That was enough to prompt at least some response; Joe lifted his arm and wrapped it around the compliant dog.

That was how they fell asleep. When Mackenzie woke up a few hours later, it was because Joe was squirming around, clearly trying to get up without disturbing either of his bedmates. "We're awake," Mackenzie said quietly. "You can just get up. But do you really need to? You should sleep more." Light streamed in through the small casement window, but the angle made it clear that it was still early.

Joe twisted around onto his back, then sat up. "I have to call home," he said. He sounded better now, much more with it. "Austin will want to know where I am."

"Just Austin? No one else will be worried?"

"I called Will last night." Joe shrugged. "Which doesn't mean he won't be worried, I guess. He's a bit of an old lady."

"You almost burned up in a fire!" Mackenzie sat up and stared at Joe. "You have cuts and burns, and I looked in that bag—there's a puffer in there with instructions for what to do if you start having trouble *breathing*! I think he has a right to be a bit worried about you without being called an old lady for it!"

Joe raised an eyebrow. "Now *you're* being a bit of an old lady."

"No." Mackenzie shook his head emphatically. "You were messed up. Don't even deny it. I'm glad you're feeling better now, but don't pretend you weren't feeling crappy last night."

Joe looked like he was thinking about arguing, but Griffin rested his head on Joe's shoulder and looked at him with his soulful eyes, and Joe relaxed. "Yeah," he said. "I was feeling crappy. Sorry for dumping that on you."

"Don't be sorry. I was glad to help. Just don't make fun of people who are worried about you when you do something that *makes* us worried."

Joe didn't respond, which Mackenzie decided to treat as a full admission of his bad behavior. "I don't have much food here," he said, willing to change the subject now that he'd made his point. "But we can go out for breakfast, if you want." He braced himself for Joe's lame excuses.

Instead, Joe looked down at himself and said, "I'm naked. And my clothes reek. I can't go to breakfast naked *or* in those clothes."

Which was technically an excuse, maybe, but a pretty damn valid one.

"You could borrow clothes, but we're not really the same size, and most of my clothes fit pretty snug."

"I've noticed." Joe's grin made it clear the man was on his way back to normal.

"Obviously that's not ideal," Mackenzie continued as if he hadn't been interrupted. He looked over at the clock on the bedside table. "Call home. Do your breakfast greetings or whatever. Then I can either lend you a bathrobe for you to drive home in, or you can tell Will to bring some of your clothes when he comes to work on the church. I think he was planning to finish with the floor in the sanctuary today."

"You got bossy overnight," Joe observed.

"Had a taste of being in charge, kinda liked it." Mackenzie grinned. "Also, I gave you a choice. Isn't that what you're supposed to do with a stubborn kid? Give them two choices, both of which are okay with you?"

"You're giving me the illusion of control."

"That's right. Pretty generous, huh?"

"You're a prince." Joe rolled his shoulders and winced, then craned his neck around to look at the bandage. "I'm falling apart." He lay back down. "Do you know where my phone is?"

Mackenzie reached over to the bedside table and pulled the two phones off it, looked at them, and handed the right one to Joe. Then he stood up and shuffled off to the bathroom, aware of his nudity in a way he hadn't been the night before.

By the time he got back, Joe was ending his call. "Will's gonna bring clothes," he said. "And probably gloat quite a bit. Just so you're ready."

"He's not going to gloat at *me*. Whatever you two have going on, that's your business."

"Wow. Supportive." But Joe didn't seem too concerned. Instead he was looking at Mackenzie with a familiar gleam in his eye. "He's going to be a while. Probably almost an hour." Joe grinned. "Any thoughts about what we could do with that time?"

"How about a conversation?" Mackenzie kept his voice light but made a show of reaching into the drawer of his beat-up secondhand dresser and pulling out a pair of underwear.

"Conversation," Joe said slowly. "Huh."

"You could always leave, if you don't want to talk." Mackenzie focused on his clothes and didn't let himself look at the man on the bed. "Oh, except for the 'no clothes' thing. That's a bit awkward, isn't it?"

"I've been naked on these streets before," Joe said nonchalantly. But he wasn't getting up and heading for the door.

"Okay, excellent conversation starter." Mackenzie pulled his shirt over his head, flopped onto the bed, and propped himself up on his elbows. "Why have you been naked on these streets, Joe? How often?"

Joe frowned at him for a moment, then sighed grudgingly. "Youthful hijinks," he said. "I used to hang out with a guy who lived down by the creek. He wasn't out, and his dad was pretty... well, his dad was not the sort of guy you'd want catching you naked in his son's bedroom."

"Better to be caught naked in the street?"

"I didn't get caught." Joe grinned. "It was after dark."

"It's weird," Mackenzie said slowly. "I've been thinking about the country as being a sort of gay desert. But I guess there's just as many gay kids up here as there are in the city."

"Gay *kids*? Yeah, probably. But I bet there's not as many gay adults. Most guys I know move down to the city as soon as they can. A few come back, once they're looking to settle down." He grinned. "But I got way more action, or at least more variety, when I was a teenager. The pool definitely dried up after high school."

"Opposite for me. I wasn't out until university."

Joe squinted at him. "I can't imagine you being in the closet. You seem so... I don't know. The way you act and everything... you just... you seem *gay*. You know?"

"Ah, stereotypes. What a charming way to start the day."

"Come on. You're pretty swishy, Mackenzie. I mean, not *way* over the top, but...."

"Not all butch and straight-acting like you?" Mackenzie was beginning to wish he hadn't started this whole 'conversation' business.

Joe frowned at him. "I'm not acting straight. I'm just not *acting* at all. I'm not putting on a show."

"The cowboy hat? That's not putting on a show?"

"That's sun protection. You want to see something scary, look at the skin-cancer statistics for farmers right about the time they stopped wearing hats with brims and started wearing baseball caps. Skyrocketed. You know where the new cancers were? Rims of their ears and backs of their necks. Areas covered by hats with brims." He leaned back in the bed, apparently confident his point had been made.

"So *you're* natural and honest, and I'm artificial and putting on a show. That's what you're saying?"

"What? Fuck, no. I'm not saying that. I just... even if you *are* putting on a show, I don't think that's the same as being dishonest. I don't think it's bad. I *like* the show."

Well, that sounded a bit better, but Mackenzie still wasn't totally thrilled. "Humans use body language to communicate," he said primly. "We add nuance with our tones of voice, our choice of words, our facial expressions. I choose to use all the tools at my disposal in order to communicate in a clear and interesting way. *You* have apparently decided to limit yourself to a much narrower range of grunts and scowls."

Joe looked at Griffin, still curled up next to him on the bed. "This conversation thing is a great idea, isn't it?" He fondled the dog's ears with his nonbandaged hand. "I bet you're jealous you can't talk and have fun like we are, right?"

"What's your favorite food?" Mackenzie blurted out.

Joe seemed to be questioning his sanity. "My favorite food?" he repeated slowly. "I don't know. Is this a trap?"

"I'm trying to find a less heated topic of conversation."

"Yeah, sure, until I say I like steak and potatoes and you say you like... I don't know... quinoa or something."

"I *despise* quinoa. And that's not a gay food, anyway. Maybe dykes like it, I don't know."

"What *is* your favorite food, then? Eggs Benedict?"

"Ooooh. Maybe. I *do* love brunch."

"Everybody loves brunch. Even straight people. How do you feel about picnics?"

"Picnics? Are picnics gay?"

"I don't know. Probably. I mean... they're a lot of work, and there's not much point to them...."

"And that makes them *gay*?" Mackenzie wasn't sure whether he was offended or amused.

"I don't know." Joe rolled over, sat up, and leaned against the wall at the head of the bed, the sheet bunching in his lap in a fairly interesting way. "Yeah. I'm gonna go with it. Picnics are gay. Do you like them?"

"I don't know. I don't think I've ever been on a picnic."

"No?" Joe was clearly searching his own memory. "I don't think I've ever been on a picnic either. Maybe they're not all that gay."

"Or maybe we're just not doing it right. Maybe we're not being gay enough." Mackenzie held his breath, waiting for Joe to jump on that with some new comment about Mackenzie being *flamboyant* or whatever.

Instead, Joe just grinned, slow and sexy. "We should absolutely be more gay," he said solemnly. "You know what we should do? Sex. With each other. Two men, having sex. In the *morning*. That'd be *super* gay, right?"

"It's more gay in the morning?" Mackenzie asked, but he wasn't totally paying attention to the conversation anymore. Instead, he was making his way up the bed, pushing Griffin to the side and swinging a leg over so he was straddling Joe's lap.

Joe's grin didn't fade. "It's more decadent in the morning," he said. "And everyone knows gay people are decadent. So, yeah, gayer in the morning." He ran his fingers through Mackenzie's hair and tilted his head a little, then pulled him in for a deep, sloppy kiss.

"I guess we'd better do it, then," Mackenzie said when he came up for air. "In the name of gay solidarity."

Joe nodded but then seemed to be pushing Mackenzie away. "Take your clothes off," he said. "Give me a little show."

Nathan had liked that, and Mackenzie had actually gotten pretty good at it. But now he shook his head. "No."

Joe squinted at him. "No? Like... you aren't going to take your clothes off?"

"No show," Mackenzie said as he lifted his shirt over his head and efficiently tossed it down to the foot of the bed.

"Too late," Joe said, his gaze appreciative as it wandered over Mackenzie's chest. "Or do you want me to close my eyes?"

Well, he hadn't, but now that it was on offer, even if only sarcastically... "Yeah. Close your eyes." Mackenzie kept his gaze locked on Joe's until his eyelids dropped. "Now keep them closed. No matter what."

"Do I have to think of England too?"

"If I do this right, you won't be thinking of anything but

me." Brave words to cover the sudden insecurity sweeping over Mackenzie. He'd never taken charge during sex before, not like this. He'd watched porn, he'd had fantasies... but actually taking action on them? He couldn't quite believe he was doing it. Then he looked down at Joe, eyes closed, waiting, and he knew he wanted to try. He trusted Joe to be understanding and patient and to laugh at him just the right amount if it didn't work out.

He looked down at the beautiful body stretched out beneath him and tried to decide what he wanted to do with it. Give it pleasure, for sure. Give *Joe* pleasure. But maybe not right away.

"Keep them closed," he warned as he swung his leg over Joe's lap and found his way upright. A quick trip to pick up a tie he hadn't worn since he'd moved north, a moment to drop his jeans and underwear, and then he climbed back up on the bed. There was no headboard to tie Joe's hands to, but that probably would have been a bit ambitious for Mackenzie's first crack at this anyway. But it was exciting to wrap the tie around Joe's face, then knot it loosely with the widest part of the silk covering the man's eyes.

Then he pulled the sheet down so Joe was completely exposed. From the front, most of the recent damage was concealed, and Joe looked as perfect as ever. His cock was just starting to fill, but Mackenzie wasn't supposed to be worrying about that, not right then. Joe would have his turn later. Mackenzie straddled Joe's lap and kissed him deeply, then pulled away and put a hand on Joe's chest when he leaned forward to pursue. "No," he said firmly. "Stay."

Joe's lips twitched. "You remind me of my nurse last night."

"Was he a hot young bodybuilder just poured into his scrubs?"

"She was an older woman, but her scrubs *were* pretty tight." Joe grinned. "But I was thinking more of the attitude."

"Don't think about that anymore," Mackenzie ordered.

"Why don't you give me something else to think about?"

Mackenzie was happy to oblige. He'd been getting hard ever since he started down this path, and his cock was more than ready for a little attention. He tugged on Joe's feet to prod him to slide down the bed a little. Joe ended up half sitting, half lying on his back, and that put his mouth at just the perfect level.

Joe seemed to know what was coming. When Mackenzie shuffled forward and rested the tip of his cock on Joe's lips, the man opened his mouth easily and slid his tongue out to tease along the sensitive skin it found. But that was letting Joe take charge again, and that wasn't the idea. Mackenzie slid his hips forward, filling Joe's mouth, pushing back toward his throat until the muscles started to tighten around his cock in the beginning of a gag. He pulled out, slid back in just as far, and Joe tightened his lips around his shaft. He felt suction and butterfly flicks of Joe's tongue, and Mackenzie was pretty sure he wasn't going to last long and pretty sure he didn't care.

He pushed a little further, and Joe shifted, changing the angle enough to accommodate a bit more depth. Damn, Joe's willingness was the hottest thing about this. Even in his fantasies Mackenzie had never thought of treating Nathan like this; it was impossible to think of the man being anything but in charge. But Joe was strong enough to be flexible and obviously willing to go along with Mackenzie's plans.

Unfortunately, those plans were pretty limited. Well, maybe it was a good thing, actually, because Mackenzie really didn't want to stop doing exactly what he was doing right then. Joe's mouth was warm and firm, his tongue was strong, and Mackenzie got to decide exactly how deep he wanted to slide into that heaven. He even got to pull right out and take a little break, rubbing the head of his cock along the outside of Joe's mouth, dipping it in just a little, letting Joe's lips wrap around it and then pulling it away like he was taking candy from a baby. The sensations were wonderful, but it was the power that Mackenzie found intoxicating: this strong man, doing what Mackenzie wanted simply because Mackenzie wanted it. It was even better that Joe *wasn't* tied up, because his freedom made it perfectly clear that he was being obedient because he wanted to be.

Mackenzie tested his boundaries, pushing in deeper and deeper, not pulling out until Joe finally gagged and moved his head back. "Sorry," Mackenzie whispered.

Joe turned his head away just long enough to swallow and say, "No you're not." Then he grinned and leaned forward, sightlessly searching for Mackenzie's cock, and that was it for Mackenzie's self-control. He wrapped his fingers in Joe's hair and pushed his cock in deep, then pulled out just as quickly before going back for more sweetness, and more and more. He could feel his orgasm building and tried to fight it off; he wanted to keep going for so much longer. But Joe was moaning softly, sending vibrations along Mackenzie's sensitive skin, and he was so willing, so ready to please.... Mackenzie came while his cock was deep in Joe's mouth, and Joe swallowed, fighting not to choke, keeping his lips wrapped tight around Mackenzie's cock as it shot load after load into Joe's eager mouth.

When Mackenzie finally pulled away, Joe reached up slowly with his good hand and wiped the spit and come off his chin. Mackenzie was still gasping as Joe grinned beneath his blindfold. "I thought for sure you were going to go full porn star and come on my face."

Mackenzie snorted as he came back to reality. "That's a two-hundred dollar tie. I didn't want it to get dirty."

Joe nodded slowly. "Martha Stewart would approve."

"You really think *Martha Stewart* is my style guide?"

"I have no idea. I get most of my fashion tips from John Deere."

"I don't know who that is."

"I didn't think you would."

Mackenzie slid down Joe's body until their mouths lined up and kissed him deep and soft. "Thank you," he said.

Joe grinned again. "I like the way you're talking like we're *done*. Really. That's cute."

Mackenzie pulled away in alarm. "Oh my God, Joe, I was totally thinking we were! I completely forgot about you!" He could feel Joe's laughter rumbling up through his chest and brought his mouth down to kiss the spot where it seemed to originate. "I'm an asshole," he whispered as he kissed his way lower.

"I'm about to forgive you," Joe promised. "Can I take the tie off? I want to see."

"Okay," Mackenzie agreed, and he lifted himself up enough that Joe was able to shift into a more comfortable position. When he knew Joe was watching, he rubbed his stubbled cheek against Joe's cock like a cat claiming its favorite person's leg. Joe closed his eyes for a moment, then reopened them and stared. Mackenzie licked a long strip from Joe's balls to the head of his cock, then kissed his way back down and sucked on the loose skin. He spit on his palm and wrapped it tight around Joe's shaft, then slid back up to find Joe's lips. "I'm going to suck your cock," he whispered between kisses.

Joe's lips twitched into another grin. "I was really hoping you were, but I have to admit, you've got me a bit worried."

"I'm going to. I just can't decide what you need to do to earn it. Do I want you to ask nicely, or do I want you to beg?"

Joe's grin didn't falter, but there was a new light in his eyes and a different tilt to his jaw as he said, "I think you're going to have much better luck with the first of those options."

And there it was. Joe's boundary, reached and announced in a clear, confident way. Mackenzie smiled at him. "Okay," he agreed. He tightened his grip on Joe's cock and watched in fascination as the man's eyes lost their focus. Then he loosened his fingers and said, "Joe, I was thinking about sucking your cock. Would you like me to do that?"

"That sounds excellent." Joe opened his eyes wide and fixed

his gaze on Mackenzie. "Would you please be so kind as to suck me off?"

Now it was Mackenzie's turn to laugh, and he chortled his way back down Joe's broad chest and washboard stomach. Once he arrived at his destination, though, he stopped laughing. Joe had asked nicely, and Mackenzie absolutely wanted to reward him for it. He abandoned his teasing and went to work in earnest, using all the tricks he knew and trying to pay as much attention to Joe's reactions as Joe always seemed to pay to his. He could feel Joe's orgasm coming almost as if it were building in his own body. He tightened his lips and pulled off just a little as Joe's body spasmed and filled his mouth. He swallowed quickly, kept sucking, and was rewarded with another bitter gush, and another. When he finally pulled away, he rubbed his cheek on Joe's cock again, but this time Joe laughed and pulled away.

"Get back up here," he ordered, and Mackenzie was happy to obey. Now they were both ready for slow kisses and a languorous descent into sleep... until a slamming door upstairs made them both jerk back awake.

"Will," Mackenzie whispered, feeling like a kid about to be caught by a parent.

Joe nodded and relaxed back into the pillows. "You think you could go get my clothes from him? He's seen me naked, but not usually while my pubes are still wet from some guy's spit."

"Ewww!" Mackenzie pushed away, laughing. "That is nasty. I'm going to have a thirty-second shower, get dressed, and go get your clothes and check in with him. You'll have a quick shower while I'm gone, I'll redo your bandage, and we'll go for breakfast. Yes?"

"Yes, master."

Mackenzie waggled his eyebrows. "I like the sound of that."

"I thought you might," Joe said, and he leaned back into his pillows. "You kinky bastard."

"You have no idea," Mackenzie promised, and he was pretty sure that was true. After all, he really had no idea himself. But he was enjoying the process of self-discovery and was looking forward to doing a bit more experimenting with his willing, and handsome, assistant.

CHAPTER TEN

BREAKFAST WAS weird, as Joe had known it would be. Only one place in town served real breakfast food; they could have gone for donuts and bagels, but that would have been just as awkward and it wouldn't have had the comfort of bacon.

But Joe was used to living in a small town and used to chatting with ten different people during the course of a meal. Of course, today was a little bit worse than usual, between Joe's appearance with a new guy and the rapidly spreading news of the fire the night before.

"Those poor girls," Denise Alcroft said. She'd been Joe's high school history teacher, but she'd retired and now ran a craft shop across the street. "Lacey was in my class a couple years ago. And now they're saying they don't know if *any* of them is going to make it?"

"I don't know," Joe said. "I haven't really heard anything." Mackenzie had been an excellent distraction, but now Joe felt guilty for enjoying himself while the girls were still fighting for their lives.

"They're collecting clothes and housewares over at the church," Tony Albano said five minutes later. "They always do that when there's a fire. But it's a bit weird this time, isn't it? I mean, the girls aren't going to be setting up a *house*. They might need the clothes, God willing, but they'll be living with family or going into foster care, right?"

"I have no idea," Joe said. He was pretty sure there was no family around, or the girls would have gone to them instead of to the Suttons when things got bad at home. But maybe there was someone farther away. "I guess people just want to be able to help somehow, right?"

"We can't all go charging into burning buildings," Tony agreed. The man owned an electronics store that was always on the edge of going out of business, and he weighed at least three hundred pounds. He definitely wasn't the type to go jumping up on roofs. "Good thing you were there, though. Any chance these girls have, it's because of you."

Joe wished that little bit of news hadn't spread quite so quickly. The radio had apparently reported that a volunteer fireman had arrived early and pulled the girls out before the trucks arrived, but hadn't given his name. Still, the small-town gossip engine had revved up instantly, and it seemed like everyone knew pretty much everything already.

After they finished their meal, the owner of the restaurant came over to say that heroes didn't have to pay for their breakfasts, and the whole place erupted into applause. Joe would rather have paid his twenty bucks and gotten out without the embarrassment, but Mackenzie was practically glowing by the time they hit the sidewalk.

"You didn't tell me all that! You didn't tell me you were the first one in, and you got the girls out! I thought you were just another firefighter doing his regular job."

"I *was*," Joe insisted. "I was just the one who happened to live closest. I got there first so I acted first, but anyone else would have done the same thing."

"*I* wouldn't have," Mackenzie protested. He stopped at the passenger door of Joe's truck and looked over the hood at him. "No way. I'm just not a hero. Not at all."

Joe frowned at him. "Neither am I," he said firmly. "People just like to get worked up about stuff. I reached through a couple windows, that's all. It's not a big deal."

"Yeah, it is," Mackenzie said fondly. "But we can pretend it isn't if it makes you feel better."

"That'd be great," Joe said with feeling. They climbed into the truck, and Joe pulled out and headed for the church. "Look, I have to get back to the farm. Ally covered my chores for me this morning, but I've got work to do, and everything's going to be way slower with my hand only half-working. But...." He wished he had better words. "Thank you. For last night. I was... like you said, I was a bit messed up. I appreciate you looking after me."

"Anytime," Mackenzie said breezily, but his voice was more serious when he added, "I mean it. Anytime. I was happy to be useful."

"And what if I'm *not* messed up?" Joe knew he was making a mistake but didn't seem able to stop himself. "What if I just want to come over?"

Mackenzie's smile was damn close to smug. "Uh-huh," he said in a happy singsong. "What if you just want to come back for some more Mackenzie-lovin'? Huh? Is that what you're looking for?"

"You were in the closet until university? Seriously?"

"Don't change the topic. We're focusing on how hooked you are and how much you want me."

It was too close to the truth. Despite his best efforts, Joe *was* hooked. Like charging into a burning building, he knew it was a bad idea but didn't seem able to stop himself. But this time there were no kids inside to save. This time it would be just him groping around in the smoky darkness until he was, inevitably, burned.

Mackenzie obviously realized Joe wasn't in a mood for joking anymore. "I'd like you to come over again," he said seriously. "But... no more booty calls. Or at least not *just* booty calls. Come play euchre with me next week. Make me dinner. Let me make *you* dinner. The sex is great, and it should absolutely continue.

But more would be good too."

"More is tricky," Joe said. "It's hard to find time. Someone has to be home for Austin, and...."

Mackenzie held up his hands. "I'm not asking you to move in. This doesn't have to be an every night thing. Just... sometime. Something." He looked out the window. "Is it really such a horrible thought?"

"It's not horrible," Joe said. "It's just hard to manage."

"I'd appreciate it if you'd try," Mackenzie said softly.

"Yeah." They pulled up in front of the church, and Mackenzie climbed out of the truck without speaking.

He looked like he was about to turn away, but then he leaned through the open window and quickly said, "Or I could take all that shit back. You can come over for booty calls. Absolutely. I know you're busy, and it's *great* that you're committed to your family. I get it. No problem."

Joe stared at him. For the first time he realized he wasn't the only one finding all of this a little scary and overwhelming. Mackenzie wasn't quite as urbane as he seemed, and it obviously wasn't easy for him to ask for things he wanted, or at least not to stick to his guns until he got them. Which meant Joe had to do a better job of looking out for him. But he still had to look after his family too. "What night is euchre?" he asked quietly.

"Thursday." Mackenzie shrugged. "But you don't have to."

"Tell Will he's babysitting," Joe instructed. "Thursday. Euchre. Absolutely." It was Monday, though, and Thursday seemed like a long way away. Well, Nick said he wanted to spend more time with Austin, and Ally was usually good as a backup. "And maybe a movie tomorrow? We'd have to drive over to Darton, but it's not that far. Half an hour, probably. Or we could go out for dinner, or see if anyone's playing music anywhere...."

Mackenzie was smiling at him. "Why don't you just come over tomorrow night? I'll cook for you. And euchre on Thursday, and maybe something on the weekend. Maybe. Okay?"

"Yeah. Okay. Sounds good." But he still didn't feel quite right driving away. Then he realized what was missing. "Hey, Mackenzie? You think maybe you could get back in the truck for a quick minute?"

"Back in?" Mackenzie looked confused, but he climbed back up on the seat and sat looking quizzically at Joe.

"See ya later," Joe said, and he leaned in for a good-bye kiss. Mackenzie seemed startled at first, his lips almost unresponsive, but then they quirked into a grin that made serious kissing pretty damn difficult before finally settling down to work. Joe made himself pull away before the kiss shifted from "good-bye" to "hello and stay awhile."

Mackenzie licked his lips, then slid out of the truck and shut the door. "What time tomorrow?"

"Can it be a bit late? Austin goes to bed around eight. I could be here by eight thirty or nine."

"Sounds good," Mackenzie said.

AND IT was good. They ate pasta, talked, had sex, talked some more, had more sex, and Joe still made it home in time for breakfast with Austin. And Thursday went just as well. It had been a while since Joe had played euchre, but the game wasn't too complicated, and he ended up having more fun than he'd expected. And going back to the church with Mackenzie was almost feeling like a routine, in the best possible way. They were getting comfortable together, learning each other's quirks, and realizing they fit together surprisingly well.

Joe was trying to keep himself under control. It was all good, but that didn't mean it would stay that way. Things happened, people changed—the world was an uncertain place. He had commitments and responsibilities and couldn't afford to be too distracted from them. All the same, he knew where he wanted to be and who he wanted to be with. So, when Mackenzie suggested they do something together on Saturday night, Joe agreed without hesitation. He'd stay home on Friday, and someone else could cover Austin-duty the next night. Not that being with Austin was a duty; it was just a pain to have to be in the house while he was sleeping. Awake Austin was fun. Sleeping Austin was just keeping Joe away from Awake Mackenzie.

"Lacey actually posted on Facebook!" Ally crowed as Joe came into the kitchen after putting the little guy to bed on Saturday night. "She's still in the hospital, but they let her use a computer! She says she's going to be fine!"

"Nice." He'd been hearing good reports about her for a few days, but it was excellent to actually hear something from the girl herself. "And the younger ones?"

Ally's face grew more serious. "Savannah's probably going to be okay. Lacey said there's some weird brain stuff, but they think it's going to go away. Kami's still...." Ally shook her head impatiently. "She's still working at it. But she's a tough little monkey! She'll be okay."

Joe wondered which one he'd pulled out first. He was pretty sure it had been Savannah, the youngest. Maybe the few extra moments without proper oxygen had affected Kami. If he'd been faster, it all could have been different. He'd played it over in his mind so many times. He could have left the first girl just outside the window and gone right back in to grab her sister. He could have left the goddamned dog where it was and maybe that would have saved half a second. Not much, but maybe enough. He could have driven faster to get there, climbed faster, searched faster, done *everything* perfectly, and maybe a little girl wouldn't still be fighting for her life.

"Joe," Ally said slowly and seriously. "Lacey's alive because of you. She knows it. Everyone knows it. Their parents were passed out in the living room; that's what people are saying. If you hadn't gotten there, *nobody* would have gotten out. You did the best anyone could have done for the little ones."

He forced himself to smile. Sometimes his family knew him a little too well. "I'm glad Lacey's okay," he said sincerely. And he was glad. But he still wasn't in a great mood as he pulled out of the driveway and headed into town. He and Mackenzie hadn't made firm plans, but Joe knew what he wanted to do. Bed. Not sex, necessarily, although that would be fine, but really just being in bed with Mackenzie, being wrapped around him, breathing him in and feeling his warmth. Yeah, he planned to make a strong case for staying in that night.

His anticipation turned to confusion when he arrived at the church and found several unfamiliar cars in the parking lot. Mackenzie hadn't mentioned visitors. Joe pulled out his cell and pressed the right buttons, but Mackenzie didn't pick up.

Joe was pretty sure his plans for a quiet evening had just fallen completely apart. A petty, childish voice in his head told him to just turn around and drive back to the farm; he and Mackenzie might not have had specific plans, but they definitely hadn't talked about a party. Joe let himself pout for two breaths, then found a parking spot and got out of the truck. It would still be good to see Mackenzie, even if he had to see other people at the same time.

His resolve weakened as he made his way up the walkway and heard the dance music playing inside and the shriek of what he really hoped was laughter. What the hell was going on?

He pulled the carved wooden door open and peered inside. There were no lights on, but it wasn't dark out yet, and the stained-glass windows were doing their job, giving a glowing, muted tone to everything inside. There were about twenty men and half as many women—or excellent cross-dressers—gathered at the front of the church, some sitting in the front row of pews, some sprawled on the steps to the altar, and a few dancing in the middle. Joe had never been religious and had never thought of the church as anything other than a great piece of architecture, but something about the scene felt wrong to him. Maybe not sacrilegious, but certainly disrespectful.

He was halfway up the aisle when one of the women noticed him. She smiled, and he recognized Kristen from the afternoon with the dog. But where *was* the dog, and where the hell was Mackenzie?

Someone else followed Kristen's gaze, and suddenly the whole group became aware of Joe's presence. The music cut off, and a man in short shorts and a low-cut tank top straightened from one of the pews and stood to block the aisle. "This is private property, officer."

Joe stared at him. Why did the guy think he was a cop? But Kristen came to her feet, a little unsteadily, looped her arm through the protector's arm, and laughed. "No, this is *Joe*." The man beside her looked at her doubtfully, and she nodded several times, her chin going right to her chest and her hair flying about. "The cowboy," she said in a stage-whisper.

"Where's his hat?" someone asked.

"Where's his horse?"

"Where's his cow?" Apparently that last one was pretty funny to at least a few of them.

But Joe had only one question he wanted answered. He stepped closer and asked Kristen, "Where's Mackenzie?"

She looked around blurrily, as if inspecting each face in the circle.

"He's not here," Joe said as patiently as he could. "Where did he go?"

She looked puzzled. Finally, mercifully, Mackenzie's familiar face appeared in the doorway to the back of the church. He was carrying a couple bottles of liquor, and Griffin was at his side. As soon as the dog saw Joe, he bounded happily over, but Mackenzie's greeting was a little less enthusiastic. He looked at

Joe as if confused by his presence, then set the bottles down on a table and looked at his watch. His face was comically surprised as he looked back. "Holy shit, it's nighttime!"

Drunk, Joe could handle. Hell, he could handle high, too, with a little warning. But this was not what he'd been expecting when he came to town.

Don't be a princess, Joe. You don't always get what you want. You need to be more flexible. You need to accept Mackenzie for who he is, not who you expect him to be.

Joe took another deep breath and smiled. "Yeah, nighttime. Kind of. Seems like you all got an early start." He wished there wasn't an audience for this particular conversation, but he wasn't sure how to move Mackenzie somewhere else. Instead, he just edged around the crowd and got as close to Mackenzie as he could before saying, "Do you want me to do anything? Go pick up pizza or something?"

"Pizza would be *excellent*," came a voice from the crowd.

"This wouldn't be *good* pizza," another voice contradicted. "Trust me, I grew up in a shithole just like this one. We're talking thick crust, pepperoni, and grease."

Joe kept his smile as fixed as he could manage and waited for Mackenzie to do something, or say something, or *somehow* let him know what was expected. But Mackenzie wasn't functioning at anywhere near his usual capacity.

"Pizza for those who want it?" Kristen said from somewhere near Joe's elbow. "We brought snacks, but not enough." She looked up into the rafters as if searching for the answers to universal questions. "Why are there never enough snacks?"

In Joe's experience, there was almost always too *much* food at social gatherings, so he didn't feel qualified to respond to anything but the first part of Kristen's communication. "Okay, I'll get food." He glanced over toward Mackenzie. "You okay, there? You want some fresh air?"

"You want another *drink*?" someone asked from the pews, and again there was general hilarity. Joe was way too sober for this.

"I'm good," Mackenzie said. He did pretty well on the first couple steps, but stumbled on the last one, fell forward, and caught himself on Joe's chest. Then he let himself sag as if trusting Joe with the responsibility of keeping him upright. "Surprise party," he whispered in Joe's ear. "They just... appeared." He leaned back a little, and Joe moved quickly to wrap an arm around him and keep him from toppling right over backward. "I am *so* drunk."

"Yeah, looks like it." Joe didn't bother mentioning that it seemed like something more than alcohol might be involved. He glanced over at Kristen, then scanned the crowd to see if anyone was in better shape. The guy in the short shorts who'd thought he was a cop seemed like the best candidate, unfortunately. "Come here," he said softly to Mackenzie, and they made their way through the group together.

The short-shorts guy looked suspicious as they approached. Joe tried his best nonthreatening, friendly smile, but the guy seemed unmoved. "I'm Joe. Friend of Mackenzie's. You're a friend of his too?"

"I've known him since he was a *teenager*," the man said pointedly.

"Great, so you'll want to take care of him." Joe smiled again. "I'm just a bit worried that this party could hurt his business if it spills out into the neighborhood. You know? He's trying to make connections and work his way into the community, and people are pretty open to the idea of a wedding chapel in the village. But the gay thing has them thrown a little. And it doesn't help that he's from the city. And it really, really won't help if they start thinking the church is going to turn into some sort of nightclub or something. You know?"

The man's smile was too sweet to be real. "That's really good news," he purred. "Because the theme of this party? It's 'Get Mackenzie Back to the City Where He Belongs.' We came up to remind him that he has friends, and he has a life, and he does *not* need to hide away in Buttfuck, Nowhere, just because he had a fight with his boyfriend." The man looked positively triumphant, now. "If we need to outrage the neighbors a little in order to make it clear to Mackenzie that he's trying to live somewhere that will never accept him, then I guess we have our plan for the evening."

"In my experience, Mackenzie usually catches on to things pretty quickly, usually just with conversation. I don't think you need to stage a big scene just to help him get your point."

"'Stage a big scene.' Yeah, Mackenzie *said* you were like that. He *said* you didn't really understand gay culture. Said you didn't accept it." The man raised an eyebrow imperiously. "Life *is* a scene. And some of us want our lives to be *big*. And, if our lives are big, our scenes must be big as well, no?"

Joe really wished he'd turned around in the parking lot, but he needed to try to salvage something from this, for Mackenzie's sake. "It'd be pretty sad if Mackenzie left here because he couldn't stay. Wouldn't it? I think it'd be a much better scene if he got to go back to the city triumphantly, not crawling away with his tail between his legs because the ignorant rednecks wouldn't accept him. Right? I mean, if people want him to leave and he leaves, then the people up here win. But if they want him to *stay* and he leaves... he's made a point, right?" For the time being, Joe tried to focus on the effect his words were having on the man in front of him, not on himself.

"And he needs to hide who he is in order to make them accept him?" The man still sounded snarky, but maybe not quite as sure as he'd been before.

"He can be who he is. But he doesn't need to be a bad neighbor. He can have a party, but it should stay inside. That sort of thing. If people don't like him, you want them to have to admit they don't like him because he's gay. You don't want to give them the excuse of saying they don't like him because he woke up their kids and his friends puked in their flowers."

Finally, Mackenzie seemed ready to join the conversation. "I'm coming *back*, Anton!" He said it like it was obvious. "I didn't move up here *forever*! It's just for a little while. Of *course* I'm coming back!"

Joe fought to keep his face expressionless. It wasn't like Mackenzie was saying anything Joe hadn't always known. Maybe he'd let himself forget it for a little while, but he had no reason to be shocked by hearing the reminder. Mackenzie was a city boy. He was just visiting. "He'll get a better price if he can sell a profitable business, not an empty church. He's got plans, and this little gathering can't get in the way of that. Okay?"

The man looked thoughtful, but finally, slowly, he nodded. "That makes sense. Mackenzie should have something of his own. A little nest egg hidden away. That'd be good."

Joe didn't really follow that part, but at least the man seemed to be getting on board with the contain-the-party plan, and that was something. "I'll get some food—it probably won't be what you all are used to, but it might help soak up some of... whatever. And you'll keep the music down, and people will stay inside? Does that sound like a plan?"

Again, the man's nod was slower than Joe would have liked, but it eventually came.

Mackenzie, meanwhile, was getting heavier by the minute. "You need to sit down, buddy." Joe lowered him down to sit on one of the pews and tried surreptitiously to gauge Mackenzie's vitals and responses. His first-responder training had made him more sensitive to the signs of alcohol poisoning and drug overdose than he'd been as a kid, but there was often a clash between medical standards and what was expected by the public, especially at a party. How many people passed out after one of Mackenzie's typical nights out? Technically, any of them who couldn't be awakened should be rushed to the hospital for treatment, but nobody really followed that rule.

Joe looked down at Mackenzie. He was going back to the city. He'd been the one who'd pushed to spend more time with Joe, but that was because *he* had the normal ability to keep things casual, to spend time with someone and share a bed with someone without thinking it was a sign of some big deal. Mackenzie hadn't done anything wrong. It was Joe who'd made the mistake, even though he'd known he shouldn't. "You're not looking too good, Mackenzie. You feeling okay?" Joe sank down onto the pew and tried to ignore the curious looks from the crowd. They were probably wondering why he hadn't gone to get their pizza yet.

"I'm totally out of it," Mackenzie said. "I don't know what happened. I mean... I drank too much. I...." He looked almost guilty, then just confused. "I took a pill. I'm not even sure what it was. They just said it would be fun."

"Maybe it was. Maybe you're just tired now, if you got an early start. You want to go sleep it off?"

"I'm the *host*," Mackenzie said, obviously scandalized by Joe's suggestion.

"It's a surprise party. You're more the guest of honor. And I think guests of honor get to do whatever the hell they want."

"And if I want to go outside?" Mackenzie sounded crafty now, and the way he slid his gaze across to see Joe's reaction made it clear he'd heard and understood at least part of the earlier conversation.

Joe sighed. "I'm not your babysitter. If you want to go outside, go outside. If you want to run around naked and singing, go for it. Take your whole band of brothers with you. Your call." It was a bit harder to fight for Mackenzie's business future when Joe was seeing it strictly in terms of Mackenzie selling out for a better price rather than Mackenzie trying to make a living. And a bit harder to fight when Mackenzie himself seemed interested in destroying it.

"What if I want to go to bed?"

"I think that would be a good idea."

"No, not to *sleep*. What if I want to go to bed *with you*?"

"With me *to sleep*? Okay. But, no, I'm not real interested in having sex with you right now. Not when you're all messed up."

"You only want me when I conform to your standards?" Mackenzie's consciousness was clearly getting its second wind, but it wasn't feeling too friendly.

Joe shrugged. "I'm just not in the mood," he said quietly. No point in having a fight that Mackenzie might not even remember the next day.

"What if someone else *is*?" Mackenzie looked around the room. "I've fucked three of the guys here. You want to guess which ones?"

"What are you doing, Mackenzie? If you want me to leave, just tell me to leave. You don't need to... whatever you're doing. It's not necessary. You don't need to pick a fight."

"You're always so *calm*," Mackenzie sneered. "So fucking *careful*. Do you *ever* lose control? Do you ever just let yourself go?"

"I think I'm going to let myself go right now," Joe said. He tried not to let Mackenzie's words echo in his head, tried not to wonder whether maybe he'd been too careful at the fire. If he'd just pushed everything a little more, if he hadn't cleared the glass as thoroughly or hadn't made that one little bounce when he checked that the roof was going to hold his weight... maybe those had cost him the crucial seconds.... He slipped away from Mackenzie and stood up. "You're a nasty drunk."

Mackenzie's expression was unreadable. Joe was giving him what he clearly wanted, so why didn't he look happier? Just another mystery of the miserable evening, Joe supposed. "I'll see you later," he said, but Mackenzie just turned away.

Joe headed for the door. He knew he should stick around and make sure everyone was okay. He should try to contain the situation and take care of Mackenzie's business future. But it seemed pretty pointless. Maybe a better man would have done all that, but Joe just wasn't that strong. He would at least order the pizza, he decided, but he'd do it from the truck, and he'd ask for it to be delivered. He could use his credit card over the phone.

He headed out into the night and closed his eyes for a moment as he barreled down the path to the driveway. He almost ran into a man coming toward the church. He was smaller than Joe, older, and wearing a suit, albeit one with the tie off and the neck of his shirt open. Joe had never seen a picture, never even heard a full description, but he knew at once who he was staring at.

"Is this Scott Mackenzie's church?" the man asked.

Joe was temporarily speechless. *Scott Mackenzie.* Joe had never asked for Mackenzie's surname; he'd never even been curious, really. Never bothered to look at any of the paperwork Will must have had for the work on the church. But all along he'd known Mackenzie's last name. He'd just never known the guy's *first* name.

It was a little thing. Just a silly detail. Except that it wasn't. "Yeah, this is his church," Joe said slowly. He thought about how Mackenzie had pushed for a fight, and it made sense now. He'd been eager to get rid of Joe before Nathan showed up. "I think he's expecting you." And then Joe got in his truck and drove away.

CHAPTER ELEVEN

MACKENZIE'S BRAIN felt too big for his skull. The pressure was even, pressing out on all sides, and it wasn't so much painful as it was nauseating. Or at least, *something* was making him nauseous.

He looked around him blurrily and saw his familiar bedroom in the church basement, a body-shaped lump in the covers next to him on the bed. He didn't have time to investigate any further before his stomach's revolt kicked into high gear and he had to race for the bathroom. He hovered over the toilet for a moment, as if his gut had suddenly changed its mind, then it took advantage of the opportunity and emptied itself, a disgusting stream of whatever the hell Mackenzie had consumed the night before. He was shaking and weak by the time it was over, but he pulled himself to his feet and flushed the evidence away. Then he stumbled to the sink and braced himself with his forearms on the enamel, gathering strength for a few moments before managing to turn on the tap and rinse his mouth out. He felt a bit better now that his stomach was empty, and he managed to feebly brush his teeth before raising his head and looking in the mirror.

The sight that greeted him was appalling. Not his own pale, drained face, although on a normal day that certainly would have been upsetting enough, but the man standing in the doorway behind him, wearing Mackenzie's silk robe... a robe that had been a gift from the man himself.

"That sound is no way to start the day," Nathan said. He sounded like a less than patient schoolteacher. "And the ventilation in here is atrocious—the smell is going to be with us for some time."

"What are you doing here?" Mackenzie stammered. The lump on the bed—it had been too small to be Joe, now that Mackenzie thought about it. And Joe didn't usually burrow under the blankets like that—he slept sprawled out and uncovered. Mackenzie looked down at himself and was relieved to see he was still wearing his jeans; someone might have been able to get those off of him while he was incapacitated, but they'd have had a hell of a time getting them back on. But his fly was undone, his underwear bunched in a way that could be the result of a night's sleep or could be... "What happened?"

"We've had the talk about your overconsumption before," Nathan said. He edged past Mackenzie and opened the robe enough so he could pee in the toilet. "It's not healthy for you, and it's not something I want to be around. You need to practice a little self-control."

Yes, they'd had that talk. Repeatedly. But not recently, because Nathan no longer had any say over how Mackenzie lived his life. Did he? "What the fuck is going on?" Mackenzie groaned. His head was in no condition for this sort of bewilderment.

Nathan nodded sympathetically as he shook off and moved to the sink to wash his hands. "That's about what I said last night when I arrived. Anton had invited me to a small gathering in your honor. I was expecting a dinner, perhaps, or some light cocktails. With an invitation from Anton, of course, I should have known better." Nathan smiled at Mackenzie in the mirror. "But it's okay. I understand my presence was a surprise for you. I'm sure you've been... unhappy lately. And when you're unhappy, you engage in destructive behavior. I've always found that the best way to keep you on track is to keep you happy. Doesn't that sound about right?"

"Where's Joe?" That was what Mackenzie had to cling to. Joe would make everything make sense.

"Who?" Nathan turned around and said, "There are quite a few people upstairs. They brought *sleeping bags*." He pronounced the words as if they were from a foreign language. "I didn't catch all of their names."

Joe sleeping upstairs while Nathan shared a bed with Mackenzie? No, that wouldn't happen. Maybe Mackenzie should stop asking Nathan questions he couldn't answer and ask the one that he could. "Where's your boyfriend? What's his name, again? Calvin?"

Nathan frowned as if the question was in poor taste. "I don't know where he is, nor do I care."

"He dumped you?" Mackenzie tried to keep the vicious anticipation from showing on his face.

But Nathan scoffed. "*Dumped* me? Of course not. But he was...." Nathan looked at Mackenzie appraisingly. "I found that I'd underestimated you," he admitted, but he made it sound like that error had somehow been Mackenzie's fault, as if he hadn't made his qualities clear enough. "I'm afraid poor Calvin couldn't quite measure up. He was just... selfish, I think. Immature. Much like you were when we first became involved, actually. And I suppose I could have put the years into nurturing him and molding him, like I did with you, but it occurred to me... why bother? I mean, when I've already *done* all that work once...."

It wasn't clear whether it was the hangover or the words, but something was making Mackenzie dizzy. "I need to sit down," he said faintly.

"You'd better go back to the bedroom, then, because this bathroom does *not* have many amenities. I suppose you could perch on the toilet...."

Mackenzie stumbled past Nathan and flopped onto the bed, face-first, burying his head in the covers and wishing desperately for a do-over. If he'd had less to drink the night before, he'd be able to respond to all this much better.

He pulled his face out of the sheets when he realized he was smelling Nathan's familiar cologne. Damn it, the man had been in the room for one night and his presence was already pervasive.

"Sleep for a bit," Nathan said softly, running his fingers through Mackenzie's hair. "I have a few things to do, and then I'll come back and we'll talk." The mattress shifted and a moment later Nathan said, "I've set the alarm for an hour. Wake up then, shower, and come upstairs." Of course Nathan knew how to set the alarm; he was the one who'd bought it when he decided Mackenzie needed to have more disciplined sleep habits.

Mackenzie stayed still until he heard Nathan leave the room, then rolled over and found his phone on the bedside table. A few quick pokes at the screen, and then he heard Joe's familiar voice.

"Hi, Mackenzie." Joe sounded tired. Hopefully there hadn't been another fire... and Mackenzie too out of it to help Joe recover?

"Are you okay?"

"What? Yeah, I'm fine. What's up?" He still sounded tired, and now maybe a little impatient.

"I'm not sure. I... I had way too much to drink last night, I guess." It was embarrassing to ask, but Mackenzie needed to know. "Did you come by? I know we had plans...."

"I was there for a bit. Wasn't really my thing, though, so I left."

"Oh. Okay." That all made sense. And maybe explained why Joe sounded less than impressed with Mackenzie. They'd had plans, and Mackenzie had screwed them up. Not good. Not something Mackenzie's boyfriends should be expected to tolerate. "I'm sorry. I'll make it up to you, okay?"

The pause was long enough to make Mackenzie's already fragile stomach churn a little more. "Don't worry about it," Joe said. The words were fine, but the tone was not.

"No, I will. That was rude of me, to be drunk when you showed up. I really am sorry."

Joe's huff of breath might have been a bit of laughter, or it might have been something else. "Don't worry about it," he repeated. "It's not a big deal. We're just casual, right?"

A flash of memory came to Mackenzie then. Joe *had* been at the party. And Mackenzie had said something about moving back to the city someday, and Joe hadn't reacted at all. He'd been fine with the idea. Because everything was casual between them. Because Joe didn't really have any attachment to any of this. It had made Mackenzie angry the night before, but now it just made him sad. He'd let himself fall for another man who didn't really care about him. They both just wanted to use him, but at least Nathan had been in it for the longer term. At least Nathan had *provided* for Mackenzie, made him comfortable in his servitude. He looked around the church basement. There wasn't a single gift from Joe, not even flowers or chocolate or something disposable. "Just casual," he echoed.

"Okay, so I'll see you around. Bye, Mackenzie."

The phone disconnected, and Mackenzie stared at it. The call had taken less than a minute. So little time, but still a pretty important message delivered. All along, Joe had been saying he wanted to keep things casual, and Mackenzie had never really disagreed. At least he hadn't *said* anything about it. He'd hinted at it when he said he wanted to spend more time together, but he hadn't made it clear enough. It wasn't Joe's fault Mackenzie was feeling so empty and alone.

He sighed and hauled himself to his feet. He was tired, but he wasn't going to go back to sleep on Nathan's command. So he showered, trying not to think about sharing the stall with Joe, and then got dressed and headed upstairs.

There were bodies strewn all over the sanctuary of the church, most of them wrapped in sleeping bags, some just laid out in the clothes they'd been wearing. People were starting to wake up. Hungover, poorly rested, and grumpy: just another Sunday morning. Except there was no trendy brunch spot to stumble to.

They'd have to drive to get to town, and the one restaurant that served a real breakfast would have trouble accommodating this many extra customers. Mackenzie wondered whether whoever had organized this little event had thought of these challenges. Probably not; after all, he hadn't thought about support services when he'd *bought* the damned place.

He snapped out of his gloomy reverie when the front doors swung open and a swarm of black-and-white clad strangers bustled in. Even through his confusion Mackenzie could recognize the traditional serving uniform, and he couldn't deny that they seemed to be setting up tables, carrying in silver trays... and there, in the middle of the action, was Nathan, smiling in satisfaction.

"What the hell?" Mackenzie managed as he stumbled toward the narthex. "Nathan... what the hell? Where did they come from?"

"I shipped them in," he said nonchalantly. "Not from right downtown, I'm afraid; they're from the north end of Brampton. The menu looks interesting. We'll have to see about the quality. But if we worked with them, they could adapt as needed, I'm sure. We'll give them a try today and see what needs to be done."

Mackenzie realized that his mouth was hanging open and snapped it shut. "They're... today's a tryout? They could.... You're thinking they could cater the weddings?"

Nathan nodded patiently. "That's right. There's always a way, Mackenzie. You should have learned that by now." His smile was almost genuine as he added, "And I'm quite excited about another one of the solutions I've found to your little problems."

"Wait. How do you even know what my little... what my *problems* are?"

"We have mutual friends, Mackenzie. I didn't show up here by *accident*. I was invited to be part of the event." He shrugged. "I had to give it some thought. You know how I feel about some of your friends. But... I came. I'm here. Everything is going to work out fine now."

Mackenzie watched in a daze as warming pans were set up and food started. After a quick consultation with Nathan, the servers started unloading tables from one of the vans and setting them up in the partly weeded gardens. White tablecloths and napkins, centerpieces, gleaming silver cutlery... the caterers were going all-out.

Lorraine came out on her front steps to stare at the proceedings, and Mackenzie jogged across the street to join her.

"Have you had a wedding already?" she asked in amazement. "I thought you were just getting set up!"

"We are. This is... it's a trial run, I guess." He looked across the road at all the commotion and tried to see it through her eyes. A nuisance, maybe, but she didn't seem resentful. More curious. "Lorraine, I'm not sure if you'll be comfortable with some of the people who'll be over there. They may be a bit...." Hung over. Drug addled. Irreverent. Indecent. "... unusual. But I'd love it if you'd join me for breakfast."

"I don't know," she said, but her eyes were dancing. "It looks very fancy. I'm hardly dressed for it...."

"You'll be in better shape than most," Mackenzie promised, and he gestured down at his own jeans and deep V-necked T-shirt. The outfit might have cost more than her fanciest party gown, but she wouldn't know it by looking.

"Well... I've already eaten. But maybe I could have a little taste...."

"That's all they give you," he stage-whispered. "The portions are *bound* to be tiny. If they aren't, Nathan will be outraged and consider it a grave flaw in their service."

"Nathan?"

Oh. That was a bit too complicated to be discussed before coffee. "He's the one who set this up."

Lorraine smiled blandly, but her eyes were still sharp and interested. "How kind of him. He must be a very good friend."

Mackenzie didn't answer that. Instead, he crooked his arm in her direction. "I'm not sure the food is ready yet, but there's juice, and I can smell coffee from here. I could really use some of both, and I'd love it if you'd keep me company."

Nathan didn't seem to love it so much. He frowned when he saw Mackenzie's chaperone and then ignored them completely. It wasn't clear whether he was actually wrapped up in the minutiae of the breakfast service or just pretending to be, but Mackenzie didn't really care either way. He needed to clear his head before he had any more contact with his ex.

The sleepers from the church started waking and stumbling out, and Lorraine greeted them with equanimity. Mackenzie made a point of emphasizing that people attending a wedding would certainly be on much better behavior and dressed more formally than this crowd had been. Lorraine just raised an eyebrow. "Dressed better, maybe. But the weddings I've been to? The receptions can get pretty rowdy."

Mackenzie supposed she had a good point. When he pictured the church's role in future events, he saw white linens, like that morning. He saw carefully dressed ladies and gentlemen circulating among the tables with cocktails or champagne in their well-manicured hands. If there were children in his dreams, they were wearing frilly white dresses with wide pink sashes that matched their shoes, and they were standing nicely off to the side, not doing a hell of a lot. There didn't seem to be any little boys in his vision at all. Then he looked at the collection of zombies shuffling out of the church into the cruel sunlight. These people were invited to weddings. They *went* to weddings. And they acted like themselves while they were there. Mackenzie's vision was not strongly connected to reality.

He was in way over his head. The chapel had been the original idea, and he could do that. Get it fixed up, help coordinate a nice ceremony, maybe fulfill a few special requests. But he wasn't a caterer, he wasn't a party planner, and he wasn't a hotelier. He had no idea how he could have found these clowns places to sleep the night before if they'd been real guests and expected something better than the church floor. Maybe if he'd worked his ass off, and had some damned warning, he could have found people willing to serve as B&Bs. But how many misbehaving guests would anyone tolerate in their home before closing the doors and going back to their quiet existence? How could this become a sustainable business, especially with a neophyte like Mackenzie in charge?

He looked over at Nathan, who was carefully scrutinizing the amount of champagne the server was pouring into a pitcher of mimosas. Nathan didn't know anything about catering or party planning, either, but he knew people who did, and he had the money to pay the experts. Now he said he had solutions to Mackenzie's problems, and he was probably being truthful. Nathan was an experienced and successful businessman, an expert at finding ways to make money. He'd know what Mackenzie needed to do, and he'd also know what he expected from Mackenzie in return for his assistance.

And Mackenzie had no reason to resist Nathan's plans. If Nathan was here to offer him his old life back, he knew he had to take it. He was failing on his own. His business was going nowhere, his personal life... no, damn it, he couldn't let himself think about Joe. He couldn't remember how safe and cherished he'd felt in Joe's arms, not if he was about to walk back into the controlling embrace of another man. Besides, the warmth from Joe had been a lie, or at least not the truth Mackenzie wanted it to be. Joe didn't care about him as anything other than a fuck buddy. Joe could move on anytime. Nathan had lasted almost six years, and he was back for more.

When Nathan glanced over, Mackenzie made himself smile and raise his mimosa glass in congratulations. The breakfast was a success. Nathan would tolerate nothing less.

By the time Mackenzie returned from escorting Lorraine home, things were starting to wind down. Party guests were rolling up their sleeping bags like good little scouts at a jamboree, and the servers were covering food and clearing away dishes. Nathan was sitting at the most distant table, the chair beside him pulled out in an invitation Mackenzie had been well-trained to notice and obey.

He slid into his seat. "This went really well, Nathan. Thanks."

"There were a few glitches, but I think we could make it work. I took some notes, and I'll pass them along."

"I guess I should see the expenses?" Mackenzie ventured. "I mean, people might want to use their own caterers, but if they don't...."

"Screw that. *You* pick the caterer, and that way you don't have to worry about amateurs messing things up. You'll get better service because you'll be a big client, and they'll know not to mess with you, and you can take a cut of what they bill *and* add a booking charge or something onto the invoice for your customers."

Oh. "It might be hard if we don't have an indoor venue," he tried. "It was beautiful today, but people will want a backup plan in case it rains."

Nathan nodded. "And there still isn't much for people to do while they're waiting for the happy couple to get their pictures taken. This might work if it had to, but I think my second plan is better by far."

"Your second plan?"

"Trains," Nathan said, and he leaned back in his chair with a self-satisfied smile.

"I'm sorry? Trains?"

"There's an abandoned CP line running by about two miles from here. Goes straight from Toronto up to Collingwood. I know a man who's working to get it set up as a weekend commuter train. He owns half of Collingwood, just started a new resort up there, and he thinks he can get more visitors if they don't have to drive so far. He wants to make the train an event in and of itself... a car for kids to watch movies or play video games or whatever, a car for adults to have cocktails... that sort of thing. Your guests could take that train up from the city, get off at a station nearby—we'd have to build that, but we could—have the wedding, then get back on the train and have cocktails while they went the rest of the way up to Collingwood to stay at one of my friends' resorts." Nathan waited for Mackenzie's brain to catch up.

"Wow," he finally said. "That... that could really work. The trip could be a part of the experience. And it would eliminate the worries about drunk-driving, or bad weather... trains can run in bad weather, right?"

Nathan shrugged. "I think so. We'd have to look into that."

"My God, Nathan, this really *would* solve my problems!" Mackenzie tried to control his excitement, but it wasn't easy. His business had a chance. The church could be a success.

"And you could run it from the city," Nathan said, clearly thinking he was putting the icing on the cake he'd already delivered. "I was thinking you could turn that little guest bedroom into an office, if you wanted. I don't think you'd need a public space; you could visit clients in their homes or meet somewhere neutral. This would give you something to keep you busy when I'm out of town or when my own business takes up my time. But it wouldn't be so big that it interferes with your time with me. I think it could be perfect."

And there it was. Nathan was too refined to actually spell out the deal he was offering and too proud to apologize for his misdeeds and ask Mackenzie to come back to him, but the setup was clear. All could be forgiven and forgotten. Mackenzie could go back to his old life as a kept man. He could stop worrying about money and just let himself be taken care of. All he had to do was agree to Nathan's plan.

He pushed his chair back from the table and stood up so quickly he almost knocked over a server who'd been hovering behind them. "I'll think about it," he said.

"What's to think about?" Nathan seemed genuinely confused. "You really think you're going to get a better deal anywhere else?"

"Probably not," Mackenzie admitted. "Look, can I give you a call in a day or two? I just need to wrap my brain around a few things."

Nathan was wearing his "I'll be patient but not for long" expression. "Fine." He stood up. "Today's Sunday. I'll hear from you by Tuesday night."

"Yeah, okay," Mackenzie agreed. He'd bought himself some time. That was good. Now he just needed to use the time and figure out what the hell he wanted. For his business and for the rest of his life.

CHAPTER TWELVE

MISERY WAS a hell of a cow horse. She worked the cattle with a serene authority, not ruffling feathers but establishing herself as an animal deserving of respect. Every now and then Joe was pretty sure she got cocky, practically daring one of them to defy her, just so she could show off her cutting skills. If she decided a steer was going in a certain direction, it would damn well go that way, and she would out dodge and out deke any animal that thought differently. And as soon as she'd made her point, she'd lapse back into placidity, like a mother cat napping while her kittens frolicked.

At least, that was how it usually went. Today, though, it seemed like everything was going wrong. It should have been a simple job, moving a herd of fairly calm steers from one pasture to another. Something Joe did practically every day with one herd or another. It wasn't usually a big deal. But today it was like the cattle were out to get him. They were restless, acting almost afraid of the horse and rider they'd always accepted. Two different animals had tried to make a break for it, trying to dodge behind Misery and run back to the old pasture. One of them had almost made it and would have outrun the mare if Red hadn't intervened, lunging at the steer and barking him back into the herd. It was unheard of for Misery to fail, and Joe could feel her body tightening in frustration.

It wasn't her fault, Joe realized. It was him. He was directing her too aggressively, and he was even transmitting his agitation directly to the cattle. He was driving when he should have been waiting. And when the steers had tried to get by, he'd been too tense, jerking from side to side instead of staying loose and easy in the middle of the saddle. He'd thrown off Misery's balance and the mood of the whole herd. He was a mess.

But he had too much to do to take any time off to deal with it. He'd already wasted too much daylight in the past couple weeks, messing around with some city boy who couldn't be expected to know that summer was the busiest time in a farmer's world. It was a time for working dawn until dusk and then stumbling into bed to *sleep*, not to mess around. Yeah, this whole situation could have been avoided if Joe had just remembered his priorities and focused on getting work done.

Yeah, he'd let himself get distracted, and now that needed to stop. He took a deep breath and exhaled, forcing his body to relax. He was doing what he loved. This was his land, his job, his life. He'd made a mistake, thinking the grass on the other side of the fence was greener. He grinned at the metaphor. "It really is greener, for you guys," he told the cattle softly. "You're heading for some tasty grazing, no doubt. I wasn't staying inside my fences— that was the problem. I broke out, and I was running down the highway, practically begging to get hit by a truck. You guys won't do that, right?"

A few ears twitched at him, and he could feel the softness returning to the herd. Even Misery seemed to be listening, swiveling her ears as if waiting for his next words. Of course, he wasn't really sure what else there was to say. "I really liked him," he admitted, and he eased Misery into a slow walk along the back edge of the herd. "I should have known better. He just snuck up on me, I guess."

Red was walking beside them now, looking up at Joe with an interested expression. "Yeah, you met him, buddy. The blond guy. He brought chocolates. Nobody's ever brought me chocolates before. I bet they were expensive too. They seemed expensive." And thinking about how much things cost made Joe think of the little man marching up the walk of the church like he owned the place. The ex. Or maybe not all that ex, because what the hell had he been doing there? "Maybe Mackenzie *didn't* know he was coming," Joe tried. The cattle looked skeptical. "Maybe he just wanted me out of there because he didn't want me around his friends. I mean... I don't know. Does that make it better or worse?" Misery twitched unhappily, and Joe made himself relax his legs.

"Sorry," he said to the horse. They were moving fairly well now, an easy walk toward the gate he'd opened on the way to get the cattle. "But you're right. There's no better, no worse. It just doesn't matter. Right? It was just casual. If he's seeing someone else, that's his business. If he doesn't want people to know he's fucking a hick, that's his business too."

Joe's pride made him wish he'd been a bit more discreet about his visits to the church. Not that there was much he could have done, really. He'd needed to make sure someone was home for Austin, and as soon as he did that, they'd figured out where he was going.

He shouldn't have started sleeping over, he realized. That was where the trouble had begun. Well, a bit before that, maybe. Yeah, it had started the night of the fire, when Mackenzie had been so quiet and accepting. Joe should have followed his usual plan that night. He should have driven until he ran out of road, then gotten out of the truck and walked until he ran out of land. He could have sat there and stared at the water and let his fear and pain and frustration wash out into whatever lake he was staring at. Instead, he'd let it go down the drain of Mackenzie's shower. Just as effective and quite a bit quicker, but there had been repercussions.

"I really liked him," he said again, but none of the animals seemed to be listening anymore.

He worked until dinnertime. It was Sunday, and Sarah and Dave were scheduled to be over. They spent one Sunday dinner with his family, one with hers, and if Joe skipped out on the meal, it would raise more curiosity than he wanted to face. So he schooled his expression as well as he could and headed down to the house. The family was gathered in the kitchen, as they usually were, helping to make the meal or at least offering a critique of other people's contributions.

"I'm going to go shower," Joe said as he pulled his boots off and set them in the mudroom.

Austin looked up from the peas he was shelling and absentmindedly shoved a few fat pellets into his mouth. "Bath?" he asked.

"Bath for me. You have your bath after dinner."

Austin looked at Nick, who'd been helping him with the peas. "You give me bath?"

Nick nodded. "Sure. I can give you your bath. But after dinner. And there's no dinner without peas. So let's keep going."

Joe kept going up the stairs and into the bathroom. Yeah, he was the one who always gave Austin his bath. Yeah, the little guy had always screamed the house down if anyone else tried to get him wet. But it was good that he wanted Nick to help him. Good that Austin was growing up and getting more independent. Good that Nick was working his way into his son's life. It was good. So what if it felt like one more piece of Joe's heart being yanked out and skewered over an open fire? He was just being selfish. Austin was happy. Nick was happy. Mackenzie was happy.

He pulled the closet door open and reached inside to pull out a towel, but his hand hit bare wood. What the hell? He'd done laundry the day before, put a whole stack of towels right there....

He wanted to storm down the stairs and start yelling. Who the hell was using all the towels, and why the hell weren't they washing them and putting them back where they belonged? Was it seriously asking so fucking much that he be able to have a shower? He just wanted to clean off some grime, wanted to stand under the spray and turn the water on so hot it burned all his thoughts away. He couldn't even have *that* little bit of fucking comfort?

Yeah, he wanted to yell. He wanted to throw a damned tantrum. Instead, he took three deep breaths and stared at himself in the mirror. He didn't want to be that angry, ugly person. He took three more breaths and tried to think peaceful thoughts. It hadn't been *one* person using all the towels. A bunch of people had used one each. It wasn't a big deal. And Austin still loved Joe. His affection was a bottomless well, not a shallow pond. He could love *lots* of people. And Mackenzie…. Joe stopped there. He wasn't ready to find a bright side for that.

He walked quietly down the stairs and through the kitchen out to the back room. Sure enough, there was a big pile of towels on the floor waiting for the washing machine. None in the dryer, none waiting on top of the dryer to go upstairs. Joe stood there for a moment, then walked back to the kitchen.

"You still smell like horse," Nick said. Austin was sitting in his lap now.

"Has something happened to the towels?" Joe asked the room at large, trying to keep his voice calm. "Is there some sort of towel shortage? Why are they all dirty at once?"

Nobody answered him. He could feel the tension trying to split his head open. He turned to Nick. "You're living here now? Full time, not visiting? Can you be in charge of laundry, please?"

Nick stared at him for a moment, then said, "Well, I can chip in. I can help out. But I'm not really loving this dynamic. You know, you being in charge and handing out jobs to the rest of us. I'm an adult, now. You need to see me that way."

"I'm pretty sure adults do laundry." Joe was proud he'd managed to get that out without any expletives.

"They do their *own* laundry," Nick replied. "They don't let their brothers turn them into a maid service."

And that was it. Joe needed to get out of there before he lost his temper in front of Austin. He turned and headed for the door, stopping only to pull on his boots.

"Joe," Sarah said from behind him. "It's almost dinner. Don't go far."

"I'm going to skip it this week," he said without turning around. He heard her saying something behind him, but he was already too far gone to make out the words. He had no clear destination in mind, but he wasn't totally surprised when he found himself on the path that led through a small pine grove and then came out at the lake. He wanted to be clean, and the lake could help him with that. It could help wash away all his mistakes. His failure to help a little girl, his stupidity in letting himself fall for a guy he knew wasn't going to stick around. His pettiness with his family, his stupid frustration at the smallest of setbacks. He paused only long enough to pull off his boots again, then headed for the end of the dock. He ran out of wood and just kept walking, letting himself fall into the cool green water and then willing his body to sink. He didn't want to drown. Of course not. He just wanted to shut it all off. He wanted to live in this peaceful solitude for as long as he could. He could barely hear anything, barely see anything, and all he could feel was the silky massage of water. It was perfect, and he wanted it to last.

But he hadn't taken a very deep breath before stepping into the lake, and he could feel his lungs starting to complain, so he let himself surface and struck out for the middle of the lake in an even, practiced front crawl, slowed only a little by the drag of his wet clothes and the complaints from the torn skin on his shoulder.

He wondered how long he could live out there without going back to the house. He hadn't come very well prepared, but he bet he could figure out some way to catch fish. And there were berries growing all along the edges of the forest. Maybe he could convince one of the cows to let him milk her; the calves were old enough to wean now, or at least to share a little nourishment. Yeah, he could stay out there for a long time.

Maybe he could rebuild one of the old buildings that dotted the property and live like a proper hermit. Just him and Red. Maybe Misery too, just because she'd fit the mood of the place.

He took a deep breath and dove under the water, pushing down until the light got murky and he was skimming along the muddy bottom of the lake. He wondered whether mermen had annoying brothers. Wondered if they got all wrapped up in self-pity and started having ridiculous thoughts about mythical creatures.

He twisted around a little while he was underwater, and when he surfaced he was facing the dock. He could see Will sitting there, dangling his feet in the water. Joe felt like a drama queen. Will was missing his family dinner because he had to come check on Joe. It was stupid and embarrassing. Joe swam back toward the dock, not because he wanted to but because it would be even more attention-seeking to not go. But he stayed in the water when he got there.

"I'm in a bad mood, and I don't want to be around people. I could go for a drive, but you don't like it when I do that. I have no idea what you think I'm going to do, but you get all worried and call me every ten minutes." Joe grabbed hold of the side of the dock because now that he'd started talking he was actually interested in getting an answer, and it was easier to concentrate when he didn't have to spend any energy on keeping himself afloat. "But if I stay around here, you track me down. I really don't... okay, I don't know two things. I don't know what you think I'm going to do that you need to keep an eye on me to be sure it doesn't happen, and I don't know how the hell to get rid of you. Can you help me with either of those things?"

Will didn't say anything for a while. Then he half-smiled. "Because you're an adult now. I need to start seeing you that way. But the thing is, Joe... adults care about each other. They keep an eye on each other."

"Or what? What happens if you *don't* come and pull one of your fucking interventions?"

"You stay out all night, and Sarah and I go crazy worrying about you. That's what happens." Will shook his head. "You are a moody son of a bitch, Joe. You always have been, but it's been worse since...." Another head shake. "There are lots of reasons that I hate you doing the firefighting. I know it's an important job, and I know you're good at it, but I just don't think it's good for *you*. You care too much. And since Mom and Dad... I can't even think about what it was like for you to go to that accident. I mean, to think you were reporting to just another call, and to get there, and—"

"That was years ago," Joe interrupted. "It sucked, but it's over. It hasn't got a damned thing to do with me needing to get away from Nick and his prima donna bullshit, and it hasn't got anything to do with you needing to follow me out here and do whatever the hell it is you think you're doing."

"Yeah. Okay." Will leaned back, abruptly disengaging himself from the conversation. "You're right. Sorry. I honestly don't know why I can't let go. I guess it's because me and Lindsey—" But he stopped then and forced a smile onto his face. "Never mind. That's not important." He jerked to his feet and strode toward shore, then headed off into the pine trees.

Joe stared after him. What the hell had that been? Had he been so caught up in his own shit, *again*, that he'd missed something important? What was going on? He hadn't seen Lindsey at the house recently, he realized. Damn, what did that mean?

He pulled himself out of the water and up onto the dock. His wet clothes tried to drag him back to his peaceful refuge, but he ignored the weight and jogged down the dock to the shore. He went right past his boots; the path to the house had been smoothed by generations of swimmers in bare feet, so he didn't need to take the time. He saw his brother ahead of him, just inside the tree line, and called out. "Hey, Will! Wait a second."

Will stopped walking but didn't turn around, his head lowered as if he was staring at the ground. Joe got closer, edged around in front, and saw that his brother wasn't looking at the ground, but at his wristwatch. He lifted his gaze and didn't seem all that upset anymore. "Sixty-seven seconds," Will said. He stepped forward and waved his watch in Joe's face. "That's how much time you gave me when you thought I was upset about something. I don't know what you thought I was going to do if you didn't haul yourself out of the lake and come stage one of your 'fucking interventions....'" He paused long enough to be sure Joe was catching the references, then relaxed into a less challenging posture. "We're a close family, Joe. It's annoying sometimes. I get that. But stop pretending it's all one-sided. It's not me and Sarah chasing after you all the time. Maybe it's *more* that direction, but that's because you seem upset more often than we do. Like I said, you've always been moody. And maybe because we know you don't have anyone else to talk to."

But Joe wasn't listening to the words all that closely. "You were *playing* with me? That was an *act*? Like I'm just your toy to wind up and let go? You think it's *funny* to manipulate me?" He turned around and stomped back toward the lake.

"No," Will said from somewhere behind him. "No, I was just trying to.... Damn it!"

Joe was on the dock by the time Will caught up to him. "Don't be a princess, Joe. I was just trying to—"

But Joe didn't need to hear whatever Will had been trying to do. Not when his brother's concern had brought him so close to the side of the dock. Joe was already soaking wet, but Will....

Joe moved fast, spinning to grab his brother and then driving with his legs, pushing them both back and off the end of the dock. They landed in the water with Joe on top, and he took advantage of the opportunity to push Will a little farther down before he swam a few strokes away and turned around to watch the show.

Will surfaced, sputtering and laughing. "Son of a whore," he said, and then the chase was on. Joe let himself get caught, and they wrestled in the water, trading dunkings fairly equally. They had the same genes, they both had physical jobs that kept them fit, and they'd had enough play fights over the years to know each other's strengths and weaknesses. When they finally separated and grabbed onto opposite sides of the dock, they were both coughing up water and gasping for breath.

Will was the first to recover. "I'm glad you see the wisdom of what I'm saying," he called across the wooden deck. "I think it's good we had this little talk. No more complaining from you, right?"

"Oh, yeah, I totally see the error of my ways," Joe agreed sarcastically.

"And you'll come up to the house? Have dinner with the family?"

But that was pushing too far. "I think me and Nick are heading for a pretty big fight. I'm just about out of patience with him. I don't want it to happen in front of Austin."

"You're pissed enough that you can't sit through a family dinner?"

"Right now? I could sit. But if he starts spouting his bullshit again? He hasn't done a thing since he got back other than babysit Austin. Child care is *not* a full-time job around here. He doesn't get to knock up a sixteen-year-old and use the offspring as an excuse to never do anything else with his time."

"We'll have a family meeting," Will said soothingly. "School starts Tuesday. Maybe Austin can go to the afterschool day care and Ally can come home on the bus, and we'll work some stuff out. Another day and a half. Two sleeps. Can you make it that long?"

"I can if you stop pushing for me to spend time with the little ass-pain."

"I'm taking tomorrow off. Lindsey and I can watch Austin tonight and tomorrow, assuming Nick doesn't want to take that over. Why don't you and Mackenzie do something? Go somewhere, even? Go down to the city for the day, let him show you his world...." Will trailed off when he saw Joe's expression. "Oh," he said softly. "Things not going well there?"

"Things are done," Joe replied. He kept his tone level and matter of fact. "It's not a big deal. It was just a casual thing. But now it's a nothing thing."

"What went wrong?" Will asked carefully. "Seemed like you two were getting along."

"Yeah, we were. Like I said, there's no big deal. Just... ran its course, I guess."

"Was that your decision, or Mackenzie's?"

"It was the will of the universe," Joe said with a sage nod. He was trying to maintain his calm, but all the good done by the swimming and roughhousing was being drained away by this fucking conversation. "You go ahead with dinner. I'm going to swim some more. I'll eat leftovers when I come up."

Will looked doubtful, but he finally nodded in reluctant assent. "I'm sorry about Mackenzie," he said as he headed for the house. "I liked him."

Joe waited until Will was out of sight, then let himself fall backward into the water like a kid making a snow angel. A little melodramatic, maybe, but it felt good. He should probably take his clothes off if he was going to do any serious swimming, but it wasn't like he was trying to get somewhere. He just wanted to wear himself out, get exhausted enough that he'd fall asleep without thinking about anything. After a long day on the ranch, it wouldn't take too much more to get him to that state, but swimming with the weight of extra clothes would definitely speed up the process. He fixed his eyes on a spot across the lake and started toward it. He felt his body falling into a rhythm. His breathing was regular, his arms were strong, and his body was at home in the water. Everything was good. And for a few blessed moments of peace, he was able to ignore the images that kept bouncing into his head: a laughing little girl who might never laugh again, and Mackenzie's blue eyes looking at Joe as if he were something special, when Joe should have known damned well that he wasn't. Swimming was good, thinking was bad. Joe stayed in the water until after dark.

CHAPTER THIRTEEN

NATHAN HAD gone back to the city, so it was strange that the words in Mackenzie's head were using Nathan's voice. "You can't make a decision in a vacuum. You need to gather your facts, interpret them, and then decide. Don't let someone else set your schedule for you, Mackenzie. You decide when *you* decide." Mackenzie could picture Nathan's predatory smile as he added, "But you'd better decide fast, because there's a lineup of other guys looking for the exact same opportunities you are, and if they get there first, you're out of luck."

He wasn't sure the last part of that really applied in this case. It wasn't like anyone else wanted to resurrect the church—it had sat empty for ten years before Mackenzie had been stupid enough to think he could make it into something. And Joe wasn't exactly cruising the market either, from what Mackenzie had seen. Maybe when you were that fine you just got to sit back and let the other cowboys come find you, or maybe Joe just had the same level of apathy toward other men that he obviously had toward Mackenzie.

Or maybe it wasn't that obvious. Flashes of Saturday night were definitely coming back to Mackenzie, but it was all being remembered through a confusing haze. All that was clear to him was that he wanted Joe, and Joe might not want him back. And Nathan wanted Mackenzie. Did Mackenzie want Nathan?

Not physically. Hard to go back to cheap ground beef after

tasting filet mignon. Mackenzie wished Nathan could hear where he placed in that little analogy. But there was more to a relationship than the physical. Before things had gone wrong, Nathan had made Mackenzie feel secure and valued. Sure, his value had been based more on his physical appearance and tractability than on anything else, but at least it was something. Nathan had given Mackenzie an easy life, and he was offering to do the same again. Mackenzie ran his hand down Griffin's side. "Did you like living there, buddy? No mean porcupines in the city, right?" Griffin didn't answer, just rolled over to expose more of his belly for attention. "Nathan didn't like you all that much, though, did he? When he was here, he barely talked to you at all. You like Joe, don't you?"

At the mention of Joe's name, the dog's ears perked up, and he lifted his head to look toward the door. "No, he's not coming over right now." He might not ever come over again. Joe hadn't actually said that, but he hadn't sounded too impressed with Mackenzie on Sunday morning, and he hadn't called since then. But it was only Monday. Nothing was definite, not really.

But Mackenzie needed to know. He needed to make it definite. He couldn't make a decision without having all the facts. He picked up his phone, then held it without dialing. What if he got news he didn't want? Or what if he got Joe to declare his interest and then decided to go with Nathan anyway? That would be an asshole move, for sure.

Except Joe had made it pretty damn clear he wasn't emotionally invested in the relationship, so Mackenzie probably didn't need to worry about hurting the guy's feelings. At least his words had made it clear that he didn't care. His actions... those were more confusing. Mackenzie punched the numbers into the phone. He needed facts, not speculation.

He heard Joe answer and realized he had no idea how he wanted to approach this. He really should have made a plan. Instead, he tried to sound light and cheerful as he said, "Hey, it's Mackenzie. I was wondering if you wanted to come over tonight.

Or tomorrow, if that works better for you."

There was a pause before Joe said, "I don't think so. I think we've pretty much run our course, don't you?"

Well, there it was. But, damn it, there had been a question in that statement, and Mackenzie was going to answer it. "Well, I don't really think so, no. I mean, obviously it's your choice. But, no, I don't think we've *run our course*. I don't really know what that means." There was no immediate answer, so Mackenzie plunged on. "I get that you're upset about something that happened on Saturday night. That's the only answer, right? I mean, unless you were coming over that night to tell me we were through. But if that wasn't the plan then, and it *is* the plan now, then I guess I'm curious about what changed, exactly."

Joe sighed. "Nothing changed, really. I just remembered a few things I'd been letting myself forget."

"That's still pretty cryptic. Look, I like you. I think you like me. If you don't want to fuck around anymore, that's your call, but it'd really help me if I could understand *why* this is happening." Mackenzie was proud that he'd managed to get that out without raising his voice or betraying the sickening lurching his stomach was doing at the thought of never seeing Joe's smile again.

"I like you," Joe said. He sounded like he was admitting he had a particularly unpleasant medical condition. "But we need to stay casual, and... I think I was having some trouble with that. You know, I was... getting a bit caught up in things. It's not your fault, it's just something I do sometimes. I don't really seem to be able to control it. So, yeah. Best for me that we end it now, instead of down the road."

"Wait." Mackenzie tried to marshal his thoughts. "You're dumping me because you like me *too much*? Is that honestly what you're saying?"

"How's your ex, Mackenzie? I was in town today, and I heard about that little show he put on with the brunch. I heard he was telling people all about his plan for some train or something.

Sounded like he was pretty invested in the situation. Not the sort of thing someone's *ex* usually does for them."

"I can't control what he tells people." Mackenzie didn't like feeling defensive about this, but he was beginning to understand why Joe had pulled away. "And, yeah, if you want the truth, he *is* interested in getting back together. But that doesn't mean *I'm* interested in it."

"And you've told him 'no'?" Joe's tone made it clear he already knew Mackenzie's answer.

"Well, no. Not really. I mean, I'm considering it. I'm trying to figure things out. That's why I wanted to know where you and I stand."

"Because why?" Joe's voice was quiet. "If I say I'm still interested, you're going to dump Richie Rich and watch your business go down the drain, just for some guy you fucked a few times?"

"I don't know," Mackenzie replied. He was starting to feel trapped and desperate. He wished he'd never picked up the phone. "I mean... no. That would be crazy, right? You and me, we're... we're *casual*. I couldn't... I couldn't throw away all Nathan's offering, not for...."

"Not for some hick in a pickup truck," Joe finished for him. "I get it. We're on the same page. But I'm not sure why you're arguing with me. Are you just one of those guys who has to be the one doing the dumping?"

"Me?" Mackenzie squeaked. "You *just* preemptively dumped *me*, asshole, so don't be a hypocrite about someone else wanting to do the same!"

"Jesus Christ." Joe sounded disgusted with the entire situation. "Fine. Let's make it mutual, okay? We mutually agree, at the same time, that this isn't going anywhere. You want to get back with your rich boyfriend, and I don't want to date someone who chooses his fucks based on the size of their bank account. So we're both happy, right?"

"Oh, I'm ecstatic." Mackenzie had more to say, but he heard a click and looked down at the phone to see that the call had been disconnected. Joe had hung up on him.

He fought the urge to throw the phone across the room. He didn't let himself drop it where it was and stomp on it, either. He'd been dumped. Joe Sutton didn't want to see him anymore. Big deal. Some stupid cowboy he'd fucked a few times didn't want to have another round. That was all.

The words stung, sure. *Someone who chooses his fucks based on the size of their bank account.* That wasn't the way Mackenzie wanted to see himself. "I'm not a gold digger," he said to Griffin. The dog cocked his head as if trying to understand the words. "I need to look after myself, yeah. But... maybe I just have a type, right? Maybe I just get turned on by powerful men!"

Except he couldn't forget the way Joe had made him feel, the way desire and intimacy had mingled so perfectly every time they'd been together. Joe had been getting a bit 'caught up in things.' That's what he'd said. It hadn't been as casual for him as he'd been making it seem, and it hadn't been casual for Mackenzie, either. But now it was over.

So, he had a piece of information for his decision making. Mackenzie tried to focus on that instead of on the emptiness that seemed to be spreading through him. Joe wasn't a factor. Mackenzie had to choose between going back to Nathan and having a thriving business, or staying away from Nathan and trying to make the business work on its own. Which meant, he was back to needing more information. He could do this. He wouldn't think about Joe. He wouldn't, he wouldn't. He'd distract himself. "Stay here," he told Griffin and jogged up the stairs and out to his car. He wasn't thinking about Joe. No Joe. No way.

He drove downtown and parked in front of one of the old red-brick buildings, then headed for the front door. Business. Business. He was focusing on business. And Dale Aithers, the man who worked in this building, was a businessman. Maybe not at the same level as Nathan, but Dale was active in the chamber of commerce and was Lorraine's contact for the bed-and-breakfast investigations. He'd told Mackenzie to drop by whenever he wanted, and Mackenzie definitely wanted to drop by right then. He wanted to focus on business. Not Joe, not his smile, not the way he touched Mackenzie in all the right places. Not his quiet heroism, his commitment to his family.... Damn it, no! None of that. Mackenzie was thinking about business.

He climbed to the second floor and could see Dale through a glass door. He was standing in what looked like a foyer, chatting with a dark-haired man Mackenzie didn't know. Would it be interrupting to go in? But Dale saw him through the doorway and waved him inside.

"Mackenzie! Perfect timing. We were just talking about you. This young man is looking for business opportunities in the area, and I was telling him that your project is about the only new thing on the horizon right now." The man turned, and when Mackenzie saw his face he wondered whether "boy" would be a better descriptor. But the kid's handshake was firm and his gaze direct as Dale said, "Mackenzie, this is Nick Sutton. You already know his brother Will, right?"

"I know both his brothers," Mackenzie said slowly. He wondered what he'd done to deserve this. "And one of his sisters too."

"It's a pretty big family," Nick said with a charming smile.

"I was telling him I'm having trouble getting anyone interested in taking a chance on the bed-and-breakfast idea," Dale said. "I think people just don't feel like they have the money to risk on something that might not work out. It's hard to get them to take a chance."

And that was it. Mackenzie stared at Dale and tried to figure out why the man was smiling as if he hadn't just crushed Mackenzie's last hope for getting the business off the ground without help. The church was two hours from the city, had only a limited reception facility, and nowhere for guests to stay overnight. It couldn't work. He needed to either give up on the idea entirely or take Nathan up on his offer. Mackenzie could be single and unemployed, or he could be the pretty part of a power couple with a small but successful business in his name. The choice should be simple, but now that it was the only option left, he realized he didn't want to take it. He didn't want to go back to Nathan, and he didn't want to rely on him for his business help.

"I had another idea," Nick Sutton said, and the excitement in his voice drew Mackenzie's attention. "My family's ranch is about fifteen minutes from the church. We have a big old barn that would be great for receptions—we have parties in the hayloft all the time, and it works really well. And we have a lot of outbuildings we aren't using for anything. They'd take some work, but my brother's a contractor—he could do it for cheap, fix them up into little guest houses or something. You'd be kind of limited to rustic-themed weddings, but maybe that could be part of your marketing, right? We could take people on hay rides or horseback riding, even. There's a lake for swimming, some great hiking. A good hill for tobogganing in the winter, cross-country skiing. Fishing. Hunting, even. Maybe Joe could get his outfitters' license or something. Right now, the property's being wasted. It's just raising cattle and growing trees. There's no real money being made. If we got a bit more active, we could do a lot, and it could really help you with your church project. People could come for a wedding and make a weekend of it, or come back for a vacation later on. We're a long way from the city for just a wedding, but we're really pretty close for a relaxing vacation in the country. Right?"

Mackenzie's mind was racing. It wasn't how he'd pictured things, but it might just work. "Kind of a theme wedding, but not totally hokey," he mused. "Just a bit of flavoring, not an overpowering thing."

"Absolutely," Nick said with a wide grin that made him look a little bit like Joe. "It's not like people would have to dress up like cowboys or anything, and we'd make sure the outbuildings had all the modern conveniences. We probably wouldn't be able to have beds for *all* the guests for an average-sized wedding, but that's okay because some of them will want to drive home anyway, and some of them might want to stay at a motel over in Darton or something. But we could fix up a place real special for the bride and... sorry, for the groom and groom, if that's how you're going to specialize... but you might want to open it up a bit? Make it a destination wedding for whoever wants it, not just for gay couples."

The kid was full of ideas. And they were good, Mackenzie was pretty sure. He felt a tiny flare of hope. "This sounds really interesting," he said, trying to keep himself from getting too excited. "But how does your family feel about it?"

"I haven't talked to them yet." He shrugged. "They'll have concerns, I'm sure. But we can persuade them to give it a chance, right?"

Something in Nick's smile made Mackenzie feel pretty sure the kid knew he and Joe had been involved, and *didn't* know they no longer were. If he was counting on Mackenzie to smooth over Joe's objections, he was going to have an unpleasant surprise pretty soon. Still, the ideas were intriguing, and Mackenzie was all out of easier options. "We should talk," he said. "I'd like to see what we can come up with."

Nick grinned like he'd just won the lottery, and Mackenzie found himself smiling back. Maybe there was hope. He needed to believe there might be.

CHAPTER FOURTEEN

WILL AND Joe had started having family meetings pretty regularly after their parents died. Two a week, for the first little while. They were all adjusting, all working out new routines. The meetings had been an important way to make sure everyone was being heard and everyone knew what was going on. But it had been months since they'd needed one. The most recent was…. Joe searched his memory. Damn, it had been back before Christmas, and it had centered on planning their festivities. This one was a bit more serious.

"We're going to try to keep it low-key, right?" Sarah seemed to be addressing the room, but Joe knew she was talking to him. Will was the only other one there, and he wasn't looking too tense about anything.

"I'll try," Joe said. "But at some point Nick and I are going to need to clear the air a little. It's possible we're at that point."

"Just don't go *looking* for trouble," Will said.

"I've never really found that I need to go looking with Nick. He always seems to bring enough of it for everyone."

"Not really the attitude we were hoping for." But Sarah sounded resigned, as if she knew it was the best she could expect. Joe and Nick had been avoiding each other since Sunday; Joe couldn't help but notice that he'd done the avoiding by working his ass off dawn to dusk on the farm, while Nick had avoided him by leaving the property entirely and spending his days who knew where doing... well, doing something that wasn't going to be putting any food on the damned table. Or any towels in the linen closet. Maybe it was a bit petty, but Joe had done a few loads of laundry composed solely of his own clothes and towels, and he'd stashed the clean towels in his bedroom for his and Austin's use. He'd shared the location with Ally, and she'd grinned at him and said maybe she'd start doing the same thing. Joe wasn't sure what it meant that his only firm ally was also the only person in the group technically still a child.

He looked out the front window and saw Ally walking briskly up the driveway. The high school got out twenty minutes before the elementary, giving her time to pick up Austin and either drop him off at day care or take him on the bus with her. On this day, he was at day care, but his afterschool schedule for the fall was just one of the things that needed to be discussed at this meeting. One more reason Nick needed to be there. Joe looked impatiently at his watch. He had hay cut and cured, sitting in the field waiting for him to bale it, and every second it was out there after it was dry seemed like he was daring Mother Nature to ruin his plans. He was always a bit antsy at this time of year. Nick was just exacerbating the situation. Nick and other issues. But Joe was trying not to think about any of that.

"Where the hell is he? He knew we were doing this at four."

"Easy, tiger," Will said. "It's two minutes past, and Ally's going to want to tell us about her day anyway."

But it turned out she didn't. She came into the living room after dropping her knapsack in the mudroom and looked around impatiently. "We're waiting for Nick? Seriously? Because he had so much else on his schedule today?"

Joe grinned at her. Yeah, it was nice to have an ally.

"How was your day? Do you like your teachers?" Sarah smiled calmly.

"I've had them *all* before. It's a small school. No surprises. And no surprise that Nick is late, either. He needs to be taken down a peg."

"Your schedule's good?" Will tried.

"I picked up my schedule last week. It's fine." She dropped a bit of the attitude when she turned to Joe and quietly said, "It was weird being there without Lacey. When the bus went by their driveway, I expected it to stop and for all three of them to get on."

"She's still down with the aunt? Is that working out?"

"She's not crazy about it. I guess the aunt... she's Mr. Walton's sister... I guess drinking is kind of a family problem. And Lacey says there's room while it's only her, but she's not sure how they're going to fit the others in once they're out of the hospital."

"That's still the plan, though?" Joe wasn't sure why he kept picking at this scab. "Both of them getting out and moving down there?"

"Savannah for sure, probably next week. Kami... they're saying maybe a special school for her? One where she'd live all the time."

The laughing little girl who'd loved to swim and climb needed full-time care. Because Joe hadn't been quick enough. His nod might have been a little jerkier than it should have been, but he was pretty sure he kept his expression neutral.

And Ally was compassionate enough to help him find a distraction. "Is the hay in?"

He shook his head. "The baler lost tension again. Spent three hours figuring out how to jerry-rig it into working, but it needs a more long-term solution. Either a permanent fix, or it's time for the equipment shed in the sky."

"Dad used to bitch about the exact same thing with the exact same baler," Will said with a grin. "It's nice to see traditions carrying on."

"Get it through this season and work on it over the winter," Ally advised.

This time it was Sarah who grinned. "And *that's* the exact same thing Mom used to always say."

"She was obviously a very intelligent woman," Ally said archly. Then to Joe she said, "I don't have any homework tonight. If you run the baler with the old tractor, I can take the bales to the barn with the John Deere."

"Thanks, that'd be great." And then, because there was nothing else to talk about, he said, "You sure you want to be a vet? I could really use a fully trained, minimum-wage-earning farmhand around here."

"Tempting. But the animals are calling to me."

They sat quietly for another few minutes, then Joe looked at his watch again. It wasn't that he was *that* impatient, it was just that he didn't want to be alone with his thoughts anymore. Thinking about Kami made him want comfort, made him want to be wrapped in Mackenzie's strong arms. And that just left him with two things he wanted but couldn't have, and it wasn't doing him any good to sit there thinking about either one.

"Here we go," Will said from his spot at the window. Joe looked out to see Nick's blue Honda speeding up the driveway. It would have been nice to believe he was hurrying, but the kid drove like a maniac every day; he was just coming at his normal speed.

"It's about time," Ally groused. Then she said, "What the hell? He's got somebody with him."

Joe turned back to the window and squinted, then let his eyes relax as the car raced past the house to park in the back. There had definitely been someone in the passenger seat, but Joe hadn't been able to discern any more than that. Nick was up to something. As usual.

Will had a better view as the car approached, and he turned to Joe and said, "You hear anything about this?"

"About him bringing someone? No."

"Did you see who it was?"

"What? No. Did you?"

Will shot a look in Sarah's direction, then started for the kitchen. "I'm just going to—"

But he was too late. The door crashed open with Nick's usual exuberance, and it was only seconds before he was in the room. "Sorry I'm late," he said breezily. "I was working on a business plan. With...." He looked behind him as if only then realizing that his companion was hanging back. He waved the man forward. "With Mackenzie. You guys know him, right?"

"Yeah, hi, Mackenzie," Will said, stepping forward to shake his hand. Then he turned to Nick. "This is a family meeting, Nick. I'm not really sure—"

"I wanted Mackenzie to be here because we're still just bouncing ideas around. I only met him yesterday; Dale Aithers introduced us. I'd like him to be here to contribute to the ideas I want to present to you guys, in case he has insight that I don't." He looked around the room, but his gaze settled on Joe as he asked, "Is that a problem?"

"You're late," Joe said. He knew his voice was tight and aggressive, but he wasn't inclined to do anything about it. "And it sounds like you've got more in mind for this meeting than figuring out who does what chores around here. You should get to it."

"Okay," Nick said, unruffled. "Great." He looked at Will and Sarah. "Do you two want to sit down?" Apparently he wanted center stage.

But Joe wasn't interested in Nick's game. "If they want to sit down, I'm pretty sure they can handle it on their own. What ideas are you talking about?"

Nick took a deep breath, making a show of being patient with his surly relative. "Well, essentially, I think there's an opportunity for this property to expand its business operations. It's already home to the contracting business and the cattle business, and each of those has a family member at its head. I'd like to use *my* interest in the property to expand into a guest ranch operation. There's a lot behind the idea: our proximity to the city; the natural beauty of the property; the unused buildings currently on site; and, of course, the presence of *another* tourist operation in the area. If people are coming up here for the church, they can stay at the ranch; if they're coming to the ranch, we can show them the church. It'd be symbiotic, like a good partnership should be."

Joe let his mind run over the ideas, and apparently the rest of the room was doing the same, because nobody spoke for quite a while. He was the first one to ask a question, and once he got started he had quite a few. "Where are you planning to get the capital for this? You're... you're planning on using *this* house as the main guest house? I mean, apart from the fact that there's a family currently living in this house, it's not set up to be a public space. You'd need so many renovations you'd probably be better off building a whole new place. And the outbuildings? Have you been in any of those lately? They're falling apart—I was planning to start breaking them down when I got the time. Again, you'd be better off starting from scratch."

"We could make it work," Nick protested. "It wouldn't be ideal, but it'd be okay for the short term. We'd need to do some work, sure, but if we market it as an authentic, rustic experience, people wouldn't be expecting a luxury resort."

"And where's the family supposed to live when this all happens?" Joe tried to make it sound like he was asking questions, not raising objections, but he probably wasn't doing a very good job of it.

Nick certainly sounded defensive when he said, "Sarah's already moved out, Will's probably going soon. Ally's off in the spring. But whoever wants to live here could still live here."

Joe snorted as he thought about the party-goers he'd seen at the church. "You want Austin raised in a house filled with drunks? You want him woken up at night by people staggering home from a reception and hooking up with random people?"

"We'd have to screen the guests," Nick said with a tight, almost patronizing smile. "And we could keep an eye on the reception, monitor behavior, if we held it in the hayloft of the barn. Lots of rustic charm, right? We've had some great parties up there. It's a waste to only use it a couple times a year."

"Are you joking?" Joe knew Nick didn't care about the farming operations, but surely he'd had some awareness of what had been going on around him his whole childhood. "We have parties in the barn once a year, in the early summer… when the hay's been eaten and the loft is empty. The rest of the time it's not wasted space, it's *storing hay*. That's why it's called a hayloft."

"People store hay outside," Nick protested.

"Top-quality hay needs to be kept dry. If you're just feeding cattle, it doesn't matter, but if you're planning to run a fucking dude ranch you need good horses, and horses need good hay. Some people store horse hay outside, but we don't and we shouldn't start." Joe shook his head. "And a guest ranch? Do you know anything about the *guest* side of that? You obviously don't know a damn thing about the ranching. Inexperience aside, you'd need capital for horses, tack, safety equipment."

"We *have* horses," Nick said with a snort of laughter. "They're the ones eating all the precious hay in your loft."

"We have two horses that are safe for beginners to ride. Two. Not enough for something like you're planning. And if you're going to keep more horses, you'd need more pens and run-in sheds. You'll have to feed them through the winter whether you've got guests or not." Joe shook his head. There were lots of details, but it all boiled down to one thing. "Where's the capital going to come from?"

"There's the life-insurance policy—" Nick started, but Joe cut him off.

"After funeral costs, there was about five-fifty left. Your share was one-ten, but you've spent almost fifty of that. Sixty grand is not going to get you far."

"Well, I'd still like to do my own math on that, but you're right. Just my share isn't going to get us far. That's why I'm presenting this at a family meeting instead of just doing it on my own."

"You start doing *anything* having to do with this property on your own, and you and me are going to have a serious problem." Joe knew he was doing this wrong; he knew he should be reasoning with Nick instead of challenging him, but it felt good to just let himself go and follow his instincts instead of his brain.

Nick, of course, was ready to go head-to-head. "What about those outbuildings you were going to tear down?" He jutted his jaw out. "I can't do anything, but *you* can decide to demolish a bunch of perfectly good buildings without consulting anyone?"

"They're not perfectly good, and he mentioned it to both Sarah and me," Will said quietly. "I think Ally might have been there too."

"I was," she said firmly. "There's general maintenance stuff that has to happen. It would be stupid for Joe to consult someone who doesn't even live here every time he cuts down a tree or fixes a fence."

"I live here now," Nick said firmly. "And things need to change."

"Okay, fair enough," Will said. "And that's what we all thought this meeting was about. This new business idea, though... Joe's right: it's going to take too much capital. Sorry, guys, I don't think it'll work."

Mackenzie nodded and seemed to be headed for the door, but Nick caught his arm. "No, it *can* work," he insisted. "If you all put in your life-insurance money... whatever's left... and if we leverage the equity of the place—"

"*Leverage the equity*," Joe repeated. "You mean get a mortgage. You want us to mortgage a farm that's been in the family for four generations... five, if you count Austin... and risk it all on a harebrained scheme that relies on someone with no hospitality or business experience starting and running a guest ranch that's supposed to be *symbiotic* with a wedding chapel that's *also* being run by someone with no hospitality or business experience? No fucking way, Nick. No." Joe was pretty sure he should stop there, but instead he added, "Mackenzie wants to be in the city, and until two weeks ago, that's what you said you wanted too. There's no way we can risk our home and our history for two people who are going to walk away from whatever wreckage they leave behind and go off and start something new in the city. No chance."

Nick frowned at him. "Look, Joe, here's the thing. I'm going to be starting my own business. That's the path I've chosen for myself. If I can do it here, that works best for everyone. If I can't, you're right, I'd be happy to move back down to the city. But you need to understand that if I leave here, I'll be taking my son with me."

It was as if Nick had punched Joe in the gut. "No way," he said as soon as he'd recovered. Every muscle in his body was tense, every instinct screaming at him to attack this intruder who was threatening his family. He needed to remember that Nick was family too, but it wasn't easy to do.

"It won't be your call," Nick said quietly. "I've talked to a lawyer. He said I've got a good case."

"And you want to do that?" Sarah was staring at Nick as if he were an alien. "You want to take Austin away from the only home he's ever known, from a loving family—?"

"No! I don't want to! But I need to make a living, don't I? If you won't let me do it here...."

There was probably more Nick was going to say, but Joe couldn't make himself listen to any of it. He pushed out of his chair with such force it fell over backward, then brushed by Mackenzie and headed for the back door. He needed to get out of there. If he stayed, he was going to explode.

He wanted to jump in the truck and drive, or at least saddle up Misery and head for the hills, but he did neither. He wasn't Nick, with no responsibilities and nothing to occupy his time.

He wasn't Mackenzie, with a sugar daddy on call to bail him out when he got in over his head.

He was Joe. And that meant he needed to get the hay baled. So he climbed into the tractor and got to work, and he tried not to think about the mess he'd left behind him in the farmhouse.

Chapter Fifteen

Nobody said anything for quite a while after Joe left the room. Mackenzie wanted to go after him, partly to apologize for his role in the fiasco, partly just to escape the tension left behind, but he was pretty sure he wouldn't be welcome wherever Joe was.

"Austin stays here," Will finally said. His voice was almost as heavy as Joe's had been. "He's not a toy for you to pick up and play with when you feel like it, and he's not a pawn in whatever game you're trying to play. He stays here, with the people who love him, in the home he knows. You need to take that threat off the table, or you can forget about any cooperation on any of this."

"It's not a *threat*," Nick said tiredly. "It's just reality. You all want me to *grow up* and *take responsibility*. Well, I'm trying to do that. Austin's my son, and I should be a part of his life."

"*A* part," Ally said. "Just like we're all parts. He's lucky to have this many people taking care of him, and you'd be... if you care about him at all, you'd be an idiot to take him away from this."

"Let's forget about it for now," Nick said. His calm manner was starting to show some strain, but he still managed a charming smile. "Let's focus on finding ways to move this business ahead for the whole family. It's not like I'd be the only one benefitting."

"If it's for the whole family, Joe needs to be part of the discussion," Sarah said. She sounded as if the whole thing was making her sad.

"*Joe*," Nick repeated bitterly. "Of course. It always comes back to Saint Joseph."

"No one's calling him a saint," Sarah responded. "But he's a part of the family, just like you are. Something this big... we *all* need to be on board."

"Yeah, right." Nick's voice was clipped and controlled, but there was something about his expression that made him seem like he was about to snap. Mackenzie wanted to escape and leave the Suttons to fight in privacy, but it was also strangely compelling seeing this side of Joe's otherwise idyllic family. And Nick didn't seem to mind the audience. Indeed, he was clearly talking to Mackenzie when he said, "*Everybody* loves Joe. He's like a fucking *god* in this family, in this town.... Joe can do no wrong." He shook his head bitterly. "You know why you're not getting more pushback for wanting to start a gay wedding chapel in a redneck little town? It's because Saint Joe performed a miracle and cured the locals of their homophobia. I mean, when he came out, they had a choice, right? They could either keep hating fags or they could keep loving Joe. They couldn't do both, so they chose to love Joe. That's the kind of power he has in this town. And don't even get me *started* on how much the family kisses his ass—"

"Bullshit." Sarah's voice was like an icy dagger. "You have no idea what you're talking about, Nick. *No* idea."

"Really? What am I missing?" Nick raised an eyebrow in clear challenge, and Sarah quietly stepped forward to meet it.

"You think he hasn't taken shit from people for being gay? Maybe he didn't get beat up, but that's just because he was one of the two biggest kids in school, and everyone knew the *other* big kid had his back. But they called him names, they shunned him. Some fucking coward spray-painted his truck, and they wrote obscenities on his locker pretty much every day. There's still people who won't talk to him. You ever wonder why he always gets his gas on the east side of town, even when it'd be easier to stop at Smitherman's? It's 'cause Smitherman won't sell him gas,

Nick. Ignores him completely. Turned off the pump one time when Joe tried to pump his own. Mary Gallagher was there, and she said Joe just stared at him, then got in the truck and drove away."

Mackenzie hated to think of Joe going through any of that, but he could see it happening. He'd seen enough ugliness from people himself, but he doubted he'd ever responded with the quiet dignity Joe could muster.

"So a few assholes don't like him," Nick said. He was clearly shaken, but still trying. "Don't tell me he isn't treated like a god in this family."

"We treat *him* like he treats *us*," Ally said quietly. "That's all."

Will was exchanging some sort of wordless consultation with Sarah, and apparently they decided there was more that should be said. "And it wasn't always easy, even in the family," Will said slowly. "You would have been just a kid. Maybe... maybe seven or eight. You remember Joe going away on an exchange that year? Middle of winter, last-minute thing?"

Nick nodded his head slowly. "Yeah, I guess?"

"It wasn't an exchange." Will looked at Ally as if wondering if she should hear the rest, then at Mackenzie, the outsider. But he kept going anyway. "When he told Dad he was gay, Dad kicked him out. Fifteen years old, on the streets, no money, no clothes. Nothing. They were driving home from somewhere, and Joe told him, and Dad just pulled the truck over and made him get out."

Mackenzie looked at Ally. Her eyes were wide, staring at Will, and Mackenzie instinctively reached down and gripped her shoulder. She didn't look up at him, but she grabbed his hand and held it.

Will shrugged and looked away, trying to break the tension. "Mom freaked out, of course. Big fight, right there in the kitchen. She said Dad had better not make her choose between her kid and her husband, because he wasn't going to like the choice she made.

She sent me out looking for Joe, all the places he might have gone. But he wasn't anywhere. Dad realized he'd been an asshole, and he started looking too, but Joe was just gone."

"I don't remember this," Nick said. "I mean... the exchange. I remember the exchange...."

"That's just what they told the kids," Sarah said softly. "I didn't know about it until Mom and Dad died. Joe was drunk after the funeral. That's the only time I ever heard him talk about it."

"He was gone for more than two months," Will said. "I don't know where he was or what he was doing." He looked at Sarah, and she shook her head to show that Joe hadn't shared that with her, either. "Somehow the cops picked him up down in the city, and they called home. Mom and me went to get him because Mom was afraid that if Joe saw Dad, he'd take off again." Will looked at Nick for a long moment as if trying to gauge the kid's reaction, and Mackenzie found himself doing the same thing. He'd stumbled into this family dynamic, but now that he was here he wanted to understand it. And Will apparently saw the same thing Mackenzie did, because when he spoke again his voice was soft, comforting a brother who'd been shaken by a family secret. "They got over it," Will said. "Dad realized he was being stupid, and Joe... well, he just sort of acted like it had never happened. They moved on. I'm not saying things were ever like they were before. But they got past the worst of it. And you and Joe can get past this too. Right now, it's just a fight."

Sarah was nodding along with her brother. "But if you try to take Austin away, it's going to be something a lot bigger. Something you may not be able to come back from."

"And don't think it's just Joe," Ally said. She leaned forward, letting go of Mackenzie's hand. "I love Austin. And I've done more to raise him than you have. Will and Sarah love him, and *they've* done more to raise him than you have. You won't just be hurting Joe if you try to take him from us."

"I'm his *father*," Nick protested.

"You're his sperm donor," Ally retorted. "Joe and Will are his dads, and me and Sarah are his moms. You stick around for a while, and you can be one of his dads too. But right now, you're just a fun visitor."

"And even when you're not working outside the home, you're finding it tiring to take care of him," Sarah said. "I've seen you. We've all been helping, you aren't working, and you're still getting more Austin time than you really want. Think about how much worse it would be if you were struggling to start a new business *and* had no family to back you up."

"I have said *several* times that I'm interested in staying up here and getting that support. But I need to find a way to make it work."

"The town needs a Tim Horton's," Mackenzie said. The whole family swiveled to look at him, but he held his ground. "I know those are expensive franchises to buy, but maybe you could get a loan. Or figure out some way to get dry-cleaning services here—I get that maybe there's not enough demand for a full shop, but if you did mobile pickup and delivery, it wouldn't be much overhead, and I bet people would be interested. Or whatever else. You shouldn't...." And probably he was crossing a line, because he'd just met the kid that morning, but that was kind of the point; they'd just met that morning, and already Nick was willing to embark on a huge business venture with him. "You don't need to be desperate. This church thing... it's probably not going to work. Not the way I've got it set up right now. But something else will come along."

"I could use your help," Will said to his brother. "You'd have a lot to learn, but if you're willing, you could start as a laborer and work your way up."

"A laborer?" Nick frowned. "That's 20 percent *my* company. Why the hell should I be starting at the bottom?"

"Because you don't know a damn thing about construction," Will said firmly. "And Joe could probably use you on the farm, but again, you don't know a damn thing about that, so you'd be starting off with manual labor. Which, as I recall, is not your favorite thing."

Nick looked frustrated, but he seemed a bit less aggressive than he'd been earlier. Maybe it was time for Mackenzie to finally get out of there. And maybe he should take Nick with him. "I can wait on the porch if you guys want to keep talking," Mackenzie said. "But at some point, Nick, I'm going to need a ride back into town."

"I'll take you," Will said quickly. "I can pick up Austin while I'm there. Sarah, you sticking around for dinner?"

"No, I think I'll go see if my husband remembers what I look like."

"Okay, so Ally and Nick, can you put something together?"

"*I* will," Ally replied. "I'm sure Nick's too important for a job like that."

"Fine," Nick said with a dirty look in her direction. "You take care of it. I'll be in my room."

"Or you could do some laundry," Ally suggested. "It must kind of suck to be showering without a towel all the time."

"Yeah, *that* was the sort of thing I thought we were going to be working out at this meeting," Will said to the ceiling. Then he shrugged and looked at Mackenzie. "Ready to go?"

Mackenzie was. They drove the first few minutes in silence until Will finally spoke. "Joe said you guys aren't seeing each other anymore."

Mackenzie nodded slowly. "I guess not, no."

Will took his eyes off the road for long enough to give Mackenzie a piercing look. "That sounds like it was Joe's idea, not yours."

Kind of humiliating to admit it, but there was no point in beating around the bush. "Yeah. It was."

Will nodded slowly. "Congratulations. I think you got to that point faster than anyone else ever has. Must mean something."

"What? Are you being sarcastic?" Mackenzie hadn't ever thought of Will as cruel, but it was hard to find another interpretation. "I can hold a man's attention for less time than anyone else?"

"No," Will said softly. "You got him to care enough that it freaked him out. It's a defensive thing—he can't get hurt if he doesn't care, right? For someone who's so brave about so much, Joe is a total fucking baby about getting his heart banged up."

Well, that was a slightly different perspective. More or less the same thing Joe had said, with a little less calling Mackenzie a gold digger, but Will's word choices made Joe sound a lot more vulnerable. "I didn't have any plans to bang up his heart."

"People rarely do," Will said. "But it happens all the same." He looked away from the road again. "It's too bad. He says he doesn't want a relationship, but he totally does. He just can't ever *trust* anybody enough to let them in. You know? And he can't trust himself to be able to recover if things go bad."

"Would he want you to be telling me all this?"

Will laughed. "Hell, no. He'd kick my ass if he knew. But sometimes... well, pretty much always, really... I know what's best for Joe."

"Wait. Are you saying there's still a chance for him and me? Like, there's something I should be doing to—" But Mackenzie caught himself. He had no idea how often Joe had gotten burned in the past, but in this case at least, he was *right* to not trust Mackenzie. Joe shouldn't open up to someone who was thinking about going back to his boyfriend, thinking about giving up on the whole country-living thing and running back to the city with his tail between his legs. "No. Joe's right. He and I have run our course. It was just going to get messy after this. Better to get out while we're both still in relatively good shape."

"He's not in good shape," Will said softly. "It's not just you. There's lots of stuff. But if he was with you...." He glanced over again. "The morning after the fire, I thought he'd be a complete basket case. He takes every rescue so personally, takes everything to heart... for a job to go bad like that... normally he'd be destroyed. But he was okay. Not great, maybe, but okay. And that was because of you. Whatever you did, it made him better. And if he had you now, you could help him with the other stuff." He sighed. "I guess I'm not making it sound too romantic, huh? I'm not saying you'd be his nurse or something. It just might help him get over some of the bad stuff if there was good stuff going on too. That's all."

"I'm probably going to get back together with my ex," Mackenzie blurted out. It sounded wrong. Sounded ridiculous. Why on *earth* would he get back together with Nathan when there were men like Joe in the world? "I'm kind of... needy, I guess. I mean, he's got money, and that's great, but it's more... I feel *secure* with him. Not good, necessarily, but at least I know where I stand. He makes his expectations clear, and I...." He trailed off. There was no way to describe his relationship with Nathan that didn't make him sound like a vacuous fool.

"Do you love him?" Will asked. He sounded genuinely curious.

"Love?" How strange. Mackenzie had never really asked himself that question. "I guess... no. I don't think so. But I think maybe I need him."

"I don't think you do," Will said quietly. "I mean, I don't know you that well. Maybe I'm wrong. But it seems like maybe you *used* to need him, and now it'd be easier to keep things the same. But *easy* isn't the same thing as *necessary*. I bet you'd do just fine on your own, if you tried it."

"Maybe Joe's not the only one who's a bit of a baby," Mackenzie suggested.

"Maybe not. But babies grow up. Or at least, they can."

They didn't talk much for the rest of the drive. Mackenzie

thanked Will for the lift and headed into the church to find Griffin waiting for him.

"What are we going to do?" Mackenzie asked the dog as they stood together just inside the back door. "What do *you* want? Do you want to go live with Nathan again?"

The dog cocked his head and seemed to be thinking it through.

"Or do you want to stay here and try to grow up? It probably won't work... not the business, not Joe... not any of it. But maybe that'd be okay. Maybe we'd get banged up a little, but then we'd get better. Do you think so?"

Griffin lay down and rested his head on Mackenzie's foot.

"That's not really an answer, Griffin." Except it sort of was, because when Mackenzie tried to walk away, Griffin pressed his chin down harder, trying to keep him from moving. "You want us to stay?" Mackenzie asked. It was ridiculous, of course, but something about saying the words made Mackenzie feel lighter and happier. "I think we have to give up on Joe. I don't think it would be fair to drag him into our mess. But...." He flopped down onto the floor next to his dog. "Nathan can go fuck himself. That's what I think." Again, the words, once spoken, felt right. "He thinks I'm too old? Well, I'm older now than I was when he dumped me, so I guess I'm still not what he's looking for. And I'm looking for someone a hell of a lot better than him!"

Griffin heard the excitement in Mackenzie's voice and danced to his feet, then leaned over for a quick kiss to Mackenzie's ear. "No Nathan," Mackenzie said. "No Joe," he said after that, and even the dog seemed to realize that the first of those statements was a celebration, the second a loss. "Just you and me," Mackenzie said resolutely, and Griffin wagged his tail in agreement. "Okay, then."

He pushed himself to his feet. "But first... I think I need to do one more thing. For Joe. Might be a mistake, Griffin. Might be. But I think I need to try. You with me?"

Griffin, predictably, thought anything Mackenzie thought of was a great idea and curled up beside him as he made his phone calls.

MACKENZIE HAD been tempted to drive out to the farm and have the conversation with Joe in person. There was no real need for it; he was just presenting an option, not looking for discussion. He just wanted to see the man one more time.

But Joe had made it pretty clear that the urge was not reciprocal. Maybe Will's insights had helped Mackenzie understand Joe's caution, but that just made it all the more important that Mackenzie respect the boundaries that had been set. Especially considering the decision he'd come to that morning.

It was only Wednesday, less than a day after the family meeting had gone so wrong, but it felt like forever since Mackenzie had heard Joe's voice. Maybe because he'd sounded so angry at the meeting, so unlike the Joe that Mackenzie knew. And there was a whole new tone of voice when Joe answered the phone this time. Even in a few simple words, Mackenzie could tell Joe was exhausted.

"Hi. I'm sorry to bother you, and I won't keep you long. I just wanted... I felt bad about yesterday. My part in that. It must have felt like an ambush, and that really wasn't the intention. Nick was just so excited about it. He said the family had capital to invest, and I didn't realize he meant mortgaging the property."

"You thought maybe I was sitting on a pot of gold from somewhere," Joe said. "Thought maybe I was worth your interest after all." There was a moment's silence that Mackenzie used to consider whether to hang up the phone, and then Joe said, "Fuck. I'm sorry. That was uncalled for. I'm an asshole."

"You're tired," Mackenzie said. "But I would appreciate it if you could lay off with those comments."

"Yeah. Sorry."

"Okay," Mackenzie said. He took a moment to collect his thoughts. "Anyway, I was thinking about how hungry Nick is for business opportunities. And those are pretty rare up here. Even in the city, they're pretty rare, unless you know the right people. Which, as it happens, I do." Mackenzie didn't think he'd bother to explain that he'd met most of them because they were sucking up to Nathan's money. "So, I made some calls yesterday. I wanted to find something that was fairly small-scale, because Nick has no experience, so he won't be a useful partner that way, and he doesn't really have a lot of capital, not by city standards. But most importantly," Mackenzie rushed to say, since he could feel Joe's resistance building over the phone line, "I wanted to find something that would be completely incompatible with raising a four-year-old. I don't know Nick as well as you all do, but it seems to me that maybe he's just got his feet dug in about some stuff, and he thinks backing down will make him less of a man. If we can just find something that would be *his* decision, I think he might do the right thing."

"What'd you find?" Joe sounded interested, at least.

"I have an acquaintance who's opening a bar. He's got quite a bit of experience in the business, but he's always been working for someone else. This would be his first ownership venture, and he's a bit tight for cash. He'd let someone buy in with him if they had enough money to contribute. And he'd also make it crystal clear that the job is not compatible with raising a child. He actually laughed when I asked about that. He said running a bar is a lifestyle; you're there all the time, or else you're off at other people's bars, seeing how they do things, networking. No time for kids."

"And he'd let Nick in for sixty grand?"

"No," Mackenzie said reluctantly. He wished it was that easy. "He said a hundred grand, minimum. I think that's fair, really, but I can call around and get some opinions. I thought maybe I'd wait to see if Nick was interested, and then I could involve him in the process, make him feel more sense of ownership of the idea."

"You sound like you've got a way better idea of how to handle him than I do."

"I'm used to manipulating stubborn men," Mackenzie admitted. Joe was well-behaved enough to not comment further. "But the real potential here... if you want to see it that way... is that extra forty grand that Nick would need. Well, probably more than that, because he's going to need something to live on while the bar's getting off the ground. And I figured... I don't know if you'd want to go this route... but you could offer him the money, from your share of the insurance, in exchange for him resurrendering Austin. He'd be an adult this time, right? No coercion or whatever. Seems like it might be more legally powerful."

"There was no coercion the *first* time," Joe protested.

"No, of course not. I absolutely believe that. And I absolutely believe that Austin is best with you and the rest of the family, or I wouldn't be suggesting this. I'm not sure I *am* suggesting it, really, I'm just... putting it out there. You know?"

Joe was silent for quite a while. Then he said, "Nick would *love* to own a bar. That's what he wants out of this entrepreneurship thing—it's not the money, it's the attention. The kid wants to be a star. And he's got the personality for it. Really social, charming...."

"I agree," Mackenzie said. "But I thought I should run this by you first. I don't know where you want to go with it. Maybe nowhere. And you know, bars aren't generally good investments. Like I said, my friend has some experience, but even so it's a gamble. Most new bars fail. I just wanted to mention it."

"Thank you," Joe said. He sounded sincere. "If this works... well, no. Thank you anyways, even if it doesn't work. But if it works, I'll owe you a lot."

"Well, you saved my baby from the porcupine. We'll call it even."

"How's he doing? Griffin."

"He's okay." Mackenzie closed his eyes before saying, "He misses you."

There was no answer for a long time. Then Joe said, "I miss him too." Another pause before Joe's tone became more businesslike. "Okay, so... can you hold off on mentioning this to Nick? Until tomorrow, maybe? I should think about it. And talk to Will, I guess. He's Austin's other legal guardian."

"No rush. My friend's still in the planning stages. And if this doesn't work out, there are other opportunities. You just need to decide what path to go down."

"Yeah," Joe said slowly. "I do."

CHAPTER SIXTEEN

It was a bad idea. Joe knew better. The telephone had been invented for a reason. There was no need to be making visits like this. He was an idiot. And he was going to suffer for his weakness.

He knew all that, but he parked the truck in the church parking lot and climbed out anyway. Griffin bounded toward him from the back of the church, bouncing and smiling and butting his head into Joe's legs like an affectionate cat. Joe rubbed the dog's ears and then crouched down for a better greeting.

"See?" Mackenzie's voice came from the corner of the church. "I *told* you he missed you."

"This dog gives the exact same greeting to the postman, people walking by...."

"No," Mackenzie said with a gentle smile. "He gives them *a* greeting, but not this one. This one's for the people he really likes."

Joe let himself look at Mackenzie then. That was what this was all about, after all. That was why he couldn't just make a phone call like a normal person. And getting to look at Mackenzie was worth the future pain of getting over it all. He was dressed for gardening, wearing jeans with dirty knees and a plain T-shirt, practical shoes... nothing fancy. But he looked good.

And apparently Joe was being a bit too obvious, because Mackenzie held his arms out to his sides and did a little spin, saying, "It's the latest in church-gardener fashion. Like it?"

"Yeah," Joe admitted. "I do." But it wasn't fair to either of them to continue like that. So he gave Griffin a good-bye pat on the ribs and then stood up and walked over to where Mackenzie stood waiting. "Have you got a minute? I just wanted to talk about that stuff you suggested yesterday."

"What, you're going to tear me away from my gardening?" Mackenzie grinned and looked skyward. "Thank you, Jesus!" He turned and headed for the back of the church, saying, "Come sit down," over his shoulder.

As usual, Joe was impressed with Mackenzie's ability to be unruffled in situations that would make Joe squirm with awkwardness. Of course, maybe it was just one more sign that Mackenzie wasn't all that emotionally affected by anything; he could joke about things because everything just *was* a joke to him. But that wasn't really fair. The guy had gone out of his way to help Joe out with the Nick situation. And that thought brought Joe back to the reason for his visit.

They settled into the canvas lawn chairs in the middle of the rose garden, and Mackenzie looked at Joe expectantly.

Joe said, "I wanted to thank you again. For finding that guy with the bar. I think... I talked to Will about that part of it, but I didn't mention the other part. I decided... I don't know. I wasn't sure what he'd say. And if I *did* go ahead with it... if I bought off Nick, used the money to keep Austin... I didn't think it was something Will should know about. I just figured it would be best to keep it secret."

He frowned, trying to replay the process his brain had gone through. "And then I realized that I'd want it kept secret because it's kind of wrong. I mean, it's for the right reasons, for sure. But...." He rubbed the back of his neck and made a face. "I'm making no sense. I know that. But... buying a kid. *Selling* a kid. That's kind of what we're talking about. Kind of. I think... I think I'd be okay with Austin knowing that I'd paid money in order to keep him with me. I mean, that could just be legal fees in a custody fight, something like that. I don't think he'd be upset knowing about that. But someday, sooner or later, he's going to realize that his living situation is a bit weird. He's going to start asking about his dad and trying to figure out why he isn't a bigger part of his life. Assuming he isn't." And Joe was pretty sure that was a safe assumption to make. He'd thought it over, and he'd talked this part of it over with Will and Sarah, and they'd agreed that, sooner or later, Nick was going to realize he didn't want to be saddled with a four-year-old. Eventually, Austin would be back with the family on the farm. It was just a question of how much the little guy would have gone through before that happened.

But Mackenzie didn't need to hear all that. "When Austin asks about his dad, I *really* want to be able to tell him the truth, and I want that truth to be that Nick realized he wasn't in a position to take care of another person, and he knew Austin would be happiest with us, so he let that happen." Joe was pretty sure he'd covered the basics with that little speech. Then he quickly raised his eyes to meet Mackenzie's. "And I want that for Nick too. He's my brother. He's pissing me off right now... he pisses me off a lot... but I love him. And I don't want him to go through the rest of his life knowing that he's the kind of guy who'd sell his own son. You know?"

"I do," Mackenzie said sincerely. "I wasn't even sure if I should bring it up as an option. I wasn't sure how desperate you were feeling."

"Pretty fucking desperate," Joe admitted. He'd worked dawn 'til past dark the past couple days, trying to exhaust himself, trying to avoid Nick, trying to figure out some damn solution to the problem. It wasn't until Mackenzie had called that he'd seen even a glimmer of hope. "Sarah says we have to give Nick all the tools he needs to make the right decision, and then just trust him to make it. I like the idea of you taking the idea to him, if you're still okay with that. And maybe letting the guy in the city be the one to make it clear there's no way the life can work for a single dad. 'Cause you're right, I think. If we push Nick, he'll push back.

If you can make him think it's all his idea...."

"I can do that," Mackenzie said calmly.

And that was it. There was no more excuse for Joe to be there. And that meant he needed to leave.

He didn't want to. It was scary to realize how strong the urge was to stay. He let himself close his eyes for a moment, let the sun warm his tense shoulder muscles.

Maybe he could stay. He could help Mackenzie with his weeding, or whatever the hell he always seemed to be doing in the damned garden; when they got tired of that they'd go inside, and maybe shower together. There was a ledge in the shower stall, just about head height, that was great for holding a bottle of beer. So they'd shower, and have a beer, and maybe they'd just jerk each other off, slow and easy, just friendly and cooperative. That wasn't too much, surely. It wasn't even real sex. It wouldn't even count. And then they'd dry off, and maybe Joe would look in the little bar fridge... and there'd be no real food, because even in his fantasies Joe wasn't going to pretend Mackenzie ever had anything useful in his damned fridge. So they'd order pizza and eat it on the bed 'cause there was nowhere else to sit, and they'd both sneak bits to the dog and pretend they weren't. And when the food was gone, well, they'd be on the bed anyway, and maybe they'd just make out for a while. Slow, lazy kisses that gradually got more intense, until....

"Joe?"

Joe opened his eyes. "I wasn't asleep," he said instinctively. He tried to remember where he was and what he was supposed to be doing.

"You were snoring," Mackenzie said with a grin. "And it's been half an hour since the last time you said anything. You looked so peaceful, and so tired, I thought I should leave you alone, but then your head kind of flopped over to the side. You were going to have a really sore neck if you stayed like that."

"Okay, maybe I was dozing a little."

"Maybe a little," Mackenzie agreed.

"I think I was having a dream." He tried to chase down the memories, but they were fading in the bright sunlight. "A good dream, I think."

"Then I'm doubly sorry I woke you up." Mackenzie made a face. "But it was only partly because of your neck. The truth is... I'm expecting someone." Another face before he said, "Nathan. I don't know if you want to be here when he arrives."

It was as effective as a bucket of cold water in terms of bringing Joe back to his senses. "Right," he said. "Yeah. Okay." He heaved himself out of the low canvas chair. "I should get going, then." He should have never come, just like he'd known. It was one thing to think of Mackenzie back together with the old man, quite another to almost witness it. And spending time with Mackenzie was doing nothing to help Joe get over his stupid crush, or whatever it was. He'd made a mistake and gotten attached, and now he needed to do the right thing and get the hell over it. Or at least cover it up. "I just came by to... well, to have a nap, I guess, but also to say thanks. Seriously, I appreciate your efforts." There, that was the right tone. Friendly, but not intimate. Not anymore.

"I'm happy to do it," Mackenzie said. He walked with Joe toward the parking lot. It felt wrong to leave. Joe wanted to stay. He could... well, it probably wouldn't be right to actually *fight* the little old man, but he could do *something*. Make a declaration of... well, no, not love. That was a little much. He could... fuck it, he could just sweep Mackenzie off his feet, carry him downstairs, and when the wizened-up troll knocked on the door, they could just ignore him.

And then what? Was Joe going to keep Mackenzie locked up somehow? Because otherwise, Mackenzie was going to leave, one way or another. He was going to leave Joe behind, and it wasn't going to be any easier to be left in the future than it was to be left in the present. It might even be worse.

Joe said good-bye to Griffin and climbed into the pickup truck. "Take care of yourself," he said to Mackenzie, although he supposed it wasn't really necessary. Mackenzie was going to have someone else to take care of him.

"You too," Mackenzie said. He stepped closer, close enough that Joe could have reached out and pulled him in for a kiss. It didn't have to mean anything... it could just be good-bye. But Joe didn't do it. He was done fooling himself. He had no business kissing Mackenzie, not anymore.

Joe pulled out of the parking lot and pointed the truck toward the ranch. He was going home. Alone.

IT WAS Sunday dinner by the time Nick finally told the family about his new plans. A great opportunity, getting in on the ground floor, gaining experience, making contacts... it was all excellent. Of course, it would be really intense. He probably wouldn't be able to give Austin the attention he deserved. And since it was so important to the family that they maintain their close bonds with his son, he'd generously allow Austin to stay with them a while longer. Or possibly forever. It was hard to foresee how things would unfold. That was what it was like, in the city. None of the boring predictability of country life. The city was vibrant, ever-changing, and you had to be willing to change with it if you wanted to succeed. Which he absolutely planned to do.

"But I'm going to need a bit more capital," he said as he attacked his slice of roast beef. "I'm hoping I might be able to get a bit of a loan."

"How much of a loan?" Will looked cautious. "And from whom?"

"Maybe you don't need one at all," Sarah interjected, her smile dangerously sweet. "Ally and I've been talking. We were thinking about the books and how you weren't sure you wanted to use the same accounting we'd been using, and it occurred to us that we've really been pretty sloppy about it all. I mean, we haven't been paying very close attention to who pays for what, or who earns what... we've just been taking it for granted. And Ally and I decided we'd like that to stop."

"Joe's working sixteen-hour days while the rest of us are goofing off," Ally said with a pointed look in Nick's direction. "And Will is working *his* butt off too. It isn't fair that they should give so much and it should all go into the family pot equally. So Sarah and I think we should divide things up. We think Joe should buy the ranch, and Will should buy the contracting business. We'd get them independently valued, right, Sarah?"

"That's right," Sarah said. "And then they could give us a down payment from their life-insurance money, since neither one of them has touched a penny of it, and they could pay off the balance gradually, with the profits from their businesses."

"And we'd keep closer track of what gets contributed to the house," Ally added. She pointed to the roast in the middle of the table. "That is prime, organic, grass-fed beef right there, and we're eating it for free because it ate our grass. But we're ignoring the part where Joe did a lot of work to raise it. In the future, if Joe owned the grass *and* did the work, then we'd give him a credit for whatever beef he contributed to the family and take that off his debt."

"Same would go for firewood, eggs, and all the rest," Will said with an approving nod.

"Or if you do work around the place." Ally beamed at him. "If you're living here, then, fine, maybe we all have to contribute a little to the upkeep. But if you move out and come back to fix something, we could give you a credit for that too."

"This sounds like a lot of bookkeeping," Joe said warily. He had no idea where Ally and Sarah had come up with this. "And, honestly, I don't mind sharing with the family. I don't *need* the ranch to be completely mine. I don't want to push you guys off the land...."

"Joe," Ally said patiently. "Ask yourself when the last time was that anyone but me expressed any interest in the farm as anything but somewhere to take an occasional ride or go for a swim. The others think of it as a park, not a farm. I assume you wouldn't try to keep us from going swimming in your lake."

"But what about *you*?" he insisted. "You love it. You love the animals."

"I'm going to be a vet," she said firmly. "I want to come back and live in the area. Maybe even in this house. But I'm going to have my own business to run. Are you expecting to get a share of my profits from *that*?"

Joe was at a loss. He looked over at Will, who shrugged his own bemusement. "We should think about it," Will said.

"It would really help Nick out right now," Sarah said sweetly. "He'd get the cash he needs in exchange for businesses he isn't too interested in being part of. Right, Nick?"

He frowned. "Well, it'd depend on the valuation, I guess. And the repayment schedule...."

"Joe and Will's two-twenty would be more than seventy grand for each of us, right off the top. Combined with her own share, that'd be enough to see Ally through undergrad and vet school, and combined with your sixty, you'd have a good start on your exciting business plan." Apparently Sarah had it all worked out.

Joe looked at his youngest sister. "Ally, you don't need to sell your shares in order to get money for vet school. If the insurance money isn't enough, we'll find it somewhere else."

"I appreciate that," she said with a smile. "But this way, it wouldn't be necessary. The money you would have found somewhere else could go toward repaying the debt, so I'd still get some of it and it would feel more fair. I don't like feeling like I'm taking advantage of you guys."

Another look between Joe and Will. "We need to think about

it," Joe said firmly. Think, and talk, and try to contain their excitement at the new possibilities. "It's... it's tempting, for sure. We just need to make sure it'd be fair."

They didn't talk much for the rest of the main course, but while Will was bringing in dessert, Nick said, "It'll be too bad to see Mackenzie go, huh? I thought he was really going to make things happen around here."

Joe focused on the plates he was clearing. It was Ally who said, "He's going? Back to the city?" She looked at Joe as if for confirmation or denial. Getting neither, she turned back to Nick. "Why? What about the church?"

"I guess he's still going to try to make it work. But he says he needs more money... it always comes down to money, doesn't it? I guess he used to model quite a bit, and he got an offer for some work, and his agent thinks he could find more, so he's going to save up and then try to do something different. Buy a house nearby and do the B&B thing himself, or—"

"Wait," Will said. He turned to look at his brother. "What about the train thing? The rich boyfriend?"

"The ex?" Nick shrugged nonchalantly. "I don't think he's going to be too interested in helping Mackenzie out after the guy dumped him. Well, does it count as dumping when you just refuse to get back together? I don't know." He paused as if pondering the issue, then shook his head to dismiss the ideas. "But, yeah, the ex is out of the picture. Mackenzie's on his own... Joe? Hey, Joe, where are you going?"

But Joe didn't answer. He dropped the plates off on the kitchen counter, grabbed his keys, and headed for the truck. He had someone he needed to talk to.

Chapter Seventeen

"I don't think you'll need your bed," Mackenzie told Griffin. "I mean, you don't really need it *here*... you just sleep on *my* bed. And you know you're going to do the same at Kristen's. And she hasn't got much space...." He dropped the overstuffed monstrosity onto the floor. "No, we're not taking it."

He looked around the rest of the room. He'd left out pants and a shirt for the next morning, but otherwise his clothes were mostly packed. He was leaving a few pairs of his grubbiest jeans behind; the dirt was too ground in for them to ever be presentable again. And there was a T-shirt he'd found when he was packing. It was Joe's. Mackenzie had been tempted to take it with him, but it was probably best to make a clean break. He picked up the shirt and held it to his nose, but there was no scent left in it. Joe was gone.

The knock at the door startled him, and he checked his watch. Only eight o'clock, but Sunday nights in the country weren't usually visiting time. When he opened the door and saw the man standing there, he held out the shirt almost guiltily. "This is yours," he blurted out. "Sorry. You left it here."

"You just happened to be holding it?" Joe asked, confused.

"Strange, but true." Mackenzie tried to collect himself. "I'm just getting packed up, and I found it."

Joe reached for the shirt, and Mackenzie had to fight a sudden urge to snatch it away and keep it for himself. "Thanks," Joe said.

He peered around Mackenzie, then crouched to greet Griffin. "You're packing?" he said, looking up.

"Yeah. I'm going back to the city for a bit. Maybe... I don't know, maybe permanently. I mean, I can make a living down there. Save up a little, maybe try another approach at this whole thing next time around...."

"But you're not getting back together with the troll? I mean, Nathan? You're not getting his help?"

"No," Mackenzie said. He raised his chin. "I realized I deserved a hell of a lot better than him."

"You do," Joe agreed slowly. He was clearly thinking something through. "And you... you deserve a hell of a lot better than me too. But...."

That last word made Mackenzie afraid to breathe. "But...?" he prompted.

But Joe, predictably, would not be rushed. "They've got a new plan at the house. The family does. They want me and Will to buy their parts of the family businesses. You know? So I'd own the farm."

Okay, slight distraction, but Mackenzie tried to roll with it. "That sounds good. Right?"

"Yeah, maybe. The thing is... when they told me about it, I wanted to talk to you. I wanted to know whether you thought it would be fair. And if you *did* think it was fair, I wanted to tell you about it and, I don't know, tell you I was happy about it."

"Okay," Mackenzie said. He really wasn't sure what was going on, but he didn't seem to be able to turn down any chance of contact with Joe. He glanced behind him at the upheaval caused by his packing, then opened the door anyway. "Come on in. I need more details before I can really give you a good opinion."

"No," Joe said with a confused frown. "That's not what I meant. I mean, yeah, I *do* want your opinion, eventually. But the thing is... I *wanted* to talk to you about it. You know?"

"No. I have no idea what you're talking about." There was no point in pretending otherwise, even if it felt like a failure to admit to his confusion.

Joe grinned then, not a full-power smile but still enough to make Mackenzie's knees a little weak. "Yeah. Sorry. I just mean... something big happened. Or something that might be big. Whatever. It happened, and you were the first person I wanted to tell about it. I wanted your opinion, because you're smart and you have good judgment and... I like talking to you. And if it worked out, you would be the first person I'd want to share it with. Because owning the farm would make me happy, and being with you makes me happy, and doing both at once would be... I'd be really happy."

"Oh," Mackenzie said. He wasn't sure if his heart was going to stop beating altogether or burst right out of his chest. "Okay. Yeah, I... I get it."

"But you don't sound happy about it," Joe said, peering at Mackenzie's face. "I screwed up; I got scared. I know that. And you're going back to the city now. You've got a job lined up, Nick said. That's great." His smile looked a little forced, but at least he was making the effort. "I just... well, I guess I just wanted to say it. And if I can be a little bit pushy... if you do end up coming back up here... you know, if that ever worked out for you...." He stopped talking and frowned, staring at the floor for a moment before looking back up at Mackenzie. "No. Fuck it. I said this much, I might as well say the rest. I want you to stay. You don't hate it here, and we can just fucking make the business work. If you can't get people to take the train, then I'll drive them back and forth from the city. You can sleep at the house, and we'll set up cots in the church basement. We'll fucking pay people to start B&Bs, or we'll get Will to offer to do the renos for free.... Or I don't need to buy the farm. I could put the money from that into doing the renos... I mean, I have to find cash for Ally's school, eventually, but she's got enough for the first chunk, at least. I want you to stay. I want you to be with me, and I want us to talk about stuff every night and eat pizza in your bed, and I want Griffin to meet Red, and they won't get along, but I'll kick Red's ass if he beats Griffin up. I want...." He stopped and took a deep breath. He actually looked like he might pass out, and he was holding onto the doorframe as if it was giving him balance. "Okay. Yeah. I know. Too little, too late. And too much about me, not enough about you. I just...." He shook his head. "I just can't figure out what I could say, from your perspective, that would make this seem like a good idea. I know why I want you. But I can't really think of any reason why...." He nodded decisively. "Okay. So, I said it. Probably pointless, but—"

"It was pointless," Mackenzie agreed with a slow nod. His heart had slowed to a healthier pace during Joe's speech. "It was nice to hear, but there was no point to it." He looked at Joe and smiled. "Because all you really *had* to say, you said right at the start. You want me to stay."

Joe stared at him for a little too long. "Wait," he finally said. "What?"

"Let's simplify it a bit," Mackenzie suggested. He felt like his whole body was glowing, like the words coming out of his mouth should float and bounce in fluffy rainbow clouds. "Joe, do you want me to stay? Do you want to be with me?"

Joe squinted as if trying to discern a trap, then nodded slowly. "Yes?"

"Okay," Mackenzie agreed. He looked around the room. "I can unpack most of this. I still need to go down to the city for a few days; I made a commitment to do some work, and I'm not exactly irreplaceable, but I'd like to not be a flake. But I'll come right back. I promise."

Joe was still squinting. It wasn't his best look. "What? Really? It's that easy?"

"Easy?" Mackenzie shook his head. "I doubt it. I think we're probably going to have to work our asses off if we want this to last. But this part? Yeah, it's pretty straightforward. You missed me, even though you didn't want to admit it. I missed you too. So let's stop missing each other."

"So... if I wanted to come in...." Joe turned his head sideways and looked at Mackenzie obliquely. The man had a surprising number of ways to express his disbelief.

"That would be excellent," Mackenzie said. He was feeling a bit like a relationship counselor, but better that than whatever the hell Joe was being.

Joe stepped forward cautiously, and Mackenzie eased back to give him room. "Really. This easy," Joe mused. He turned sideways and stretched his arms out, wiggling them around experimentally.

"What, are you looking for trip wires now?" Mackenzie shut the door and looked at Joe in amusement.

"I was just seeing how it feels," Joe said. "And it feels pretty good."

"I bet we could make it feel a little better," Mackenzie said in his best sex-kitten purr.

"Really?" Joe grinned, full power. "Sex too? I mean, this is going *much* better than I expected."

"This dweebish side of you is new and not entirely welcome," Mackenzie said. "I guess I appreciate the honesty, but could you try to be a *bit* less of a nerd?"

"I'll try," Joe said sincerely. He looked over at Griffin, curled up by the door, then stepped forward and rested his hands on Mackenzie's hips, like a nervous boy at his first dance. Then he didn't do anything else. Just as Mackenzie was about to throw his arms up in despair, Joe grinned again, but this time it was his wicked, sexy smile, and he flattened his hands and ran them slowly up over Mackenzie chest. "Still no chance of you putting on a show for me?" he asked softly.

"Someday, maybe. But not today. Today, you should just undress me and show me who I belong to."

"I'll undress you," Joe said, and he pulled Mackenzie's shirt over his head with one fluid movement. "But I don't need to show you who you belong to. You already know that, right?"

Mackenzie knew the answer Nathan would have wanted to hear to that question, but he was pretty sure Joe didn't have the same expectation. Joe just wanted Mackenzie to tell the truth. "Yeah," he said quietly. "I belong to me."

"You do," Joe said softly, scratching his stubble against Mackenzie's. Then he made a warm trail along Mackenzie's jawline with his lips, finding all the sensitive spots as if Joe had some sort of special radar. "But I really appreciate you giving me access." He kissed his way down Mackenzie's chest as he worked Mackenzie's fly and then slipped his fingers inside the fabric to find the warm, sensitive skin inside.

Mackenzie gasped at Joe's firm grip and leaned his shoulders back against the wall, letting his hips jut forward wantonly. Joe was keeping himself busy pulling off Mackenzie's shoes and socks with one hand, then using his mouth on Mackenzie's cock when both hands were needed to deal with his pants. Mackenzie was about to suggest that Joe lose a bit of his own clothing when his words were interrupted with another deep kiss. Then Joe slid his hands down Mackenzie's body, cupped his ass, reached a little lower, and suddenly lifted Mackenzie up. No warning, hardly any strain, not even a break in the kiss. Mackenzie was not small, and he'd never been manhandled like this, but he wrapped his legs around Joe's hips in enthusiastic support of the idea. Joe grinned into the kiss, then started moving them toward the bed, massaging and playing with Mackenzie's ass muscles as they went.

When they reached the bed, Mackenzie let his legs relax in anticipation of being set on the floor. He gasped when he found himself flying through the air, instead, as Joe tossed him into the middle of the bed as if he were a feather pillow. Mackenzie landed softly and stared at Joe, who grinned back at him, then slowly, tantalizingly, lifted his T-shirt up over his head. Mackenzie's mouth watered in anticipation as each inch of skin was revealed, but his impatience really grew when Joe's face was covered with fabric. He wanted to see Joe's eyes, his smile, and he wanted Joe to see *him* too. When the shirt was gone and Joe was looking at him again, Mackenzie brought the flat of his hand over his chest, down his stomach, then wrapped it around his cock and jacked himself, slow and tight.

Joe's grin showed his appreciation, but he didn't speed up his own routine. Another slow peel of fabric as his jeans were shed, and then he ran his hand inside his boxer briefs and wrapped it around his own cock.

"Striptease a la Joe," Mackenzie said musingly. He was almost too turned on to think, but not quite. "Not quite a performance, right? Reality and nature, just slowed down for my enjoyment."

Joe shrugged. Apparently he was totally comfortable taking his clothes off while Mackenzie stared at him, but too bashful to talk about it. At some point, Mackenzie would work on that. He wanted to hear dirty words coming out of this man's mouth. Then Joe slipped his underwear down, and Mackenzie stopped thinking anything that could possibly be missing from his current experience. Damn, the man truly was beautiful all over. Mackenzie didn't realize he'd frozen until Joe grinned and nodded his chin at Mackenzie's stilled hand. Mackenzie slid his fingers experimentally along his cock and watched Joe mirror the gesture on his own body. Mackenzie brought his other hand up to his chest, tweaked his nipple, and watched Joe do the same to himself.

But then Joe moved, crawling up the bed, sliding along Mackenzie's body until they were lined up perfectly and Joe's lips hovered over Mackenzie's. "We should do more of that sometime," he said softly. "But for now, I really want to touch you."

Mackenzie tried not to squeak his answer. "Okay," he managed, and then Joe kissed him, and all the tension left his body. They stretched out next to each other on their sides and stayed like that for quite a while, kissing and touching and laying claim to each other. At some point they became more mobile, shifting and remolding their bodies into new, more sinuously connected shapes. When Mackenzie finally found himself facing away from Joe, his ass rubbing into Joe's cock, it seemed only natural to arch his back a little, inviting a more intimate connection. And Joe seemed happy to oblige, sliding his hand down to line himself up....

"Wait," Mackenzie forced himself to say. Damn, he didn't want to. But it was necessary. "Condom."

"I'm clean," Joe said quietly. "Got tested a couple months ago. And I...." He shifted around so he was looking straight at Mackenzie. "I've always used condoms. Ever since I was a teenager. Always."

Always had, but was willing to change now. Because of Mackenzie. Because whatever they were doing was real, and serious, and Mackenzie felt exactly the same way, but he couldn't let the sentiment get in the way of what he needed to say. "I haven't," he said quietly, "and Nathan... he slept around. I'm not really sure how much or how careful he was." He sighed and twisted around so he could kiss Joe without disturbing the arrangement of their lower bodies. "I really, really want you inside me, skin on skin. I want that a *lot*. But it's more important to me that you're safe."

Joe looked at him for a long moment, then nodded. "Okay. If you've got some. Otherwise we're going to need to renegotiate...."

"I do," Mackenzie said quickly. He even knew where they were; he'd packed up his toiletries right before Joe arrived. But the bag was so far away, and Mackenzie felt *so* perfect where he was... "Griffin!" he called. "Griffin, come here!"

"What are you doing?" Joe asked. He sounded like he wasn't sure whether to be amused or alarmed.

Mackenzie ignored him, focusing on the fuzzy head that peered at him from around the corner. "Get it, Griffin," he ordered, waving his hand in the direction of his toiletries bag. "Get it!"

Griffin looked a little doubtful but trotted over to the bag and looked back at Mackenzie for confirmation. "Good boy, Griff. Get it! Bring it here!"

Griffin's shoulders might not have gone up, but his shrug was as clear as it could be. He picked the kit up in his jaws and walked slowly to the bed, stopping once to adjust his grip.

"Good boy, Griffin!" Mackenzie said, ruffling the dog's ears. "Clever boy."

"Good dog," Joe agreed from right beside Mackenzie's ear. "Now go lie down." He kissed Mackenzie's shoulder, then nipped it gently. "Call off your dog," he whispered.

"Good, Griff. Go lie down." Mackenzie waved toward the door, and Griffin reluctantly turned away, clearly unimpressed at being used like some sort of servant.

"Red would have chewed that kit up and then puked it on the rug," Joe said with a grin.

"That would do nothing for the mood," Mackenzie said as he burrowed through the bag and came up with a familiar cardboard box. "Jackpot."

"Still sealed shut," Joe mused. "Should we check the expiration date?"

"You should stop talking." Mackenzie quickly opened the package and handed a condom back over his shoulder, then burrowed a little more until he could pass back a bottle of lube. "Now get to the action."

"Wow. That's a sexy sales pitch you've got there."

Mackenzie didn't complain about Joe's continued chatter because he could feel the man was moving around behind him. "The sale's been made. I'm just waiting for delivery."

Joe was quiet for a moment, then said, "I'm trying to decide between saying something about having your meat delivery right here, or something about coming to your back door...."

"Neither, please." Mackenzie squirmed around again so he could look at Joe. "But I would really like it if you'd kiss me some more."

Joe apparently agreed. They stopped talking then, Joe focusing on Mackenzie's body, and Mackenzie... well, he was focusing on his body, too, letting himself get lost in the sensations Joe seemed able to elicit with the slightest touch. When Joe finally slid inside him, it was almost disappointing, not because it didn't feel perfect, but because it meant they were getting closer to the end, starting to read the final chapter of a book that had kept them enthralled throughout. But as soon as Joe started moving, the disappointment faded away, and Mackenzie let himself go. Joe was there: he was a solid presence against Mackenzie's back, a strong arm wrapped around his chest, soft lips on his neck, and a glorious, masterful presence inside him. They moved together in perfect unison, never speeding up, just sliding and working together in a slow, ancient dance. When Mackenzie felt his orgasm building, he clutched Joe's arm, pulled it into his chest, and held on as if it were the only solid thing in a world suddenly made of light and music. He felt Joe arching into him and knew his pleasure was being shared.

They lay quietly for a while as their bodies relaxed, then Joe pulled away a little. Mackenzie rolled over so they were facing each other, their knees slightly bent, their mouths in perfect kissing range. But Joe frowned slightly, then turned his head away. "Hey, pup," he softly called. "C'mere." It was only a moment before the bed dipped as Griffin jumped up, and then he immediately curled up just below their knees, his body warm as it pressed against them.

"Does Red sleep on your bed?" Mackenzie asked.

"Red is a filthy beast," Joe muttered. He kissed Mackenzie then. "He's lucky he's allowed in the house."

"That's not really answering my question."

Joe grinned. "On Christmas Eve," he admitted. "Just once a year. He protects me from Santa."

"Santa's dangerous?"

"Hell, yeah." Another kiss made Mackenzie not care about the nonsense Joe was coming up with. "Breaks in, eats your food... steals shit...."

Okay, no kiss was sweet enough to make that acceptable. "Santa doesn't steal shit!"

"Maybe not from you," Joe said with a shrug. "But all those toys he gives to the good kids? He *steals* them from bad kids."

"He makes them in his workshop," Mackenzie corrected. He really wasn't sure Joe should be trusted to raise a four-year-old.

"That's what they want you to believe." Another kiss, and then Joe pulled away and looked serious. "I want to buy you a Christmas present," he said quietly.

"What? Right now?"

"It would just be a present if I bought it for you now. I want it to be a *Christmas* present." He looked down at the sleeping dog, then back at Mackenzie. "I want you to still be around at Christmastime."

Mackenzie smiled at him. "I want that too," he said. Then it was his turn to grin. "But I don't want Santa to steal my shit, so we'd better be really good until then, okay?"

"I'll try," Joe agreed. And then they faded off to sleep together, Griffin snoring happily at their feet.

CHAPTER EIGHTEEN

"MAYBE HE doesn't realize Griffin's a dog," Will suggested from his spot on the porch. "Red's always been really good with the cats."

"He doesn't think Griffin's a cat!" Mackenzie protested.

"It's because Griffin was immediately submissive," Ally said wisely. She was sitting beside Joe, sipping on a cup of cocoa, watching the dogs trot happily through the autumn leaves, Red in front, Griffin close behind. "He didn't challenge Red, so Red doesn't have to beat him up."

"That's how Mack works too," Joe said from his spot on the porch steps. He knew he was pushing his luck, but it was kind of fun to get Mackenzie almost mad. "He just immediately saw my superiority and dominance and never challenged me at all. Just rolled over and showed his belly... peed on himself a little...."

The clod of wet leaves came from behind Joe, someone's hand rubbing them into his face so hard some little bits of half-decayed vegetation went in his mouth and up his nose. "Hey!" he protested once he'd pulled away. Mackenzie was still in front of him, and the hand had been strong, but not *that* strong... "Sarah," he said in disgust. "You two are ganging up on me." It was true. Just the night before, Joe had said something Sarah didn't care for, and Mackenzie had splashed him with dishwater in retaliation.

"I think of it as more of a universe-wide effort to keep you in line," Sarah said smugly. She sat down on the steps next to him and snuggled in, brushing a little leaf detritus off his cheek. "You're kind of obnoxious when you're happy," she said, softly enough that only he could hear. "But in a good way."

Austin trotted over with an orange leaf in his outstretched hand. It was apparently his autumn version of giving flowers to people; it certainly saved the family some money. He looked thoughtful, then edged past Sarah and made his way onto the porch to give the leaf to Will. "Bye-bye," he said sadly.

Will's guilty expression gave Joe a quick stab of satisfaction before he rearranged his emotions to something more appropriate. "You know it's not a *big* bye-bye, right, buddy? Will's going to sleep somewhere else more often than he does now. That's all. He'll still be here lots. He'll still see you all the time."

"And if he doesn't watch his step, he'll be back before Christmas," Sarah muttered into Joe's shoulder. The family's concerns about Lindsey seemed to have crystallized lately, mostly centering around the idea that she wasn't friendly enough to the family and didn't appreciate Will's good qualities. It was nice for everyone to be picking on someone else for a change, but Joe generally kept his opinions on the matter to himself. If things *did* go badly, Will would need someone neutral to talk to. Even if Joe had to chase his brother down and *force* the conversation.

And Austin didn't really seem all that worried about any of it. The family watched him as he jogged down the stairs and leaped off the second-from-the-bottom tread, his new feat of daring. He glanced around to be sure everyone had seen and admired it, then headed for the leaf pile.

"Not there, little man," Mackenzie said as he grabbed Austin's shoulders and steered him around the more glistening leaves. "The doggies peed there. It's a bit dirty."

Austin allowed himself to be diverted, and Mackenzie picked up his rake again. The family had told him not to bother; they might run the lawn tractor over the leaves to mulch them up before winter, but that was about as far as they ever went. Raking and piling and burning leaves? Who had time for that?

But Mackenzie had it in his head that this was an authentic country activity and hadn't allowed himself to be dissuaded. He'd at least agreed to compost the leaves instead of burning them; Joe was pretty sure there would be another struggle when he had to convince Mackenzie that loading them into the bucket of the tractor and dumping them on the manure pile counted as composting.

Austin had found himself another leaf, and this time he brought it to Mackenzie. "Coals to Newcastle," Sarah muttered, but Mackenzie accepted the leaf as if it were a rare treasure.

"It's *beautiful*!" he gushed. "I really like the colors—green *and* orange, and there's a bit of yellow right there! And some pink up around the top!"

"Let's see if he can keep that up after the twentieth leaf," Ally said with wry affection.

"It's for 'hello,'" Austin said to Mackenzie, then frowned as if dissatisfied with his word choice. "Not 'hello.' For... for sleeping here now."

"Welcome?" Joe suggested. "When somebody comes and you're happy they're there, you say they're 'welcome.'"

Austin squinted at him suspiciously. "You're welcome?" he said. "That's for after 'thank you.'" They hadn't been playing the Joe-suggests-ridiculous-things game lately, but apparently Austin still wasn't sure he could completely trust his uncle on these issues.

"Same word," Joe agreed. "Kinda the same idea, but a little different. You can leave the 'you're' off and it just means you're happy somebody came."

Austin still looked a little unsure, but he turned to Mackenzie and nodded in strangely formal way, like a tiny ambassador. "Welcome," he said.

"Thank you," Mackenzie replied with feeling.

"You're welcome?" Austin said with a dubious look in Joe's direction. He obviously wasn't a fan of the repetition.

"Yeah, that's it, buddy! Not my fault it's kind of weird."

Austin returned to his leaf-hunting and Mackenzie to his own, larger scale version of the activity, and the rest of the family sat on the porch and watched them both. It was mid-October, and things had finally slowed down a little on the farm. There were certainly things Joe *could* be doing, but he'd shipped a good number of cattle off to market over the past couple weeks, the hay was in, the machinery that needed repairs wasn't going to be used until the next spring…. He could afford to take a Friday afternoon off to enjoy his family. Will was supposed to be packing and moving into his new house, but he wasn't taking anything but his clothes with him, so he had some time too. Ally and Austin had just gotten home from school, and Sarah had dropped by with some paperwork on the ranch sale and decided to stay a while. It would have been better, in theory, if Nick had been there, just to make the family complete, but he would have just been bragging about the new business, letting everyone know how important and successful he was going to be… it was easier to miss him than it was to deal with him.

And Mackenzie was there. Sure, it was mostly because he was trying to distract himself from the next day's wedding… the clients were doing the decorating and had made it clear they didn't need any help, so Mackenzie was on call in case anything went wrong with the building but otherwise superfluous. He wasn't handling it well, and Joe caught him taking another worried look at the sky.

"It's not going to rain," Joe reassured him. "And if it does, that's *their* problem. The joy of not holding the reception is that you don't have to worry about that crap. The church doesn't leak, so rain won't affect your part of things."

"The whole *wedding* is my part of things!" Mackenzie protested.

"If this event gets messed up, no one's ever going to want to get married in that building again!"

"No, the rest of the world isn't insane like you are," Sarah said kindly. "They won't blame you for some bad weather."

Mackenzie didn't look convinced, but he went back to his raking anyway. He had the front of the property almost cleared when a car stopped at the end of the driveway and let two people out, then sped away down the road.

"Who's that?" Will asked, squinting. Nobody answered, but they all turned to watch.

The visitors were halfway down the driveway when Ally squeaked, "It's Lacey! And Savannah!" She dropped her mug and skipped off the porch, then ran to greet her friends.

"What the hell are they doing here?" Will asked quietly. Again, he got no answer.

Mackenzie set down his rake and came over to stand by the family, and together they cautiously took a few steps toward the new arrivals.

"Hey, guys," Sarah said cautiously. "It's good to see you, but... what's going on? How'd you get here?"

"We took a bus to town and then caught a ride with Donny Travis's brother," Lacey said matter-of-factly.

"That's the second question answered," Joe said. He smiled and tried to sound nonthreatening. Mostly, he tried not to think about the sister who was missing, the little girl who was living in a care facility she might never get out of. "But what about the first question? What's going on?"

Lacey straightened her shoulders and looked dead at him. "You said we should come here if things got bad at home. You said if people were drinking too much or if we didn't feel safe, we should come here. You said it didn't matter what time—we should just come."

Joe stared at her. Yes, he'd said that. Of course at the time they'd been living a five-minute walk away, not a five-hour drive. But he'd said it, and he'd meant it. And he still did. "Okay," he said slowly. "Yeah. Okay." He'd need details, eventually, but for the time being, he supposed this was enough. He looked at Will, who just looked back at him, then at Mackenzie, who smiled as if he was sure Joe had a plan for just this situation. "Are you guys hungry? Ally, why don't you take them inside and get them something to eat?"

Ally raised her eyebrow as if she knew she was being removed from the adult conversation, but she did as Joe had suggested. When the girls were out of earshot, Joe said, "We need to call Andy. He felt bad about not getting them out of that house before the fire. He'll help us now."

"Help us do what, though?" Sarah was frowning at him. "What are we supposed to do with them?"

Joe didn't know the details, but he definitely had a good idea about the general principle. "He'll help us keep them safe," he said. "He'll help us help them."

Mackenzie stepped closer and took Joe's hand, looking at him with a concerned expression.

"I can't let them down again," Joe said quietly.

"You didn't let them down last time," Mackenzie corrected. "But we can try to help them. Absolutely."

It wasn't fair to him. Mackenzie hadn't signed on for this. But he was smiling at Joe now, his agitation about the church completely gone. "We'll help them," he repeated. "We'll make it work."

Joe made himself nod. This wasn't Mackenzie's problem, and Joe wouldn't let him take responsibility for something so unrelated to him, but at least he wasn't trying to keep Joe from helping out. "Thank you," Joe said with feeling.

"You really don't make things easy on yourself, do you?" Will

The Fall

smiled ruefully at his brother. "I can't decide whether I should offer to stay and help out or hurry up and get out so you'll have more room."

"Hurry up and get out," Joe said with a smile. "We'll be fine." He looked down at Austin, who was standing at his feet with a brightly colored leaf in each hand. "Who are those for, buddy?" he asked, even though he was pretty sure he already knew the answer.

Sure enough, Austin waved toward the house. "Lacey and 'Vanna," he said. "To say 'welcome.'"

Joe sighed. Somehow the arboreal tribute made it seem a bit too real. "Okay," he finally said, stepping aside so Austin could get by. "Go for it."

The little boy scampered up the stairs, and Sarah and Will trailed after him, going inside to give their own greetings to the girls.

Joe kept a tight grip on Mackenzie's hand. "This is more than you signed up for," he said carefully.

But Mackenzie just grinned at him. "You *always* give me more than I expect," he said, and he leaned in to kiss Joe, his nose cold but his lips warm. "We'll make it work," he said again.

And Joe believed him.

ABOUT THE AUTHOR

Kate Sherwood, Cate Cameron, Catherine Dale... and probably a few new names, eventually. They're all one person.

One person who's lucky enough to get to live a bunch of extra lives through all the characters in her books, and who's trying desperately to keep all the lives organized into some sort of categories... so each name writes a different type of story.

But really, beneath the genre categories? All the stories will have some kind of humour, even in the darkest times. They'll all show characters who are far from perfect, but who are trying to be better.

Basic bio stuff? Kate/Cate/Catherine lives in Cottage Country, the water-filled world north of Toronto, Canada, the land where summers are sunny and crowded with visitors and winters are snowy and isolated. She loves it there. Not that she doesn't sometimes miss the city, especially when her internet is acting up or she wants something delivered!

She works full-time at a non-writing job but would love to shift into a more writing-centred life. There's a five-year plan. It might work....

Other Books by Kate Sherwood

For details, see www.booklives.com

Writing as Kate Sherwood (m/m)

All That Glitters – contemporary romance

Long Shadows, Embers, Darkness, Home Fires – four book contemporary action

Feral, Lap Dog, Twice Shy, Pure Bred – four book NA contemporary romance

Sacrati – fantasy/alt history

In Too Deep – NA contemporary romance

Chasing the Dragon – angst and adventure!

Mark of Cain – contemporary romance

The Fall, Riding Tall – two book contemporary romance

The Shift – contemporary fantasy novella – monster hunters!

Room to Grow – contemporary romance novella

The Pawn, The Knight – two book futuristic romance with plenty of angst

Poor Little Rich Boy – contemporary romance

More than Chemistry – light contemporary novella

Dark Horse, Out of the Darkness, Of Dark and Bright – three book contemporary romance with extras

Shying Away – NA romance

Lost Treasure – contemporary romance

Writing as Cate Cameron (m/f, YA)

The Billionaire's Forever Family – contemporary romance

Center Ice, Playing Defense, Winging It, Breakaway – contemporary YA hockey romance

Just a Summer Fling, Hometown Hero – contemporary small town romance

Shining Armor – contemporary romance (originally published under "Kate Sherwood")

Writing as Catherine Dale (YA, contemporary fantasy, general fiction—everything but romance!)

Dark Houses – Speculative YA

www.ingramcontent.com/pod-product-compliance
Lightning Source LLC
Chambersburg PA
CBHW051431170626
46809CB00006B/2421